INTENDED ENEMIES

BOOKS BY D. LIEBER

Minte and Magic

The Exiled Otherkin

The Assassin's Legacy

Intended Fates

Intended Bondmates

Intended Strangers

Intended Enemies

Council of Covens

Dancing with Shades

In Search of a Witch's Soul

Also by D. Lieber

Conjuring Zephyr

Once in a Black Moon

A Very Witchy Yuletide

The Treason of Robyn Hood

INTENDED ENEMIES

BOOK THREE OF INTENDED FATES

D. LIEBER

Copyright © 2023 by D. Lieber

First edition January 2023

Ink & Magick, LLC
Kenosha, Wisconsin
contact@inkandmagick.com

Hardcover ISBN: 978-1-951239-25-1
Paperback ISBN: 978-1-951239-26-8
Ebook ISBN: 978-1-951239-27-5

Cover art by Maria Spada
Edited by Jennifer L. Collins
Proofread by Julie Chyna Editing

ACKNOWLEDGMENTS

Thank you to my beta readers: John, Amy, Joyce, and Aunt Debbie.

And a very special thanks to those who helped me with German and French language translation — Jügen, Chloé, Karen, Edouard, Marcel, Caz, Veronica, and Kathleen — as well as those who connected me with them — Bonny, Belle, April, and Kass.

PROLOGUE

A lot has happened. I wasn't here for all of it, but I can tell you what I know. I know that my brother, Rowan, was heartbroken when his promised mate left him for the fae she wasn't allowed to be with. I know that he went to the human realm so our parents wouldn't pressure him to mate someone he didn't love. And I know that that's how he met Yuti, the human he eventually mated.

As for me, I've spent the last year preparing to leave Faerie. After I completed my rite and played my part in upholding the treaty by protecting my bondmate from vampires—who love nothing more than fae blood—I went to a fae university to learn more about humans. Now I've come to live amongst the were-wolves of the human realm, to stay with the Northern Pack and learn what I can about being an alpha from Lia, my brother's alpha. Not that I want to lead a pack...just the opposite. I want to learn everything I need to know about being an alpha so I can avoid the whole thing altogether. I can't have my alpha influence inadvertently drawing unclaimed wolves to me while I'm just trying to enjoy a peaceful, undisturbed life.

My parents say I'm running away from my responsibilities,

but it's my life. Just because I was born with alpha power doesn't mean I owe anyone anything.

In any case, things are going to be pretty strange here in the human realm. I've been living under the treaty my whole life. It's going to be so different living with the wolves who decided to stay in the human realm rather than go to Faerie to avoid humans. But then again, I'll do whatever I have to in order to get out from under the fate I never asked for and never wanted, the fate that makes me an alpha.

This is what it feels like to be in another alpha's territory.

I rolled my shoulders, trying to adjust to the new feeling pressing on my skin—like with a heavy blanket, I couldn't quite decide if it was comforting or oppressive. I'd had only a taste of it when I'd come for that one night last summer, but facing months, possibly years, of it seemed to make the sensation a little heavier.

Staring out at the evergreen forest beyond what was now my bedroom window, I smiled to myself. My window was at the back of the house, where pines and firs, dotted with maples and white oaks, grew in uneven waves on the tumbling foothills. The cheery sight of so many shades of green under the cobalt blue sky of summer blotted out any anxieties over what was to come.

I was finally in the human realm, or "the realm of origin," as the werewolves here called it. I didn't put much stock in the distinction, but it mattered to some.

For an entire year, I'd studied and read everything I could about humans to prepare for this moment. I relaxed into this small accomplishment, letting go of the expectations that had hung over me in Faerie—expectations that I'd never planned on fulfilling but nagged me nonetheless.

I was safe here. And though I hadn't even started my alpha training yet, I was one step closer to my goal.

My brother, Rowan, entered through the already-open bedroom door, a small box wrapped in polka dot paper in his hands.

As I looked at him in the bright summer sunlight filtering through the window, I knew that I needn't have worried about him. Happiness sparkled in the bright tropical waters of his blue eyes. His black hair was thick and windswept from our drive with the windows down. He looked healthy and fit, all well-fed lean muscle. And I knew it was all thanks to his mate. She'd saved him, and I loved her for it.

"Here." He held the box out to me with a smile. "A welcome present."

I glanced up at him. "What is it?" The box was heavier than its size suggested.

He smirked. "Well, it's wrapped in paper so that it's a surprise. Open it."

The thin paper was unexpectedly loud as I tore through it.

"It's a cellphone," Rowan told me while I stared down at the gift.

I scowled. "I know what it is. Jeez... You showed one to me last time I was here, and what do you think I've been doing over the last year?"

He chuckled and held up his hands. "How do I know how much you know? You could have just been partying the whole time."

I clicked my tongue at his complete lack of faith in me. Then I turned to place the box on the nightstand.

"Thanks," I said. I knew what a cellphone was, but I didn't know how to use one. I hoped there wasn't a big learning curve.

"I want you to keep it with you wherever you go..."

A flash of pink caught my eye outside the window, and Rowan's words filtered into the background as he continued.

I watched the movement making its way through the trees, finally appearing on the small lawn between the tree line and the house. The pink turned out to be Yuti's hat, a baseball cap with her dark ponytail pulled through the back. Yuti looked over at the man accompanying her, her face lighting up as she laughed at something he said. She reached out and gave him a joking push, to no effect.

A tingle ran over my skin, and my heart gave one hard thump as I stared at the man my sister-in-law walked with. He was taller than Yuti—though most people were—with the lithe build of a surfer. His brown hair was warm and sun-kissed as the summer breeze played in it. A dimple peeked out from the side of his mouth as he gave Yuti a tight-lipped smile, all the more striking because of his high cheekbones and sharp chin. I couldn't tell the color of his hooded eyes, but I very much wanted to know.

"Who's that?" I asked my brother, only barely aware that I'd interrupted whatever he was saying.

He moved to stand beside me and looked out the window. "Oh, that's Adrian, Yuti's best friend. Lia will be telling you all about him when she gives you the rundown."

I smiled in appreciation of the beautiful human. *I don't think I'll have any trouble adjusting to this realm after all.* "I'd rather find out about him myself, thanks." And with an excited flutter in my stomach, I made for the bedroom door just as Yuti and Adrian entered the house.

Rowan rushed after me. "Uh, maybe you should wait up here. Lia still has a lot to explain!" he called as I bounded down the stairs.

Right when my bare feet hit the cool wood of the ground floor, I froze. I was still getting used to all the sights and smells in the realm of origin and hadn't yet memorized the scent of each of Lia's pack. But just as I recognized Yuti's unique sweet and spicy, just as I clocked the new hints of hay and bergamot, a much darker scent smothered all the rest.

Earth. Soil, rich and damp.

Vampire.

Every bit of reason—of self—flew from my mind, and I was left with only one word: *protect*. I clenched my jaw, my limbs seizing involuntarily. Fabric tore as my snarl echoed in the front hall. Never before had I shifted on instinct, no thought put into the action...but I did now.

I surged forward, knocking into the hall table beside me. A vase tipped over, water spilling into my fur, followed by a crash as it hit the floor behind me.

Less than a second later, I was in the dining room, the vampire staring at me wide-eyed from the other side of the table. My muscles bunched to spring.

"Adrian, run!" Lia barked.

The vampire took off, heading for the back door.

I lunged to the left, my nails slipping on the floor as I tried to close the distance. But just when I rounded the table, a heavy weight piled onto me.

I twisted and writhed, trying to escape the two sets of arms that grabbed at me.

"Enough!" Lia commanded from across the room, her voice laced with alpha power.

The pressure I'd felt upon first arriving in Lia's territory became heavy and almost unbearable—the crushing weight of an established alpha's command.

Lia walked over to where Ashwin and Rowan held me down. She knelt, her eyes blazing with power as they burned into mine. "I can see we have a lot of work to do."

My lungs fought to expand against the steel in her voice, and my jaws snapped together while I still struggled to pursue my prey.

*M*y limbs shook like I was shivering from intense cold as I paced the backyard of the main house. I could still smell the vampire. His damp earth scent—accompanied by the tangy smell of his fear—filled my nose as if he were right beside me as opposed to watching me from the other side of the screen door, four werewolves and a human in between us.

"You're just going to have to get used to him," Lia called from the porch, her arms crossed over her chest. She was the last wolf I'd have to get through if I wanted to take a bite out of him.

I scowled. "Why would I have to do that? What's he even doing here?"

Rowan, Ashwin, and Noire flinched at the steel in my voice, but Lia was entirely unaffected.

"Do you want to learn how to be an alpha from me?" Lia raised an eyebrow at me.

"Of course, I do!" I snapped. I wasn't trying to be rude, but I didn't seem to have control over the rage rushing through my veins.

"Then you'll follow my orders. We don't hurt Adrian. He's too important."

I growled. *How could that thing possibly be important? Why is everyone so calm about all this?*

My brother frowned at me, and I'd never seen such worry in his eyes while looking at me. "There's a lot you don't know, Willow. Adrian is doing very important research. And we watch him carefully to make sure all of the humans are safe."

My eyes flicked to the vampire. He flinched under my gaze, frowning but standing his ground. Yuti stood beside him, her arm wrapped around his waist as if her small human body would be any sort of protection from me.

"Yeah? What could be so important?" I didn't take my eyes off Adrian, and he froze, seemingly trying not to activate my chase instincts.

"Adrian is trying to prove that vampires were created by the fae," Lia's beta, Ashwin, said.

I stilled, my eyes widening as I sucked in a breath. "What was that?"

Lia nodded. "He's right. Adrian still needs to uncover more details, but from what we can tell, vampires were created by the fae."

"That can't be true! That would mean…"

"It would mean that the fae created vampires, then lied to the werewolves in order to effectively enslave them to have them act as guard dogs," Adrian murmured.

My mind whirled at his words. I felt like I'd been hit over the head, and at that moment, another scent reached me—a faint undertone that was hard to pick up against the strong smell of terrified vampire…hay and bergamot.

"So you see?" Lia continued. "You'll just have to get used to him. He's far too valuable."

"Gee, thanks," Adrian muttered.

Yuti gave me a weak smile. "Besides, he's my best friend, and he's just as human as he is vampire."

I let out a heavy sigh. This was crazy. Out of all the things I'd expected upon coming to the human realm, having to play nice with a vampire—or half-vampire, as it were—hadn't even occurred to me. But if what they said was true, then this really was an extenuating circumstance.

"I'm sorry I tried to kill you," I mumbled, wrapping my arms around myself. It was humiliating enough that I'd lost control of my instincts. But having to apologize to a vampire was a new low for me.

He didn't say anything.

Yuti nudged him with her elbow.

He sighed long and loud. "Yeah, sure. We all make mistakes."

Mistakes? Kind of a strong word for trying to kill your mortal enemy. But I let it slide. I wanted to stay here, and it was clear learning to deal with Adrian was one of Lia's stipulations for training me.

"Good," Lia declared with a nod of approval. But as she turned to go back inside, she put a hand on Ashwin's shoulder. "Don't leave them alone. Just in case."

Ashwin accepted his orders with a nod, and from then on, he kept his word.

Over the months that followed, Adrian and I were never allowed to be alone. There were always at least two other wolves present when we were around each other.

I knew that the practice was for his safety, but it didn't take long to annoy me. I got used to his scent and my urge to rip his throat out. Still, whenever he met my eyes, the smell of his fear would reappear, and I would be reminded of the lack of control I couldn't seem to live down.

"Um, Willow?" Coral peeked into the stock room, and the number I was about to write down on the inventory list flew from my mind.

I glanced over at the younger woman. When I met her olive eyes, she quickly lowered her gaze and ruffled her ginger hair into her face. I stifled a sigh. The Rapids Café's newest project was still skittish around me, and I didn't want my frustration making it worse.

"Yes, Coral?" I asked nicely.

Despite my best efforts, she flinched. "Well...I filled the bucket with hot water and cleaner like you asked me to, but...I think I put in too much soap because the bubbles overflowed, and I can't seem to clean them up."

I stared at her. And the longer I did, the more upset she got. Her anxiety crashed into me like the waves of a turbulent ocean. Taking a slow breath in through my nose, I held it and counted three heartbeats before letting it out steadily through my mouth, blowing her feelings from my mind with the puff of air.

The exercise Lia had been teaching me over the last year and a half worked, and the only emotions left in me were my own.

"Coral, you've been here for almost a month now, and I've shown you how much detergent to put into the bucket multiple times already," I said reasonably.

Coral's lip quivered, and her eyes filled with tears. "I know. I'm sorry," she whimpered. "I don't think I'm cut out for the human realm. Maybe I should just go back to Faerie."

The longer she talked, the more hysterical her voice became.

I put my clipboard on the shelf next to the bags of sugar and approached the younger wolf. "Listen," I soothed her, "I'm not saying all that. You know how tough it is for us to get the hang of living here. That's why Camille and Andi started this internship program. Don't you think they'll be disappointed if you leave without giving it your all?"

Coral sniffled and nodded.

"I don't want to upset you, but you need to learn to do this stuff yourself. So I'll finish everything else that needs doing to close for the night, but I'm going to have to insist that you clean up the mess yourself. All right? If I keep doing it for you, you won't learn."

Coral didn't respond.

"Okay?" I asked gently.

She nodded.

"Good. So let's get this done before Camille and Andi come back from their date night."

Following Coral out of the stock room, I halted at the threshold. The kitchen was a disaster. Fluffy, white suds overflowed from the sink onto the counters and floor. It was clear that Coral had tried, and failed miserably, to clean up the soap bubbles because they were splattered in places they couldn't have reached on their own. Tufts of foam were smeared onto the glass display case and into the trash can. I looked up, tilting my head in awe.

How did she manage to get it on the ceiling?

Even with me helping with everything else, we left an hour later than usual. Once again, I bemoaned Camille and Andi making me a shift manager. But I didn't wonder why. I knew that they'd conspired with Lia, that together they thought placing me in such a position while I learned to control my alpha power was the quickest way for me to complete my training. And it didn't hurt that the unclaimed werewolves under me couldn't really help but want to follow my lead.

After locking the door behind me, I wished Coral a good-night. She went around to the back of the building, where a set of stairs led up to Camille and Andi's apartment.

I pulled my winter coat closer, shoving my chilled hands into my pockets for the short walk to my vehicle. The truck I shared with the Northern Pack, one of the few owned by the ski resort, screeched as it sputtered to life. It liked these freezing tempera-tures about as much as I did.

I shivered while I waited for the cab to warm up, my teeth chattering as puffs of air hissed from my lips. This was the part I hated most about staying with the Northern Pack. Though I didn't harp on them or give them voice, I had tons of complaints: not getting much time to myself, working in customer service, and training as an alpha were all pains. But the winter cold was the absolute worst.

Still, when spring did come, I would have the wildflowers to look forward to. I let that thought cheer me and hoped tomorrow would be just a little warmer, though January in a mountain town meant that was highly unlikely.

The light in the upstairs apartment turned on.

"I wonder if she'll make it," I muttered to myself.

Unlike some of the other interns I'd worked with at the café, Coral was by far the most absent-minded. I was surprised she hadn't just outed herself and all of werewolf kind to the humans in the short time she'd been here. She was sweet and kind, but her head was full of rocks.

How did she even manage to see a fae through her awakening? She must have lived in a very well-protected area of Faerie. I couldn't imagine she would have survived in a border town where there was always the threat of a vampire slipping through a portal.

Breathing hot air onto my fingers, I glanced at the dashboard clock, cheering a little at how late it was. If I was lucky, Grant would be the only one awake once I reached the secluded ski resort. I put the truck into gear and started to make my way home.

The roads were white with packed snow, lined by the naked trees of winter. Now that the cab was nice and warm, I could appreciate the beautiful view. A snowy road winding through the foothills, a waxing moon enchanting the scene with glittering magic. I longed to be a part of it and vowed to brave the cold tomorrow to do just that. My daily walks had gone untread as of late. I bundled up from head to toe, but the moment I felt the slightest goose bump, I lost my nerve and retreated inside. I could have gone out in wolf form, of course—the cold wouldn't bother me at all with my thick fur—but it was too risky to go in the daytime, and I was generally too tired from work to go out at night.

Once I'd arrived, I made my way into the main house. The porch lights of the resort's cabins twinkled, dyeing the snow a warm gold in the distance. With the lift's lights off, the stars were clear and bright overhead. I still didn't slow down to admire them; I shuffled my boots on the walk as quickly as I could while still being wary of any ice the salt crystals might have missed.

I smiled when I entered the hushed hall. *As expected.* Quietly, I made my way to the living room, where I found Grant reading on the couch.

He looked up at me as I entered, his gray eyes glowing in the firelight.

"Hey," I greeted him softly, not wanting to wake the rest of the pack.

"Long night?" he asked. Fine lines formed around his mouth as he smiled at me.

I nodded, removing my winter things and sitting on the other end of the couch.

"Rowan called. He wanted me to tell you to turn on your phone."

Of course he did. I focused my attention on the hearth fire. It wasn't that I didn't miss my brother or that I didn't want to talk to him. It was that I didn't like my cellphone. It made me feel like I wasn't in control of my own time and environment. I could be interrupted or redirected at any given moment. I couldn't fully enjoy where I was or what I was doing in the present knowing there was an intrusion box in my pocket.

"Okay. Thanks."

With nothing else to say, Grant and I fell into a comfortable silence. Most nights were like this for us. He usually stayed up late, well past the park crew who had to clean up after the last run of the night. Knowing his natural tendencies, Lia had made him the night clerk—not that the tiny resort needed a night clerk, but it didn't hurt to have someone awake and ready to help the few guests. For me, this was the only time I could find to unwind and be alone...well, mostly alone anyway.

But in a pack, one never really got to be alone, as demonstrated by my evenings with Grant. That was the point of a pack. And one of the many reasons I would never lead one.

4

I found my phone charger shoved into a desk drawer when I retreated to my room for the night. The moonlight was so bright through my window that I could easily see the socket behind my nightstand, not that my werewolf eyes needed much help. I couldn't remember the last time I'd plugged the device in.

It took a few minutes before the screen came on, bright and blinding in the dark room. The phone carrier's startup sound was way too loud, and I clenched my jaw, certain the noise had awoken the entire pack. I hurriedly pressed the button to put it on silent as one message after another popped up on the screen. Texts, emails, voicemails, and missed calls—all from Rowan— flashed insistently.

I sighed and called my voicemail first.

"You have ten new voice messages," the computer's voice informed me. "First message: 'Willow? It's Rowan. Why isn't your phone on? I've called you like five times, and it keeps going straight to voicemail. Are you even charging it?'"

My brother's voice continued to nag at me until the message cut him off. I patiently listened to the rest of the messages. They were all the same. He was annoyed that I wasn't answering his text messages, that I wasn't looking at the pictures of his and Yuti's trip around the country while she traveled to conventions and fairs for her art.

He knew I was all right from talking to Lia and her pack members—just like I knew he and Yuti were all right because Lia had told me—but that didn't stop him from worrying.

I frowned at myself, plopping onto my bed, the springs squeaking softly under my weight. I couldn't promise to keep the phone on all the time, but I vowed to try to remember to charge it and carry it with me. It was a small inconvenience to make my brother feel better, though I didn't know how much he would appreciate my effort. He would likely still be annoyed when I didn't answer.

I opened the text messenger and shook my head. There were messages going back weeks, everything from little updates to demands that I answer him to pictures of their travels.

Even from just skimming, I could feel how happy Rowan and Yuti were, and my heart warmed at seeing their smiling faces. Yuti's hair had grown even in the time she'd been gone. I knew she'd been trying to grow it out for a while, and I told myself to compliment her on how good it looked when I saw her next.

I lay down on my bed, angling my neck to be able to see the screen while the phone was plugged in, and started reading from the beginning. Eventually, my eyes began to burn. I turned off the phone and put it on my nightstand to finish charging. I'd look at the rest tomorrow.

The winter wind howled like my ancestors outside the little mountain cabin. The windows rattled, and the wood creaked. I couldn't hear the bell, which hung around the neighbor's goat—a bell I could hear on still, quiet nights, even as far away as it was.

Despite the blowing snow and freezing wind, I didn't feel the bite of winter's cold. A cheery fire flickered in the hearth, easing down from the blaze of hours before. My eyes lost focus as I watched the dancing flames from my cozy bed, heavy blankets piled atop me.

A pleasant tingle ran through me as someone nuzzled my neck from behind, the warmth of his chest burning my back while his strong arms held me to him.

"Are you awake?" he whispered, his breath tickling my ear.

I smiled a sleepy, satisfied smile and hummed to tell him that I was.

"Are you feeling all right?"

I felt good, better than I could ever remember feeling. And it wasn't just the languid gratification my body felt from our thorough lovemaking. I felt full—whole—the golden thread of our mate bond singing like a string plucked. My world was everything it should be, and I needed nothing more than him to be near me.

What had my life been like before him? Had I even had a life before him? I must have. But whenever I thought of it, it seemed as though I was watching a film of someone else's story. I could place names to emotions, but I couldn't remember feeling anything.

"How could I be anything else when I'm with you?" I asked.

He tightened his arms around me.

I reached up and slipped my hand into his soft hair, arching my back to press my ass against his cock.

He let out a shaky breath as a shudder ran through him.

I smirked, but the smile didn't last long. He trailed his fingertips down my torso at a maddeningly slow rate. With every inch, my body warmed until I was trembling with anticipation. I wiggled against him—his dick jumping as it grew. I couldn't help but let out a small whimper when he teased me, so close now.

And, as always, he didn't disappoint. I gasped and jerked when his fingers finally found the sweet spot between my legs.

"Say my name," he whispered, hot in my ear.

I moaned, my mind spinning—too fuzzy to form words. I

looked back at him. I knew how much he liked to see my face when I came.

The dim light from the fire made his eyes glow.

I raised my voice while he continued to stroke. "Ah —Adrian!"

5

_____

I was jolted awake when a shattering sound crashed through the house. My eyes flew open as my heart hammered in my chest. A flurry of sounds mingled in my ears.

"Sorry," I heard Braylyn's cracked voice mumble from downstairs in the kitchen.

"It's fine, honey," Lia told her son. "You're not hurt, are you? Good. Please, go get a broom."

I immediately relaxed my tensed muscles. Braylyn breaking or bumping into something was practically an everyday occurrence. The teen had experienced a major growth spurt in his human form the last few months, and he wasn't quite used to his new body yet.

I looked at the wall near the window. The complete lack of light told me it wasn't even close to sunrise, and the clock said it wouldn't be for another hour and a half.

I groaned. I didn't want to be up this early. But as I stared into the darkness, images and sensations from my dream resurfaced.

What the hell was that? I'm having sex dreams about Adrian now?

I blew out a heavy breath. The whole thing was outrageous

and more than a little uncomfortable. Sure, I'd thought Adrian was attractive the first time I'd seem him, but that was before I knew what he was. And even though I'd overcome my instinct to kill him, I wasn't about to forget anytime soon—not that he'd let me forget. Every time he saw me, even though we still weren't allowed to be alone, he reeked of fear.

It's clearly been too long since I've had a good romp. I frowned. *Has it really been three years since I attended the Wolf Moon Festival?* Counting on my fingers, I cringed at the thought. That was right. The last time I'd tested out a potential mate had been a few months before I'd found out I was an alpha.

Even so, am I so desperate that I'm dreaming about sex with a vampire?

I pushed away the reminder that I'd thought Adrian was attractive. It appeared my body and subconscious mind were hungry for someone. I tried to shove my lingering desire aside, but his voice still whispered in my ear. *"Say my name."*

I gritted my teeth. *It was just a dream. It's not like it was actually him.*

I closed my eyes, picturing the scene. I could still see it all so clearly: I could see the fire, hear the wind, and feel his fingers stroking me. I trembled as if he were still with me.

I wanted someone to touch me, needed it.

Thinking that, I tried to imagine something else—someone else—so that I might relieve myself. But I couldn't seem to get Adrian out of my head.

I wanted to go back to sleep, but I was too keyed up, and I wasn't about to touch myself with Adrian still whispering in my ear.

Sighing, I stared fixedly at the thick sweatpants and hoodie folded over the back of my desk chair. I wished I was able to wear pajamas without getting tangled in them from tossing and turning in my sleep. The warm clothes were too far away to reach from the bed even if I wiggled down to the other side.

Tentatively, I slithered my hand out from under my covers,

then immediately pulled it back with a whimper. It would be cold again today.

Bracing myself, I thrust the blankets from my nearly naked form, my underwear doing absolutely nothing to protect my bare skin from the cold.

With a long hiss, I pulled on my clothes as fast as I could, promising myself that I would keep them under the blankets with me from now on. I stuffed my feet into the light-up unicorn slippers Yuti had gotten me for my birthday and let out one big shiver.

At least the cold had done a good job of rooting me firmly into the waking world; it didn't do a bad job of cooling my leftover lust either.

I knew everyone would be at breakfast, though some pack members didn't live on-site and weren't there at the moment. Still, I tried to avoid going anywhere the pack was gathered all at once. The fact of the matter was that I was in another alpha's territory. As kind and understanding as Lia was, her instincts told her I was a threat. And the closer I came to completing my training, the more of a threat I posed. She would never say that aloud, but I could feel how uneasy she got when I entered a space where the pack was gathered. So, as a courtesy to her, I worked late and ate at different times from the pack.

I made my way to the bathroom. This was the perfect time for a shower since everyone was still eating. As I stepped under the hot spray, I thought about what I needed to do that day. My weekly meeting with Lia, to evaluate how my training was going, wasn't for a few hours.

My mind drifted to the meeting I'd had with her the week before. She'd complimented me on how much I'd progressed in controlling my compulsion over other werewolves—the unclaimed in particular. But she was disappointed that I couldn't yet smell lies. She'd also told me to work on my shift speed. I wondered if she wasn't nitpicking at this point. How important was it to shift in two seconds or less? Could two seconds really make that big of a difference? I was still faster than all of the nonalphas in her pack. I had been practicing shifting back and forth between my wolf and human forms over the last week, but I didn't think I'd made any progress in that short amount of time.

At this point, I felt I had learned everything I needed to know about being an alpha. My training was complete. And as I slipped my arm out of the steamy shower to bring the towel in to me, I decided to tell Lia as much. She'd been a great teacher, and I appreciated everything she'd taught me. But I'd sacrificed my freedom to do things the "right" way for far too long.

I'd spent a year learning about how to live in the realm of origin because she hadn't thought I was ready to leave Faerie at the time. And I'd been staying with her for nearly a year and a half now. It was about time I struck out on my own and became the lone wolf I wanted to be, unfettered by the expectations of completing my rite, of leading a pack, of finding a mate and birthing pups.

I was ready to be my own being, free to go where I wanted when I wanted without having to answer to anyone, my only responsibility looking after myself.

I smiled as I hung up my towel. I was ready. Now I just needed to convince Lia of that fact, not that she could really stop me from leaving.

This wasn't Faerie, and there was no requirement that I get her to sign off on my training in an official capacity.

I frowned, turning on the blow dryer and tilting my head so my long, gray hair hung freely to one side. She couldn't stop me, but I wanted her approval. I wanted her assurance that I could make it on my own.

I only hoped that all the progress I'd made and the confidence with which I'd present my case would convince her.

6

_B_y the time I went downstairs, most of the pack had cleared out for the day, off to either school or work. Noire stood near the front door, pulling a knit hat over her black hair as I reached the landing.

"Good morning," I greeted her.

She glanced over at me. "Morning."

Noire's terse responses never bothered me. She wasn't one to speak much, and she hardly ever smiled. Rowan had warned me early on not to take offense, and I knew he and Noire had some sort of special understanding between them. But what my brother didn't know, couldn't know, was just how much pain Noire carried around with her. He wasn't an alpha.

While it was part of being an alpha to know what one's pack members were feeling and what they needed, it was unusual for an alpha to pick up on the emotions of another alpha's claimed wolf. But Noire's sorrow couldn't be avoided. I could hardly imagine how Lia dealt with it, let alone how Noire lived with it every moment of every day.

Even as her deep heartache seeped into me, I gently pushed it aside. There was nothing I could do for her, and I'd gathered from Lia that this was not a grief Noire wanted to share or even have acknowledged most of the time.

She pulled on her gloves and opened the door, a gust of freezing air blowing in.

I went to the kitchen to stuff down a granola bar for breakfast before returning to my bedroom. It took me fifteen minutes to sufficiently prepare to leave the house. I put on multiple layers under my coat before wrapping my thick scarf over my face and pulling on my hat and mittens. Then I shoved my feet into my snow boots and waddled downstairs.

It was annoying to have to prepare so much just to go outside when I could have simply shifted, but being careful was one of the costs of living in the realm of origin. As such, I didn't get nearly enough time in wolf form these days.

"Come on, Willow," I muttered to myself when I stood at the back door, staring out at the snow. "You promised yourself a walk, now go."

I shook myself and went out onto the porch before stomping into the path of virgin snow leading away from the house. The snow wasn't too deep, only just above my ankles, but I was glad I'd worn my snow boots so it wouldn't seep into my socks. No one liked cold, wet socks.

Once I'd committed to my walk, it was pleasant, especially as I got farther and farther into the forest and away from the resort. The crunch of the snow beneath my feet, the way the naked limbs of the oaks and maples twisted and mingled with the fluffy, laden evergreen boughs, and even the chill of the air on the skin around my eyes—the only skin not covered—was nice in its contrast to how cozy I was in my layers of wool and fleece.

I lifted one mittened hand to my mouth and pulled down my scarf, sputtering as I tried to get the knit fuzzies off my lip balm. The freezing air stung my nostrils when I took a breath, and I felt like I might sneeze. But then the feeling passed. The scent of the winter forest was completely different from that of summer. Under the mint-like feel of the cold, I could smell the fir, spruce, and pine. The ground was frozen and covered with a mask of wetness. I could smell a little of the musty damp of wet leaves. But mostly it was fresh and clean.

I smiled to myself, glad I'd decided to brave the weather. Then my nose started to run, so I covered it with my scarf again.

Farther along my route, not a designated trail but a path my feet already knew, I stopped at a fallen tree. It was a giant walnut, or had been before its demise. I don't know why it had cracked and toppled to one side, but it had been this way since before I'd ever come around. I brushed snow off a section near what used to be the top, which was now lying on the forest floor, and climbed up to take a seat.

The forest closed in around me, quiet and peaceful. I could hear the distant scratching and skittering of some small creature too far off to see and too downwind to smell, but the sounds only amplified the atmosphere. The sky hung low, gray clouds felted together like a fuzzy blanket.

And there I sat, not moving, not talking, not thinking of anything but the sensations of the present moment. I breathed, I blinked, I let my eyes lose focus, and I existed.

These were the times I liked the best, when I didn't have to worry about anything. All I needed to do was just be. My body took care of breathing, and my heart beat all on its own. I had no worries at all. No past. No future. Only this exact moment. Nothing bad could ever happen in the present. Those things were all future problems.

Tomorrow? The next hour? The next minute or second? That was all later. None of it was now.

Unfortunately, such a state wasn't sustainable in perpetuity, especially not in the real world, where I had to plan a little to maintain existence, such as making food to eat or getting enough sleep to work...and, currently, heading back so I wasn't late for my meeting with Lia.

Still, as I climbed down from my now very cold seat, I kept what I was doing at the moment in the front of my mind. Yes, I had decided to head back so I could be on time for my meeting. But that was already the past. Now I was thinking about each step I took toward the house, each scent I smelled, each sound I heard, each breeze I felt. It wasn't something that I could keep up for very long, but even a few minutes a day could nourish my soul and fortify me to deal with the rest of the world and its expectations of me. Because in these present moments, there wasn't even a me to expect anything of.

Who was Willow but a compilation of past experiences and future aspirations? Who was anyone?

I found that sort of thought comforting. So many things had lived and died well before me. I wasn't special. I didn't have to be anything extraordinary, no matter what others said. I could live quietly and then be forgotten. Because, in my view, even recorded history had expectations for us all, and that was far too much pressure for any one person to live up to.

But, regardless of my personal opinions, others did have expectations of me. There wasn't anything I could do about that. However, if they were disappointed when I didn't live up to those expectations that they formed for me purely on their own... Well, that wasn't my problem.

7

I was halfway between the tree line and the back door when the snow's crisp scent turned warm and moist like the soil of a freshly watered garden. I looked in the direction of the new scent just as Adrian's violet eyes met mine.

At that moment, I saw the Adrian from my dream, his eyes glowing in the firelight as he asked me to say his name.

"A-Adrian." My face flushed, and my heart leapt into my throat, causing me to stumble over my greeting. I groaned internally at my reaction to his sudden appearance. *What are you getting so flustered about? It's not like he knows you had a sex dream about him. Just forget about it.*

His half-vampire scent—having the hints of wet earth but lacking those of decay—soured in fear.

I frowned, and my heart sank. *I guess he's still afraid of me then.* The reality of the situation washed over me, but I was grateful to be pulled back from the awkwardness the dream had elicited.

He glanced over his shoulder at the back door, some ten feet away, much too far if he was hoping to outrun me.

"Are you here to see Ashwin?" I asked.

"No, I came to water Yuti's ivy plant."

I snorted into my scarf. *I may not be able to smell lies yet, but he's not fooling any wolf with that front.*

I might have believed that he wasn't afraid with his smooth response; his tone didn't betray anything but politeness. But the stench of his fear was unmistakable.

I looked at him more carefully. His violet eyes appeared all the more striking due to the dark circles under them. His brown hair had grown long enough to curl around the hem of his knit hat, though he'd swept his too-long bangs to one side in order to see. He even had a shadow of stubble on his face. I couldn't tell whether he'd lost weight because of the bulk of his winter coat, but I knew he'd at least be consuming the amount of blood he needed to stay in control.

He hasn't been taking care of himself. How hard have we been working him? Yuti isn't going to be happy about this.

Adrian's was a tenuous relationship with the Northern Pack; he wasn't quite a prisoner, and he wasn't quite free either. They needed his extensive research, and he needed their financial support to continue that research, not to mention that they weren't about to let a half-vampire roam around their territory unmonitored. Still, everyone tried to keep the relationship civil and productive, at the very least for Yuti's sake.

Just as I was about to make small talk and ask him if he was glad his best friend was returning from her trip soon — we were likely the two people who'd missed Yuti and Rowan the most after all — Ashwin slid the door open with a jerk. His panicked gaze flicked between Adrian and me, and he stepped outside without even bothering to put on a coat.

Adrian let out a little sigh of relief, his shoulders relaxing.

"Going out to Yuti's studio, Adrian? I'll go with you," Ashwin said.

I gave the pack's beta a wry glance, but he didn't so much as flinch.

I stifled my sigh. *I suppose I'll never live my lack of control down.*

I started toward the house again; it was clear there would be no exchange of pleasantries between Adrian and me for a while.

Both of the men tensed at my movement, and Ashwin quickly placed himself between us.

I rolled my eyes and clicked my tongue. "Oh, come on. I'm fine. Jeez," I muttered as I stomped the rest of the way to the house.

You lunge at a vampire one time, and you're in the doghouse forever.

After tapping the snow from my boots, I went upstairs and removed most of my many layers. Then I returned downstairs to eat before my meeting with Lia. When I'd been in Faerie, breakfast had always been my biggest meal of the day. But since I'd come to stay here, and didn't want to eat with the pack, an early lunch was usually my main meal.

I opened the refrigerator and settled for leftovers: meatloaf, mashed potatoes, gravy, and maple-glazed carrots. And to top it all off, I had a cup of chocolate pudding. Eating was such a sensory pleasure, even leftovers. There were so many smells, textures, and tastes to get lost in. And I had to admit humans were particularly talented at crafting sweets. Though the food in Faerie was likely far more delicious objectively, I didn't miss it. There were too many new things to try; I couldn't be sad about what wasn't there.

Ashwin returned while I was washing my dishes.

"You didn't need to do that," I said, not even looking over as he passed by the counter.

He didn't respond for a moment, which told me he was thinking carefully about what to say. "Lia hasn't given us the all-clear yet. We can't afford to take chances."

A flash of anger rushed through me, and my face flushed. *I said I was fine. Why won't anyone take my word for it?*

But the irritation was gone as quickly as it had come. *It's because I'm not their alpha. They don't trust me the way they trust her word.*

The only indication Ashwin gave that he'd even registered my indignation was the slight widening of his eyes. He didn't take a step back or look away. I could see why he was Lia's beta. As frivolous and silly as he usually seemed on the outside, he was quite hardy, and he had that loyalty every good beta has.

I dipped my head at his words, acknowledging them. "How is that going—the search for the origin of vampires? Does Adrian have any proof it was the fae yet?" The very question felt strange on my tongue. To think that the fae had betrayed the werewolves so thoroughly...it was still too much for me to wrap my head around.

Ashwin shook his head. "I've borrowed every book from Faerie he's asked for that I could reasonably get ahold of. None of them seem to have what he's looking for. But we knew that could be a long shot to begin with. If the fae created vampires, they wouldn't just have that information lying about in some corner bookstore or local library, would they? Otherwise, we'd all have known about it already."

"Right. But is there nothing? No clues at all?" I turned off the water and dried my hands on a dishtowel.

Ashwin shrugged. "He's asked Lia to gather the alphas for a meeting. I don't know what he's found, but he has something he wants to say to them."

8

I knocked on the door to the study at exactly the time of our scheduled meeting, and Lia called for me to come in not a moment later.

Straightening my spine, I entered the space. She stood in front of an armchair. The stack of papers on her desk farther into the room had grown, and I wondered if we shouldn't reschedule our meeting because of her increased workload.

I met her eyes straight on, then dipped my head and lowered my gaze, showing deference to the fact that I was a guest in her territory.

"Good morning, Willow," she said kindly.

"Good morning," I returned, looking up again as she smiled at me.

Lia sat in the armchair, and I sat on the nearby couch, but I didn't relax.

She tilted her head, her sandy hair rippling as she did so. "Something on your mind?"

I frowned. Even without Lia being my alpha, she knew me quite well at this point. There would be no hiding that I had something to say. *Now is my chance.* "Yes, there's something I want to say before we get started today."

"All right." Her tone didn't give away her thoughts.

I lifted my head, meeting her eyes. "I think I'm ready to be a lone alpha," I declared, pleased that my voice sounded confident but not frustrated or arrogant.

She didn't say anything, nor did her expression.

"I know I haven't mastered everything," I continued. "But I think I know enough to be on my own. If I was trying to lead a pack, maybe I'd want to stay longer. But since that isn't the case, I don't see that it's necessary. And…"

Lia raised an eyebrow. "And?"

"And I think you can feel that the tension between us is growing. The closer I get to being fully trained, the more our instincts tell us we're at odds living in the same territory." Over the last few months, that pressure I'd felt upon arriving in Lia's territory had gotten more and more bothersome. I was starting to feel uneasy.

Lia sat unmoving for a moment, then dipped her head slightly. "That's true. I'm pleased you're even picking up on that. It tells me a lot about what you've learned so far."

"So…?" I asked hopefully. "I don't want to seem ungrateful, Lia. I appreciate everything you've taught me and everything you've done for me and my brother and Yuti as well. You're a great alpha and a wonderful pack leader. And, out of respect for that, I'd like your blessing."

Lia sighed through her nose, and a tendril of dread clenched my stomach.

"I still think you have a lot to learn if I'm being honest. But I hear what you're saying. And perhaps my desire to make sure you're the very best you can be before you strike out on your own has made me slow your training and departure a bit longer than I should have."

I held my breath.

She frowned, pausing in a silence that seemed to drag out.

"All right, Willow. How about this? Let's have a test. The

Wolf Moon Festival in Faerie is next week, right? Ashwin mentioned that he was thinking of attending. As a wolf raised in the realm of origin, I've never been, but it's my understanding that there's a gathering of alphas there. Is that correct?"

I nodded. "It's more an event for bound wolves and nonalphas to find mates, but yeah, at least some alphas go every year. The Wolf Council goes and any alphas who are looking for successors. And younger alphas who have completed their training and are looking for packs in need of a successor also go."

"I thought as much. So there will be other alphas as well as many claimed and unclaimed nonalphas. If you can go to the festival and hold your own—not be swayed by the presence of alphas much older and more established than you while properly controlling your impact over the nonalphas—if you can stand firm within yourself without being influenced, then I'll give you my blessing."

I wanted to throw my head back and groan. I didn't *want* to go to the Wolf Moon Festival. I couldn't search for a mate there now that I was an alpha—no alpha could. And I knew that any alphas wanting successors would try to convince me to stay and take over their packs. That wasn't even considering all of the unclaimed wolves who may take it into their heads that they wanted me to be their alpha.

I frowned. Despite all that, this was my chance to prove to Lia I was ready, and I didn't know how many months of extra training it would cost me if I didn't take this opportunity to prove myself.

"Agreed," I said with a sharp nod.

Lia smiled. "Excellent."

I sighed, but I didn't quite feel the relief I'd hoped for, and likely wouldn't until I'd completed this final test.

With that settled, Lia changed the subject. "I don't know how involved you're planning on being with the wolves in the realm of origin. Even as a lone alpha, you're entitled to input when the other alphas gather. Of course, your opinions don't carry as much weight as leaders of packs, but that's to be expected."

I thought about it. "I may want to be more involved later on, but right now, I just want some time to be myself—by myself."

Though she nodded as if she understood, I couldn't imagine she did. Lia not only had that alpha drive to lead, she also had that nurturing personality that wanted to take care of everyone.

Now that she mentioned alpha gatherings though, I was reminded of what Ashwin had said. "I heard Adrian has called for a meeting of the alphas. What's going on with that?"

"I'm not entirely sure, but I've sent an email to all of the alphas who've been following this closely. We're going to have a video conference next week. You're welcome to join us if you'd like, especially if you're a lone alpha by then."

Adrian's declaration that vampires had been created by fae had been as earth-shattering to me as to all of the other wolves. Of course I was interested in how his research was progressing. But unlike the others involved, I had to hear everything second-hand since I wasn't really allowed around Adrian. This was the first time I'd been invited to this type of meeting for that reason, so I wasn't about to miss it.

"Thanks," I answered. "I'll be there."

My meeting with Lia gave me a lot to think about, and I carefully considered the challenge she presented as I left her office.

To hold my own with the other alphas, I would need to project just the right amount of my own alpha power—not so much that they would take it as a threat, but not so little that they thought they could influence me. I also needed to consider the social pressures, which were different from the alpha powers at play but nearly as influential.

I wasn't as worried about being bombarded by unclaimed wolves looking for an alpha. Their drive to find a mate would far outweigh any pull they felt toward me. And, given the norms of how wolves joined packs in Faerie, dealing with unclaimed wolves was a far bigger problem in the realm of origin.

As the Northern Pack began gathering for lunch, I went upstairs to my room. I still had a couple of hours before my shift at the café.

Once I was sitting on my bed, I looked around my space. Most everything wasn't mine. I didn't have any knickknacks or personal decorations. All the furniture had already been there when I arrived. I didn't even have a computer, just the cellphone Rowan had given me. When I left, it would be with a suitcase of clothes and the sketchpad I used for my pressed flowers.

The impact of that thought settled into me as I sat in a space not really my own.

I don't belong here. Where will I go when I'm finally free?

The possibilities were endless. Well, not endless. I'd have to either travel from territory to territory—asking permission to stay from the alpha who claimed it—or I could settle in an unclaimed territory. I wouldn't need a large territory since I wouldn't have a pack. My heart glowed as my options floated up in my mind. I hadn't really thought about them until now. It had seemed best to concentrate on the step I was currently working on: completing my alpha training. But now that the end was so near, I let my imagination roam.

Would I want to stay close by, so I could see Rowan and Yuti whenever I wanted? Or perhaps I would travel for a while and settle down later. Only a small portion of my wages from the café went toward the pack fund to cover the cost of my stay, so I'd been able to save quite a bit of money. How far would it get me?

9

"I'm sorry you have to make a second trip," I said to Ashwin from the passenger seat of his truck. We'd been driving for a while but hadn't had a moment of silence until now.

"It's not a problem," he replied.

It was a shame he couldn't just come with me. Even though he was planning to go to the Wolf Moon Festival, which started the following day, I had to head to Faerie the day before. The alphas always made this big entrance at the festival. They gathered the day prior at a wolf mystic monastery nearby so they could all arrive together. Personally, I thought they just wanted more time to show off amongst themselves, but there was probably some alpha business to discuss.

In any case, Ashwin couldn't come with me to the monastery. Like other nonalphas attending the festival, he'd arrive at the caverns the following day, which meant that he had to drive me all the way to the portal today and have someone drop him off the next day. I supposed he could have stayed the night in Faerie, but he was being weird about leaving Lia for three whole days as it was. This was the busy season for the resort, and she had a full plate even without dealing with a half-vampire living in her territory.

"So where do you think you'll go once you pass Lia's test?" he asked.

It never failed to amuse me how different Ashwin was from his sister. Noire never felt the need to fill up space with talk when we could just as easily enjoy quiet. I wondered if people thought Rowan and I were similar or different.

"I'm not sure yet," I answered, then changed the subject. "Why did you decide to go to the festival this year?"

Ashwin grinned a suggestive little smile. "You don't believe I'm just looking for a mate?"

I stared at him for a moment. "Are you?"

"Sure, I am. It's not so easy to find a wolf mate in the realm of origin, what with us having to hide from the humans. Plus, there just aren't tons of us here, and it's a much bigger space. Getting involved with a human comes with a lot of risk. And I completed my rite in Faerie, so why shouldn't I take advantage of the perks?"

I quirked an eyebrow. "And...?"

Ashwin shrugged. "If I also happen to gather some information about what's going on with the wolves in Faerie, so much the better."

I snorted. "Your partner is going to feel neglected."

His grin returned. "Oh, I'm a very good multitasker."

I chuckled, shaking my head.

Because the portal nearest to the resort required a few miles of hiking both on- and off-trail in the snow-buried mountains, Ashwin had to take me to another portal farther away. As with most portals between the realms, it was in the wilderness. But this one was easier to get to in the winter, even if it was a pain to use.

Pulling off to the side of the road, Ashwin put the truck in park and turned to me. "You got everything?"

I nodded. "Yep. So we'll meet on Wednesday morning at the depot, right? Then we can make our way back together?"

"Right. Someone will be here to pick us up."

I unbuckled my seat belt, pulled my hat tighter over my ears, and adjusted my scarf to cover my nose and mouth. "Got it." Gloves on, I grabbed my backpack and the rope, which sat on the seat between us, before climbing out of the truck. "Good luck," I told Ashwin. "I hope you find whatever you're looking for."

Ashwin grinned that easy grin of his. "You too. See you in a few days."

I closed the door.

I didn't bother watching as Ashwin turned around on the deserted road to head back home, instead starting into the trees. The thick pines surrounding me meant that most of the snow had never reached the ground. I spent more time dodging limbs than stomping through piles. Not a hundred yards from the road, I came upon a wide hole in the ground, some fifteen feet across. At the bottom of the open-ceiling cave lay a thick blanket of leaves untouched by snow.

After hiding my cellphone—which I'd made sure to charge in accordance with my promise to my brother—in the hollow of a thick oak, I took the rope and tied it securely around the trunk, just as Ashwin had shown me, then shown me again, and finally made me show him five times. Then I grabbed the rope with my gloves and backed up toward the opening.

With my toes on the ground and my heels hanging off, I looked over my shoulder. I really hated this portal, but I hated trudging miles through the snow and ice more.

"Here we go," I muttered to myself before springing backward.

The rope slowed my fall but did nothing to stop my stomach from rolling as the ground on the other side of the veil spit me out. I grunted when I hit the ground, then lay there staring up at the gray skies of Faerie. With a sigh, I sat up and tried not to look at the rope standing straight up from the smooth ground. It was too freaky, knowing the world had turned upside down; it made my head spin just glancing at the rope.

I staggered to my feet, pointing myself toward town. Even in Faerie, it was cold this time of year, though this region wasn't nearly as cold as where I'd just come from. There was no snow on the ground here, but it was dry and frozen. I took off my gloves and hat and shoved them into my pockets. I loosened my scarf as well but didn't remove it.

The border town's depot was a mile's hike away from the portal, but I didn't mind in this warmer weather. I didn't bother stopping at the post office for any messages, already knowing what any letters would say—they'd be pleas from Efren and my parents, begging me to come home and live the way they thought I should. I was too close to getting everything I wanted to deal with that, and I had my plate full with Lia's challenge.

The small depot wasn't nearly as busy as I'd expected it to be. There should have been tons of wolves arriving to take the place of the wolves here still bound to faelings, especially in a border town. Having someone fill in to protect the unawakened faelings was the only chance bound wolves had to find mates before they completed their rites. But the depot was empty except for the conductor.

I approached the fae. "Where is everyone?" I asked. "Surely, there are faelings in this town whose bondmates want to go to the festival."

The conductor tilted his head at my question. "Sure there are," he said. "We've had a few show up, but there aren't enough wolves to go around. It's all anyone can talk about these days." His eyebrows scrunched together as he eyed my human attire. "Where have you been?"

His words and their implications made me feel like I'd swallowed a rock. "I need transport to Louparest, please."

He stared at me another moment, and I wondered if he was going to refuse me service. "Step into the circle," he instructed with a jerk of his head.

There was a flash of yellow light, and I stood in another transportation circle in another depot. The new depot was much bigger than the one I'd left in the border town; this one had five permanent circles, but that was to be expected with it being so close to where the Wolf Moon Festival took place.

The depot was bustling, though not with new arrivals. Older werewolves flitted about decorating the space in expectation of tomorrow's event. Despite the place being busy, my arrival did cause a little stir. All the wolves in the large building froze and glanced at me. Such was the effect of an arriving alpha.

Their attention made my skin itch. I straightened my shoulders and stepped out of the circle, frowning. Thankfully, their eyes weren't directed at me for long. The moment they realized I wasn't one of their alphas, most of them went back to their tasks. One did not.

"Welcome," a female greeted me with a smile, bowing her head in respect. "You've come for the alpha gathering at the monastery?"

I nodded once, unable to muster a smile to mirror hers. Despite the wolves not focusing on me, their very presence affected me. These were not wolves I knew. Was that where this feeling was coming from? A little tug in my chest made me feel uneasy, like the anticipation just before one breaks into a sprint.

"Excellent," the woman said cheerfully. "If you'll just follow me, I'll give you directions to the monastery." She led me to the exit and stopped at the threshold.

Her directions were concise and simple: follow the road out of town, and I would eventually run into the monastery. I thanked her and left the depot as swiftly as I could without breaking into a run.

Outside, I released a long sigh. The little annoyance that hummed within me was still there, and I wondered if putting some distance between myself and the wolves in the depot would help. Taking a deep breath through my nose, the cold air tickling on its way in, I started down the stone road.

The paved surface of the road was mostly clear of snow. But as my foot slipped and I awkwardly stopped myself from falling, I discovered that there were still icy patches. I slowed my pace and took more careful steps forward.

The town of Louparest was small considering it was closest to both a monastery and the festival grounds, though not as small as a border town. It had a very long main street with shops and restaurants. There was the depot, a post office, and a meeting hall. But as I continued down the wide avenue, the town soon gave way to fields and farms.

I concentrated on the soft tap of my footsteps on the stones beneath my feet. The sky was clear and blue in this part of Faerie, and the sun sparkled off the snow on either side of the road. It wasn't so cold out that I could see my breath, and I smiled to myself. This type of cold, I didn't mind so much. I wasn't fond of it, but the air wasn't bitter or biting. It was the mellow sort of winter that brought delightful scenery. The breeze carried the scent of farm animals and frozen hay.

The electric hum under my skin eased a bit while my other senses took the forefront, though the uncomfortable sensation didn't completely subside. My mind drifted as I considered what could be causing it. *Is it really because there are werewolves I don't know around? Most of them are claimed. Are there unclaimed wolves nearby? Am I picking up on them? Maybe it's anticipation of the unknown and what's going to happen once I arrive. Then again, this is an unclaimed territory. No alpha has a claim to the festival grounds or the monastery. Is that why? Lia did mention once that I would feel the difference between claimed and unclaimed territory.*

I prodded the feeling, different from when I was in Lia's territory around claimed wolves I was familiar with. But even before I'd known the Northern Pack, I hadn't felt this way while in Lia's territory.

Then again, I hadn't felt this way while at the university in Faerie either. There weren't many werewolves on that campus. Back then, I'd felt restless most of the time...confused. I'd been randomly bombarded with feelings not my own, and the only way I'd known how to deal with them was to remove myself from all contact with others. I'd spent most of my time reading. I'd read about the human realm; I'd read about being an alpha—

not that there were tons of books on the subject, given that we were expected to learn from a mentor.

It had been a relief when I'd come to stay with Lia. And we'd spent much of my first year of training working on separating my emotions from others'.

But as that little tug in my chest nagged at me, I wondered if staying in another alpha's territory hadn't shielded me in some way.

10

*D*espite the uncomfortable nagging in my heart, my walk through the snowy landscape was pleasant. I wasn't in a hurry to get to my destination and deal with the other alphas. But after a while, I knew I had to be getting close. If it had been too far away, they would have sent a carriage or had their own transportation circle.

Up ahead, I could see a wooden fence on one side of the road and a high stone wall on the other. I could only see the very top of a spire above the stone wall, and I wondered what was hidden inside the secretive barrier.

Though the road was wide enough for two carts to pass each other, it didn't feel that way once I was walking between the two enclosures. The wide avenue suddenly felt narrow and very private.

I turned toward the fenced side of the road when I heard a shout and an insistent barking. Two faelings, still very young, ran as fast as their short legs could take them toward the fence, a barking dog in pursuit.

"Hurry!" the boy yelled, pulling the younger girl by the hand.

I could already see that the dog would catch them. Even if

they reached the fence first, they wouldn't have enough time to climb over. I burst into a sprint and hopped over the fence.

From behind me, I heard someone shout. "Agatha! Elwood!"

I spared only a glance for the man running across the road toward the children.

I turned my eyes back to the dog and let an alpha's growl climb up my human throat. The dog froze.

I jerked my head at the now-terrified hound. "Get!" I ordered. He ran in the opposite direction as fast as he could, his tail well between his legs.

The man had lifted the children over the fence and was clutching the little girl to him as she cried. "Elwood, are you all right?" he asked the boy, who stood before him.

Elwood nodded, though he seemed shaken. The man pulled him into an embrace despite the child's words.

After a few moments of comforting the children, the man scolded them. "I told you two to stay off Farmer Maegut's land. You could have been hurt."

"But they're going to die, Alasdair!" the little girl wailed.

"Who?" I demanded. "Who's going to die?"

The man sighed and stood from his crouch. "Aggie is talking about the farmer's sheep." He patted Aggie's head. "She has a soft spot for animals." With that, the man turned to me. "Thank you for—"

I blinked at the look on his face as he cut himself off mid-sentence.

He couldn't be more than a year or two older or younger than me, likely in his low to mid-twenties. He was taller than me by a head, with wide shoulders that spoke of manual labor. His charcoal-gray hair swooped and swirled in perfect, loose curls about his forehead and ears. He had heavy eyebrows over his orange eyes, and his jaw was sharp, with only a shadow of stubble. His scent was masculine and clean like clary sage, iris, and a campfire of lemon and pine. And his pink lips were full and parted in an expression of awe.

"Um, are you okay?" I asked.

But he didn't answer my question. Not a heartbeat later, he dropped to his knees and lifted his head. His eyes shone with a desperate devotion.

"Will you be my alpha?" he asked without preamble.

My heart raced as goose bumps rose on my skin, so startled was I by his sudden request to join my pack. But that feeling was overshadowed. I stared down at this man, his eyes pleading and his heart laid bare to me.

His emotions rushed into me, and my inner wolf instinctively analyzed them with a leader's calculation. *Would this wolf be a good fit for my pack?* His heart held no deception, at least at this moment. I felt his joy, his overwhelming jubilation. I felt his unflinching loyalty.

I shivered, and not unpleasantly. And I knew what I wanted to do, or rather what my inner alpha wanted to do. She wanted to lean down and kiss this man on his forehead, accepting him as a member of her pack.

"Alasdair, I'm hungry. May I have a cup of peaches, please?" Aggie asked politely, seemingly unaware of the seriousness and magnitude of the situation playing out before her young eyes.

I could have given the young faeling all the sheep and peaches she could ever want right then. Her words jolted me from my instincts, bringing me back to my own reality.

I breathed out a shaky sigh, closing my eyes as I pushed Alasdair's feelings out of my head. *I don't want a pack.*

I turned to the children. "You be more careful in the future, all right?"

They nodded their heads solemnly but didn't give any verbal promises.

I didn't even spare a glance for Alasdair, still on his knees on the road. I knew I should formally reject his request, but I feared that if I looked at him again—if his orange eyes were fixed on me in that same desperate way—I wouldn't be able to wrestle my wolf back under control.

So I left without another word.

Relief washed over me as I got farther away, and I felt

grateful to this unknown man for not calling after me. My steps were rushed at first, trying to make distance between myself and the uncomfortable situation I'd just fled. But once the man and children were out of sight, I forced myself to slow down.

I can't deal with other alphas in this state. I tried the breathing exercise Lia had taught me to little effect. *What was that back there?* I shook my head at myself. *The first request I've had to join my pack, and I can't even put the words together to refuse? Am I not ready after all?*

But he took me by surprise. Who in their right mind requests to join the pack of an alpha they just met?

Up ahead, the monastery finally came into view. Louparest Monastery wasn't just one building. It was a cluster of stone structures dotting a large hill—practically a town in itself. The very top of the hill held the biggest of the buildings, which bore a black flag with the symbols of the wolf mystics of Faerie: a four-sided knotwork design with five different colored circles adorning it.

I stopped walking. I needed a second to clear my head—likely many seconds, in fact.

I took another deep breath and let it out slowly, losing count of how many times I'd done this and failed to reach my desired effect.

It's fine. It's totally fine. That was just a little hiccup. I've never seen him before, and I probably won't ever see him again. In any case, none of that matters right now. He's not an alpha, and he won't be at this gathering. I may have utterly failed to control the situation back there, and I'll tell Lia when I return. I haven't even gotten to the festival yet. And now that it's happened once, I'll be ready should it happen a second time.

I straightened my spine and strode forward with feigned confidence.

The closer I got to the monastery, the more it loomed over me.

There's nothing to fear here. No one can make me do anything I don't want to do. I'm also an alpha.

Despite my inner reassurances, it wasn't the alphas or any

other unclaimed wolves I might encounter that worried me. If I was being honest, it was me—my inner wolf—I was concerned about. I clearly didn't have as much control over her as I'd thought I had. But I couldn't think about that now. If I did, I knew I would turn around without even trying to see this test through.

The archway that led into the monastery grounds was hung with banners welcoming the visiting alphas, and two wolf mystics stood near the entrance.

"Welcome," one of the mystics greeted me with a bow of her head, her smile warm and bright. "The alphas are gathering in the refectory for dinner at seven, but you're free to wander around the monastery grounds as you wish until then. The kitchen is open if you'd like a snack before dinner. If you'll just follow me. I'll show you to your room."

I followed her with a word of thanks.

11

The monastery grounds felt like a small town, similar to how my university had been. There weren't any shops or restaurants; it was the way the buildings looked and fit together. There was no clear use for the buildings we passed. They could have been storerooms or cottages, but everything was constructed with the same sturdy, gray stone—smooth and angular with clean-cut lines—and topped with terracotta roofs. Snow covered the surrounding landscape, which was flat farmland sparsely dotted with trees for as far as I could see, but it didn't seem to have reached the monastery. There were only a few small piles here and there, pushed to the sides of the cobbled pathways.

The mystics we passed moved about with clear purpose of task. They were mostly younger, newly unbound wolves, likely there to train in the mystic arts.

I glanced over at my still-smiling guide. She appeared very young, and if I hadn't known that she must have completed her rite to be a mystic, I might have thought her sixteen. The knot-work pendant around her neck held no stones in it, indicating that she was still a novice.

"How long have you been at the monastery?" I asked her.

"Oh, I've only been here for a few months now, but it already feels like home," she answered in a light, cheery tone.

The tug in my heart told me this wolf was yet unclaimed. *Is it wise to have her escorting alphas in this state?* Curious, I gingerly reached out with my alpha sense. A tingle of pure and simple tranquility seeped into me. And I gently pulled back after that little taste of her feelings. Her smile was as easy as it had been before. Either she hadn't noticed my little intrusion, or it hadn't bothered her. *Is she unaffected by an alpha's presence?*

I soon realized that it wasn't just this mystic who seemed unaffected by me, it was all the mystics we passed, even the unclaimed ones. They didn't stiffen or flinch as I approached. They greeted us with a smile and a nod of respect. *What makes them different? Is it in their training? Something about this place?*

Finally, my guide stopped at a building nestled cozily among the others, no markings to distinguish it. "This is where the young alphas are staying," she said, opening the thick, wooden door.

The dormitory seemed to be one large room furnished with couches and chairs facing a fireplace. Upon closer inspection, I noticed that there were recessed doors—eight as far as I could tell—along two of the parallel walls. The place felt empty.

"Am I the first to arrive?" I asked.

"No, the others are probably just walking around the grounds," the mystic answered.

"How many have come before me?"

"Three young alphas arrived before you. I don't know how many older alphas have come because that isn't my task, but none of the Wolf Council have arrived yet."

I nodded, though her back was to me now as she led me to one of the doors.

"You can use this room tonight." She opened the door and stepped aside.

I entered the small but comfortable room. The cream-painted walls were trimmed in warm wood. There was a double bed and a desk with a chair. There was also a bookshelf and a wardrobe. I took off my backpack and set it down on the desk.

"There are two bathrooms," she said from the doorway. "One at the end of each row, the doors farthest from the entrance."

"Thank you."

"Is there anything else I can do for you?"

I shook my head. "No, thanks. Dinner is at seven, you said?"

She nodded. "Yes, in the refectory. That's the large building next to the temple, second to the top of the hill. Enjoy your stay."

I thanked her again as she took her leave.

Left alone in the empty building, I breathed easy. I could still feel that little nag that had started upon my first arriving in this unclaimed territory, but it had dulled well into the background.

I walked to the bed and flopped onto the thick, white blanket. *Can I just stay here until dinner? Who says I have to wander around looking for trouble?*

But my stomach growled its protest. I hadn't eaten since early that morning, and a granola bar wasn't enough to deal with everything I'd already dealt with that day, let alone what could happen between now and dinner.

I sighed and sat up. *She said I could get food in the kitchen, but she didn't say where the kitchen was. I probably should have asked.* My stomach grumbled again. *Well, I'm not going to find it sitting here.*

I decided that the best place to start would be near the refectory. It didn't make a lot of sense to have the kitchen too far from where people would eat. Stepping out of the dormitory, I looked up the hill. A neat, cobbled street curved upward and split, the buildings on either side hiding exactly where each branch led.

As picturesque as the many winding avenues were to look at, guessing which one led where was impossible. I paused at the fork and chose the path that looked like it rose a little, hopefully leading up the hill and closer to the kitchen.

My footsteps were slow but steady, the stone road solid and dry beneath my boots. The sky was blue, and I lifted my face to the sun, which warmed it despite the cool temperatures. But I couldn't fool myself into believing that I was alone. Every few minutes, a mystic would pass me. Each one would nod their respect to my status, though none of them even slowed their pace. After this happened a handful of times, my tension eased. I eventually asked a woman if I was heading in the right direction to reach the kitchen, and she graciously told me the rest of the way.

Not all of the wolves I encountered were unclaimed, though most of them were. Still, they seemed almost unaffected by my alpha status. The weight in my chest lightened a little. I didn't know what it was about these particular wolves, and I didn't really care. I just knew that I liked it here. These mystics didn't seem to have any expectations of me, at least not at the moment.

To be amongst my own kind, to not have to hide like I did with the humans, and to have them effectively ignore me was something I hadn't known I needed.

12

*W*hatever peace I felt was shattered when I entered the monastery's kitchen. The space wasn't nearly as large as I would have expected to provide food for the many residents and visitors of the monastery. Still, there were multiple wood-burning stoves and two long tables in the center of the room, which acted as work surfaces. A young mystic looked up from chopping parsley at one of the tables.

"Here comes another one," she pronounced.

An older man, wooden spoon in hand, chuckled. "Never fails," he said. "Every year, you young alphas remind me of how important my work is. Go on." He waved his spoon toward a corner where a table, much too large for the space, had been stuffed. "Have a seat."

The table was occupied by three young alphas, who quieted as I approached. The hair on the back of my neck stood on end, and my shoulders tensed. Three packless alphas in an unclaimed territory could only mean trouble.

I froze and held my breath, waiting to see how they would respond.

After a heavy moment, the only other female smiled. "Seems

my mentor needn't be so worried about whether there are enough young alphas to go around. Four already this year. The elders will be pleased. I'm Shri, and this is Baishan and Damjan." She indicated the two males sitting on either side of her.

I reached out my hand. "Willow."

Shri stood and grasped my forearm. "Nice to meet you, Willow." Her light brown eyes were clear and friendly and put me at ease. I knew immediately that she was the peacekeeper type.

Baishan took my arm next, his face stiff and business-like.

Damjan grinned when I turned to him, his eyes sparkling with mischief as he looked me over. "You've been to the other side," he said, no doubt marking my human clothes. "Can't wait to see what the elders make of you."

I stiffened, his words playing into all of my fears. *How difficult will the older alphas and the Wolf Council make the next few days for me?* I'd almost started to believe it wouldn't be so bad, wandering around the monastery having lulled me into a false sense of security.

"Oh, leave her alone," Shri censured Damjan lightly. "You're always trying to stir up trouble."

I raised my eyebrows and took a seat at the table. "Do you two already know each other?" I asked.

"Sure, sure," Damjan said with a nod. "Shri has been pulling me into her schemes most of our lives."

I found that hard to believe, and Shri scowled at him. "Don't pin your shenanigans on me. But, yes, I've known this fool my whole life. He's my cousin."

Two alphas in the same family? Upon closer inspection, they did sort of look alike. They were both petite in build with dark hair and skin, though Damjan was much lighter by comparison. Still, their faces didn't share many features.

I obviously didn't hide my surprise because Damjan chuckled at me. "Yeah, we get that expression a lot."

The older mystic who'd directed me to sit brought over a

plate of sandwiches. "Nothing so fancy at the moment, I'm afraid," he apologized. "Saving that for tonight's dinner."

We assured him that the sandwiches were fine and thanked him for the food.

But as he walked away, we all stared at the platter in the middle of the table. Who was served first, who ate first when werewolves were together, had serious implications. I'd never eaten with more than one other alpha around, and even that had been when I'd been in that alpha's territory, so they'd had clear preference.

The tension mounted, and I wondered if dealing with all this was worth a few pieces of bread with meat and cheese between them.

It was my understanding that disputes such as this ended when the strongest made themselves known. I frowned at the thought. "I doubt the good mystic who so kindly made us this food wants to have a brawl in his kitchen." I tried for my best neutral tone. "I see two reasonable ways forward. One, we all grab a sandwich at the same time. Or two, we go by age, eldest first."

I knew that, in Faerie at least, alphas were given preference by strength first, then class, then age, and I didn't want to bring class dynamics into an already tense situation.

"Age sounds like a reasonable way forward," Shri seconded.

Damjan sighed. "And I was so looking forward to a fight."

"You only would've cheated anyway," Shri mumbled.

"Cleverness is its own strength," Damjan countered.

I ignored their bickering. "Baishan? Is age all right with you?"

The silent alpha was taller and broader than all of us. If going by looks alone, he would win by strength easily. But he nodded without a word, giving in to my proposal.

After a few minutes spent comparing birthdays, we found that I was the eldest by well over a year, followed by Damjan, then Baishan, and finally Shri. The distribution of sandwiches went forward without so much as a growl.

"So," Damjan started, his mouth still full as he turned to me. "Didn't you find an alpha to succeed last year? It was my understanding that young alphas are in short supply. I would've thought the elders would be fighting for successors. Weren't there any good prospects?"

I chewed slowly and swallowed. "I didn't come last year."

Even having known Damjan for only a few minutes, I could tell he wanted more information and was going to push for it.

I changed the subject. "The dormitory seems nice."

Shri nodded.

"Nice big beds, too," Damjan agreed. Then he smirked. "What do you think, Baishan? Do you think I could entice Olwyn to join me tonight?"

Baishan squinted his displeasure at Damjan.

I tilted my head. "Who's Olwyn?" I asked.

Shri smacked her cousin on the arm. "Stop it. Olwyn is the mystic who showed us to the dorms."

I raised an eyebrow.

"Damjan is just being a jerk—as usual—because Baishan was clearly interested in her," Shri explained. "Don't let him get to you, Baishan. He isn't serious."

I turned my attention to the silent giant beside me. He frowned in an expression that seemed more uncertain than anything else.

Once an alpha was unbound in fae magic, finding a mate became complicated. That was one of the reasons the Wolf Moon Festival even existed. The hope was for alphas to find a mate well before their alpha power made consent a murky issue.

"Olwyn is a mystic, so it's not a problem," Shri said. "I shouldn't be surprised if the elders don't try to set you all up with mystics while you're here."

"Why is that?" I asked.

Baishan spoke in a deep but quiet voice. "Mystics aren't as influenced by our alpha power. The Wolf Council and the elders always push for the political and spiritual leaders to mate. There's a formal matchmaking program."

I hadn't known that, not having trained as an alpha in Faerie. I wondered how they dealt with this issue in the realm of origin and told myself to ask Lia upon my return.

Shri nodded. "So why not go for it?"

Baishan still hesitated, and I couldn't help but wonder why.

"Well, if you won't," Damjan said, shoving the rest of his sandwich into his mouth and standing from the table, "I will."

Baishan's eyes widened, and he rose to follow after Damjan.

Shri just shook her head as the men left.

"You don't think Damjan will really get in his way, do you?" I asked her.

Shri took another bite and chewed slowly. "No," she said finally. "He's a jerk, but he's not that much of a jerk. If anything, he's trying to help Baishan out, pushing him to act."

"Have you two known Baishan for long?"

"Just met him today."

I smirked. These two cousins certainly had a way of making quick friends. "You said the elders would be pushing the rest of us toward mystics. Why not you?"

Shri smiled, her eyes glimmering. "I'm already promised."

My chest warmed, and I returned her smile before taking another bite. I could almost feel the love she had for her promised. *I wonder what the mate bond feels like.* Just like that, Adrian's violet eyes as he stroked me in the dark suddenly flashed to the front of my mind. I coughed, nearly choking on my sandwich.

Shri reached out and patted my back. "Are you all right?"

I nodded, clearing my throat.

What the hell? Will that dream just die already?

13

In some ways, being around Shri was easier than being around nonalpha wolves. Yes, there were little potholes we had to navigate, like who would eat first, but she was on equal footing with me. There was no pressure for me to lead her, and there was no innate desire for her to follow. For a short while, I was glad that Lia had given me this test. And I hoped I might cultivate a friendship with Shri when all was done.

Shri was studying with Elva of the Mountain Meadows Clan. She was not Shri's birth-pack alpha, but since Damjan was older, he had dibs on studying with their previous alpha. Apparently, Elva wasn't old enough to want a successor, so Shri would be courting elders during the next few days; or more likely, they would be courting her. I was grateful that Shri was such an outgoing person and so perceptive. Over the course of the afternoon, she asked me only a few questions before realizing that I didn't much want to talk about myself or my situation.

I wasn't shy by any means. I just thought explaining my views, my goals regarding my alpha state, would take more time and energy than I had at the moment. But I didn't discourage her outright. I did want us to be friends once this test was over and I was settled on my own.

Later in the evening, we returned to the dormitory. Damjan was lounging on the couch reading when we arrived.

"Where's Baishan?" Shri asked, pushing Damjan's feet off the couch.

Damjan smirked. "Getting to know Olwyn, of course."

Shri smiled. "I suppose your shenanigans can be helpful from time to time."

"I'm wounded, dear cousin. I'm always helpful," Damjan said dramatically.

Shri rolled her eyes, and I couldn't help but smile.

"Well, I'm going to get changed," Shri said. "If I'm lucky, maybe an upper-class alpha will be desperate for a successor, and I can make a good impression."

"Maybe fish can sing and trees can dance," Damjan mumbled.

Shri frowned. "Don't try to pull me into one of your theoretical discussions. I'm going to get ready."

I sank into an armchair near Damjan.

"What about you?" he asked. "Aren't you going to change out of your human clothes?"

I looked down at my outfit. It positively screamed human: jeans, snow boots, plaid button-down under a sweater. "Nope," I answered simply. *Maybe they'll just leave me alone if I'm dressed like this.*

Damjan grinned a grin that looked forward to the commotion I would cause, and I wondered if I shouldn't change after all.

I wouldn't say my attire created a stir. But as the four of us entered the refectory half an hour before seven, I certainly got a choice collection of strange glances.

The refectory was a huge room with a high, sculpted ceiling. Four long tables spanned the length of the room, each pristinely decorated with a jewel-hued tablecloth and flickering, black candles. Even with the tables, there was room for the attendees to roam and chat.

In truth, there weren't many alphas there at all. The thirteen members of the Wolf Council were there, of course, but other than the four of us, there were maybe ten other alphas in attendance. There certainly weren't enough people to warrant the grand decor the monastery had put together.

I wondered where the mystics would be eating and if they'd be joining us as I scanned the gathered alphas. To my great displeasure, I spotted Efren talking to a female alpha who wasn't yet old enough to want a successor. My heart jumped into my throat, and a shiver ran through me. *What in the world could he be doing here? He's not old enough to want a successor.*

The woman looked over at us and smiled. "This is Shri, the young alpha I was just telling you about," the woman said, beckoning Shri toward her with a wave of her hand.

Shri obliged, and I turned on my heel to head in the opposite direction.

"Willow," Efren called in that commanding tone that I recognized from my early childhood.

I froze by reflex, a thrill running through me as I felt his alpha power yank on something inside me. I pushed the feeling away, blowing an angry snort through my nose. Still, I turned to face him.

"Hello, Efren," I said, not quite as politely as I should have. "I'm surprised to see you here."

My former alpha stepped in far closer than was comfortable. "I was hoping you would come," he said low. His eyes traveled over me from head to toe, and I stiffened. He gave me a rare, yet still small, smile. "I'm glad to see you're well. Your parents will be relieved."

I didn't respond, didn't even change my expression. A little flutter in my stomach told me that he was reaching out to me again, trying to taste how I was feeling. I tried to shut him out, but he was finished before I could properly react.

He frowned. "You're still rough," he pointed out, as if I'd asked for his critique of my training thus far. "You're not ready to be here."

My stomach dropped, and all the confidence I'd felt while making my case to Lia shriveled up. This was a man I'd trusted my entire life, the alpha I'd been raised to respect and obey. If he said I wasn't ready after only a few moments, maybe I wasn't.

I shook my head, pushing the doubts from my mind. *No, Lia sent me here as a test. She thinks I'm close enough to being ready to test me.* "Then it's a good thing your opinion doesn't matter, Efren. You aren't my mentor."

His eyes widened at my disrespect. Never had he experienced it before, not even when I'd been brushing him off while at the university.

But before he could respond, I continued. "If you'll excuse me." Then I made for the other side of the room.

My heart hammered in my chest, and I took a deep breath. It came out ragged and too shaky for my liking. I separated myself a little from the gathered alphas—still in the room but far enough away that I wasn't easy to talk to. The space swirled with power, and my head spun from the pressure pushing on it from all sides.

I reached for a pitcher of water on a nearby table and poured myself a glass. At least I managed not to spill it, despite my shaking hands. I swallowed with difficulty, having to force the action that should have been a reflex.

I took another breath and cast my eyes about the room, trying to concentrate on something—anything—other than my pounding heart. Shri and her mentor had moved on and were talking to a very well-dressed elder alpha. Baishan and Damjan were also talking with a group of elders, who were no doubt trying to convince the young alphas to take over their packs when ready.

A snippet of a conversation not far from me pulled at my attention.

"—the treaty?" one elder asked a Wolf Council member, whose unmistakable power bespoke his status.

The younger alpha patted the elder on the back in a gesture of reassurance, but his expression did not carry the same message. "To tell you the truth, our last meeting with the royal family was rather tense. They're not pleased that so many of their faelings are going unprotected."

The elder bowed his head. "But what can we do? We can't stop wolves from leaving. And the packs in the human realm play an even bigger role in fighting the vampires than we do in some ways."

The council member nodded. "Yes, but if we aren't keeping up our end of the treaty, the fae could very well dissolve it and send us all back to the human realm."

"But if the vampires are changing their approach, how is that something we can affect? How are we expected to take responsibility for that?" the elder asked.

The council member frowned and sighed a long, exhausted sigh. "I don't think they much care for what is fair. The fact is: faelings are dying."

"But so are the pups!" the elder countered, raising his voice. "Are we not just as upset by the loss of our children as they are?"

How different would this conversation be if these alphas knew about Adrian's research?

The council member looked around him at the elder's outburst, and his eyes met mine. "The only way forward I can see is to entice more wolves from the human realm into Faerie. I can't see how we can avoid rewriting the treaty."

I stiffened at the attention. His words seemed directed right at me. I tried to swallow the lump that rose in my throat and failed. The power this council member had could not be denied. He was an alpha. He was an upper-class wolf from one of the original thirteen families. And he was coming toward me.

He smiled, but it did not put me at ease.

I felt the urge to drop to my knees before him. Thankfully, I only wobbled. But I gave him a deeper bow than he was warranted.

"I don't believe we've met," he said genially as he offered me his arm. "I'm Judoc."

As my hand grasped his forearm, a rumble of power ran into

my shoulder. "Willow," I said much too quietly, glancing up for less than a second before dropping my gaze.

"It's nice to meet you, Willow," he continued, as if he could hold some sort of normal conversation with me. "I couldn't help but notice that you're wearing human attire. Did you leave Faerie after completing your rite, or is this just a fashion choice?"

I took a deep breath and raised my head, despite the feeling of a great weight pushing me down. "Yes, I completed my rite, and I'm training under an alpha in the realm of origin."

Judoc dipped his head lightly. "As I expected. Do you mind telling me why you decided to leave Faerie for the *human realm* rather than take over a pack here?" His tone was still friendly and conversational, even with his emphasized correction.

Still, his words pressed on me with urgency. I resisted the feeling, concentrating on something real around me: the hard floor beneath my boots.

He continued, "You can see for yourself that we have more packs in need of young leadership than young alphas to go around. Since you grew up here, you know how important the treaty is to us. Whyever would you leave?"

His easy tone was getting harder with every word, and the floor beneath my feet wasn't enough. I focused on the glass of water still in my hand, the smooth coolness under my fingers. It gave me the respite to cast my gaze around the room for something else to center me or distract me from the effect of his presence and questions.

Our little group of alphas was now outnumbered by an influx of the monastery's mystics. I didn't know when they'd arrived. And they weren't mixing with the alphas, instead talking amongst themselves.

I scanned the room for Olwyn, just as a way to focus my mind for a moment.

But before I found her, another young mystic approached us. He bowed deeply at Judoc before dipping his head at me.

"Excuse me," he said, his eyes on me, "I don't wish to interrupt, but the archmystic would like a word with you before dinner if you don't mind."

I blinked at the novice. "A word with me?" I asked incredulously.

He nodded. "Yes, he's asked that you meet him in the private dining room for a moment."

I couldn't imagine what the archmystic of the monastery would possibly want to see me about. But as I glanced at Judoc, I didn't much care.

"Of course," I told the novice, setting my glass of water on the table nearest me.

Then I excused myself from Judoc and followed the mystic from the main dining hall, breathing a sigh of relief.

14

Our footsteps echoed in the wide, stone hallway, though we didn't go far. The private dining room sat just next door to the grand hall. The young mystic held the door open for me, and I entered the much smaller room. It was simply furnished with an unclothed table and only six chairs. There were no glittering decorations or festive tapestries—just a neat room with modest furnishings.

An elderly werewolf in human form awaited me, his wrinkled hands laced before him. His very short hair was gray with age rather than natural werewolf coloring, if his black eyebrows were any indication. Despite his aged face, his yellow eyes were still bright. He didn't sit at the table but stood before it as if he had no plans to stay. His face was clean-shaven, and his knot-work pendant held not only the five colored stones of the highest order of mystics, but the outer circle of an archmystic.

The young mystic who had guided me there closed the door without a word.

Despite holding such a prestigious position, the elder dipped his head at me. It was his place to show respect to me regardless of age and station simply because I was an alpha and he was not.

"Hello," he greeted me with a kind smile.

"Hello… Was there something you wanted to see me about?"

The archmystic chuckled. "Yes. I suppose you would be wondering why I called you here, wouldn't you?"

I waited for him to explain.

"I wouldn't normally call a young alpha away from such a gathering, especially with the elder alphas so desperate for successors. But he was so insistent that I couldn't refuse."

"Who?" I asked, trying to piece together what he was getting at.

He sighed as if longing for days gone by. "Youth is so impatient. Or perhaps the old are just long-winded. In any case, one of our mystics has requested to match with you."

I blinked. "Excuse me?"

"You are aware that, once an alpha has risen, it becomes difficult for them to find a mate. The monasteries and the older alphas work together to match mystics and alphas as best we can."

I waved my hand for him to go on, having heard it only hours before.

"Well, one of our mystics would like to meet with you with that end in mind. Will you meet him?"

I stood dumbfounded. *This day is ridiculous. Who could have seen me long enough to even make this request? I didn't talk to any mystics other than Olwyn.* I squinted in thought. *But if I meet with this mystic, at least I'll have a little break from being around the other alphas.*

I nodded at the archmystic. "Sure. Why not?"

His polite smile widened in genuine joy. "Excellent. He will be pleased."

I hesitated at his full stop. "Um, where will I be meeting him? Will he be coming here?"

"Oh, no. We want to give you two some space to have a proper talk. He's waiting for you in the library."

"And where is that?"

"It's on the opposite side of the hill, past the temple. Would you like me to send a guide to show you?"

"No, that's all right. I can find it. Thank you."

The archmystic dipped his head again. "I do so hope it works out between you."

I didn't have a response for that, so I excused myself and left the way I'd come.

The monastery seemed even more peaceful than earlier in the day as I stepped into the night. The nearly full moon had yet to rise, but the stars shone brightly overhead. The night was cold, and my wolf's eyes could see my breath even in the dim light.

Unlike Mysraina, the capital city of Faerie where I'd spent most of my life, there were no fae lights or lanterns here. The mystics simply didn't need them to see after dark. Meanwhile, it seemed that everyone was at the feast; I could hear the low hum of faraway voices as I followed the cobbled path, and I didn't meet anyone on my way.

The directions the archmystic had given me were easy enough, and the library wasn't very far away. Still, it was far enough that I had time to order my thoughts.

I wasn't really looking for a mate at the moment. The fact was that I wanted to be by myself for a while. But as I considered that possibility, the sense of completion I'd felt in my recent dream of Adrian scratched at my mind. *We weren't just doing sexy stuff in my dream. We were mated, too.* I certainly didn't want to mate Adrian; that much was obvious. However, it was possible that, now that I neared the end of my alpha training, something within me pushed me to that end. *I haven't thought of mating anyone since I was last at the Wolf Moon Festival. Maybe my subconscious longs for that connection. Have I been neglecting some need within me?*

I'd been so worried about getting past all this alpha nonsense that whether or not I'd mate in the future seemed a very far-off possibility.

But is it really that I'm ready to find a mate? Or is it that I've been told my whole life that this is what I'm supposed to do? Is that expectation just playing on my mind?

In any case, I couldn't imagine that a mystic from Faerie would be a good match for me. He'd be very ensconced in the whole setup of werewolf society in Faerie. But as I breathed in the fresh night air, I was grateful to him. He'd given me a moment's peace by even asking for this meeting.

The monastery's library looked much the same as the rest of the buildings I'd seen thus far. It was stone and sturdy with a thick, wooden door, which opened into an antechamber. This small entrance area had doors on either side and a staircase leading to a second floor. I paused, wondering which way to go first. But the faint crackle of a fire and the comforting scent of burning wood beckoned me through the doorway on the left.

The room I entered was much deeper than it was wide, with floor-to-ceiling bookshelves stuffed with volumes of all sizes. At the far end, a fire flickered in a great, stone hearth. It offered the only light in the room and shined off a covered dish on a nearby table, set simply for two.

A man's broad form blocked most of the firelight. His hair looked dark in his silhouette, the tips curling at the ends. And then it hit me: that masculine scent I'd so recently experienced — clary sage, iris, and the burning wood of lemon and pine.

"Are you serious?" I crossed my arms over my chest.

His broad shoulders jumped at my voice, and he spun to face me. His orange eyes seemed to glow in the dim light. "You came."

I hadn't noticed when I'd met him earlier, but he wore the pendant of a mystic around his neck. It held only one stone, a blue tourmaline, denoting that he wasn't a novice, but he still had a while to go before he reached a higher order.

I took a step back. I didn't want to feel the force of his emotions again, didn't want to feel my alpha desire to accept him. I wasn't in a stable enough frame of mind to refuse him right now.

"*You're* the one who wants to talk to me about mating?"

"Yes — well, no."

I raised an eyebrow.

He held up his hands in surrender. "Just hear me out, okay?

I don't want to be your mate. But the archmystic wouldn't have let me call you out for anything less than that."

I sighed. "So you lied to the archmystic? What is it that you want then?"

"I want to join your pack. I know I startled you at the orphanage. I just…couldn't think of what else to do. I couldn't stop myself."

I frowned. "The orphanage?"

Alasdair tilted his head at the question. "Yes, that's where Elwood and Agatha live—in the big house across from where we found them."

Usually, faelings without families stay with werewolf families until they awaken. Are there so many orphaned faelings that they need orphanages? Have so many pups been lost? Is that why they didn't have bondmates with them?

"My family funds it, so I often go there to check in on them."

I blinked, then looked him up and down again. *His family has that kind of money? He must be from the upper class then. And they let him become a mystic rather than mating and providing heirs?*

I pushed away my curiosity. Him, his motives, and his family weren't any of my business. Lia had told me over and over that unclaimed wolves who wanted to join my pack would feel compelled to follow me. *But shouldn't his mystic status have given him some kind of immunity?*

I raised my chin. "You don't know what you're asking. I—"

He rushed to stop me from rejecting him a second time. "Look, it sounds weird to me, too. But I've never felt so sure of anything in my life. You're *meant* to be my alpha. It's like the ancestors are screaming in my ears, 'follow her.'"

Like every wolf raised in Faerie, I knew the yearly rites to honor our ancestors. I had been lucky enough—since I hadn't lived in a border town while bound—to attend the ceremonies of change, where the mystics thanked and celebrated the land and its cycles. I'd been taught to respect the mystics and the wisdom they carried.

So, despite my mind shrinking from the idea, I didn't take his words lightly. The ancestors had never spoken to me, and the mystics had never had any special messages for me. But as I looked into Alasdair's pleading eyes, I wondered if they did now.

"I think fate brought us together," he pressed.

My breath hitched, and it took a few moments for my mind to start working again. I huffed out a laugh. "You actually made my heart flutter there for a second." But as I took in his all-too-serious eyes, I frowned. "You're joking, right?"

"I'm not."

My stomach clenched. Fate and I didn't have a great relationship. "There are so many reasons why this won't work. Look at my clothes; I live in the human realm. You're a mystic in Faerie. Are you planning on leaving all of your aspirations behind?"

He frowned and went still. For a brief moment, the only sound was the crackling of the fire. But then he met my eyes. "The ancestors' call is clear. If you're going to the human realm, then so am I."

I sighed out an exasperated breath. "I hate to disappoint you. At the very least, you seem like a nice guy. But I'm not accepting pack members. Ever. As soon as I finish my training, I'm going to be a lone alpha."

His brow puckered; I couldn't tell whether he was confused or just upset.

"So...thanks, I guess. I mean, it's nice to feel wanted. But I'm going to go now. Good luck." I turned to leave.

I didn't look back, but just as I reached the threshold to the antechamber, he called out, "Your name. Please, if nothing else, at least tell me your name."

With all the rejections I'd given him that day, I didn't see a reason to deny him that. "Willow."

"Willow." He nodded once.

"Goodbye, Alasdair."

In the cold winter night, I blew out a steadying breath, which puffed in a white stream from my lips. For once, I was glad for the chill. It was a shock to my senses, a shock that forced me back into reality, away from the surreal exchange I'd just lived through.

But as I turned in the direction of the refectory, I halted.

My emotions were all a-jumble. Too much had happened that day...way too much.

I employed Lia's breathing exercise for a good thirty seconds before I gave up. My heart sank. I wasn't ready to be a lone alpha.

With slow steps of defeat, I trudged down the hill toward the dormitory. I was in no state to deal with the other alphas. And my earlier interactions with them had made it clear to me that I'd already failed Lia's test. I could stay. I could stick it out and force my way through the festival. But I only saw that ending in disaster. If I wasn't ready, wasn't stable enough, to hold my own against the other alphas, then I may end up causing an incident. That wouldn't be good for anyone.

The dormitory felt emptier than it had upon my arrival, though I knew it was only that I felt even more out of place than before.

I was disappointed at my utter failure. I'd gotten ahead of myself. I should have just trusted Lia's gauge of things. But as I shouldered my backpack and started toward the depot in Louparest, I tempered my dejection. Sure, I'd failed this test, but it wasn't the end of the world. I still had Lia to mentor me until I was ready. I still had Rowan and Yuti; they would be glad I wasn't leaving right away. I still had my job, where I could keep helping the interns. I wasn't homeless or heartbroken.

This was just a delay, a small hiccup on my journey to my goal. And though things hadn't gone the way I'd wanted this time, they could have gone a lot worse.

*a*s I sat in the snow where I had climbed out of the portal, cold meltwater seeping into the fabric of my jeans, I thought about whom I should call. I wasn't supposed to meet Ashwin for a few days. There'd be someone along tomorrow morning to drop him off at the portal, but that was still a long way off.

It was late, but not so late that most everyone at the resort wouldn't still be awake. After pulling my cellphone from the hollow of the tree, I turned it on and scanned my contacts. Finally, I settled on Grant. He was the night clerk, so I wouldn't be keeping him up for the long drive, and he wouldn't pressure me to talk on the way back. He would, of course, need to tell Lia he was coming to get me, but at least I wouldn't have to face her just yet.

After making the call, I settled against a bare tree to wait, kicking myself for giving up that warm, fluffy bed in the monastery dormitory. I could have stayed the night and headed out in the morning. I could have been waiting for whoever dropped Ashwin off in the comparable warmth of daylight.

Instead, I was hunkered down in the woods, shivering my tits off.

I pursed my lips. *Maybe I should shift.* But I left that option as a last resort. If I didn't want to rip my clothes and my thick, winter coat, I'd have to get naked first. And I did *not* want to take my clothes off in this weather.

Standing from my crouch, I shouldered my pack and started walking toward the road. Moving around would make me warmer. I pulled out my phone, reluctantly removing one glove to search for the nearest shelter. At best, a car would pass by and pick me up. At worst, I could walk the two-and-a-half miles to the all-night diner the map suggested. I sent a quick text to Grant, telling him my plan.

I wasn't lucky enough to get a ride. The few cars that passed me were either going in the opposite direction or didn't slow down to help. But at least the walk gave me time to think.

As much as I wanted that warm bed at the moment, I knew I wouldn't have been able to stay at the monastery overnight. I'd already failed, and I didn't need any more chances to fail harder. And what if the other alphas had pressured me to stay longer? What if Alasdair had found another opening to do something even more outlandish?

No, it was better to deal with my walk of shame, deal with the consequences of my actions, and come clean with Lia sooner rather than later.

But as prepared as I was for that discussion upon my return to the resort, Lia didn't pressure me to talk about what had happened.

She kept to her routine, and we didn't even see each other over the following few days, not that we didn't know the other was there. I didn't have work because I'd requested those days off for the Wolf Moon Festival, so I used the time to double down on my training. I practiced everything she'd taught me with the gusto of a new recruit. Gone were my arrogance and vanity. I was a novice, and I would start from scratch if I needed to. Lia would tell me when I was ready.

A few days after I'd failed my test, on the day I should have arrived back in victory, I heard a gentle knock on my bedroom door. I stood naked in my room, my eyes fixed on the clock while I kept shifting from one form to the other.

"Come in," I sighed. I still wasn't down to two seconds.

Lia entered a moment later and held out a granola bar. "You didn't come down for your breakfast."

I took the offering and put it on my desk. "Thanks."

She made no move to leave. I shivered in the cool air and pulled on the clothes that I'd piled onto the bed.

Lia crossed her arms and leaned her hip against my desk. "Are you ready to tell me about it?"

I dropped my gaze and shrugged. "There isn't much to say. You were right. I wasn't ready. I'll stay as long as I need to in order to get it right. I…don't like feeling that out of control, like my instincts can just override my rational mind at any given moment. Even if I don't lead a pack, I need to be able to handle myself when I come into contact with other alphas or unclaimed wolves."

I glanced up at Lia. Her expression was smooth but soft. Whatever she thought of my declaration, she didn't say. "We're having that video conference tomorrow afternoon. Do you think Camille will allow you to go to work late?"

My eyes widened. "Am I still allowed to come? I thought I'd only be invited if I'd passed my test."

"I'd like you there," Lia said simply.

"All right."

We both looked toward the door when our keen hearing picked up the sound of the front door opening and closing.

"Ashwin is back from the Wolf Moon Festival. I better go see how it went," she said. "Don't forget to eat something."

I nodded and thanked her.

I was also curious about how Ashwin had fared at the festival. The pool for potential mates when I'd gone a few years before had been mostly younger wolves, too young for Ashwin.

Still, there was always a chance that there were unmated older wolves like him still looking for mates.

More importantly, though, I wanted to hear how the nonalphas were feeling. Were they as nervous as the alphas about a potential rewriting of the treaty? Did they even know that it was a possibility? How upset were they about the pups and faelings who were being hunted down by vampires?

How much unrest was there?

But it wasn't my place to question him. Lia was his alpha, and she would let me know if there was anything she felt she needed to share with me. I took off my clothes again and stared at the clock before shifting to wolf form.

16

*T*he following afternoon, I entered the study just as Lia turned her computer to face the larger room rather than the desk chair. Adrian shot to his feet, glancing around for an escape route as if he could get past me to the only door. Ashwin moved to stand strategically between us.

I stifled a sigh and drifted toward the back of the room. We played out a little dance where we adjusted our positions so Adrian was closest to the door and I was in the corner. The fear in his scent eased once he had a clear means of escape. Ashwin's tense shoulders also relaxed, though he remained between us.

I leaned against the wall next to the armchair, trying to look as at ease as I could, and crossed my arms. I took furtive glances at Adrian, not wanting to alarm him. He'd shaved in preparation for this meeting, though his hair was still shaggy, too long for the style it was cut in. Without his coat on, I could see that he had indeed lost weight. He had the slightness of someone who spent his time with dusty tomes rather than the taut muscle of an active sportsman.

"All right." Lia stepped back from the computer to make sure all four of us were in the frame. She looked over her shoulder at Adrian. "You ready?"

He nodded.

When Lia joined the video conference, a collection of five other alphas—some with betas hovering over their shoulders—stared back at us. I was surprised to see how many on the continent had come. There were only seven packs in North America, a pittance compared to the clans in Faerie. And they weren't organized in any sort of council of authority, which was why I couldn't help being surprised so many had joined.

Lia smiled at the camera. "Hello, everyone. Thank you for coming—especially you, Guillermo. I know you've got some territory disputes on your hands right now."

An alpha with dark skin and yellow eyes nodded at her acknowledgment.

"You've all met Adrian before." Lia gestured toward Adrian. "He's got some news for us. Go ahead, Adrian."

Adrian stepped closer to the camera, clasping his hands behind his back. I wondered if he was nervous. By all outward appearances, he seemed calm and collected. Still, I got the impression that was just a façade, though I wouldn't have been able to point out why.

"Good afternoon," he started. "I'm sure you're all busy, so I'll try to make this quick. As you know, I've been working with Ashwin and Lia to find out more about vampire origins. In my research prior to our collaboration, I'd discovered a reference to the idea that vampires were initially created by the fae."

"A claim you have yet to substantiate," one of the alphas on the screen interrupted him.

A few of the others shifted in their seats.

Adrian frowned but continued. "Ashwin and I have been concentrating our efforts on books from Faerie. My initial source referred to a fae by name, so we thought we might be able to track down some record of that fae in Faerie."

"Have you found something then? Why have you called us here?" another alpha asked.

Adrian's expression tightened. "We haven't had much luck. But I think I have a lead. I found a source that might be helpful. But...there's a hitch."

"What kind of hitch?" Lia asked.

"I can't get access to it here. It's in an archive in France. If I want to look at it, I have to go there."

There was silence for a second, followed by a burst of speaking on all fronts. The alphas all tried to talk over each other, none of their opinions coming through.

Lia waved her hands for attention. "One at a time, please."

"We cannot allow you to just wander around by yourself," Guillermo said.

Adrian's back stiffened. "I think I've proven myself by now. You can't expect me to live the rest of my life under these circumstances, every move I make watched. I spent years researching this on my own before ever meeting a werewolf."

"That's not what he means," another alpha said. "He means it's too dangerous for you to go around by yourself. Your research is important. What if you're attacked by another wolf, one who doesn't know you?"

"That is a little what I meant..." Guillermo muttered.

"But my research won't go any further if I can't go to where the information is," Adrian argued.

"We will need to send someone with you, someone to keep an eye on you and make sure other wolves don't attack as well," an older alpha with cloudy, deep-set eyes recommended. "Does anyone have a wolf they can spare?"

"I have a suggestion." Lia raised her hand. "I think Willow should go."

My heart leapt into my throat, and I choked on my own spit. "What?" I coughed.

"It's the perfect solution," Lia continued. "She's an alpha without a pack. She'll be far more qualified than anyone else we could send because she'll be able to stand up to any other wolves she encounters, even other alphas."

"But, Lia," I argued, "I failed my test. You said I'm not ready to go off on my own."

Lia turned to me, kindness and patience shining in her jade eyes, and smiled indulgently. "You passed the test, Willow."

My breath hitched, and my mind spun in confusion.

"You thought I was testing you to make sure you could hold your own against other alphas, but that wasn't the case. The real test was how you handled your failure. We all reach a point in our training when we're confident in our abilities. More accurately, we're *overconfident*. It's a pitfall for alphas. And when faced with our first real-world challenges, we all fail."

I stared at her hard, not daring to hope at what her unbelievable words meant.

She rested her hands on my shoulders. "You responded to that failure with humility and a determination to be better. That's what made you pass my test. The fact is that there are some things you can only learn by doing. Holding your own against other alphas? Dealing with unclaimed wolves? Those are things you get used to the more you're exposed to them. It's time for you to leave the resort. You're too sheltered here. The only alpha you deal with is me, and we don't have many unclaimed wolves here. To fully complete your training, you need to be consistently tested, consistently exposed to those things you cannot yet handle. This is my final task for you. I want you to go with Adrian. You're in the best place to do this, and I know you'll learn a lot along the way."

A thrill ran through me. *I passed? Lia thinks I'm ready?*

I had but one task before me, and then I'd be free.

"I'll do my best," I promised.

"No!" Adrian protested, his tone strong and clear. "I'll go with anyone but her."

I scowled at him.

"She almost killed me."

"I didn't even touch you," I muttered.

"Not from lack of trying!"

"After all this time, what do I have to do to prove myself to you?"

I surged toward him, and he didn't take one step before I grabbed him by the shirt. His violet eyes went wide with panic. He glanced over at Ashwin, but Lia had stopped him with a simple gesture of her hand.

I sniffed Adrian exaggeratedly. I got the sting of vinegar, rich earth, dry hay, fruity bergamot, and something I'd never noticed before: a slightly floral scent that I couldn't place. "Look. See? Your smell doesn't even affect me anymore. What do I have to do, huh? Do I have to kiss you just to prove my point?"

I leaned toward him.

"N-no, I got it," Adrian stammered.

I loosened my grip and released him. He took a step away but didn't run. My point had been made. I turned my attention back to the alphas, who were making various expressions of dismay and disgust.

"All in favor of Willow escorting Adrian on his research trip to France?" Lia asked, raising her hand.

The decision was unanimous.

17

I was feeling pleased with myself when Lia ended the video conference. My heart was light, and I vibrated with determination. *So close now.*

Lia turned to her beta. "Ashwin, I'm going to need you to get all of the paperwork in order. How long will it take for you to get Willow a passport?"

Ashwin smirked. "Not long."

Lia nodded. "Good. Schedule their flights for early next week then."

My stomach clenched. "Whoa, flights? I have to get on a plane?"

Ashwin snorted. "What did you think? Did you think you were going to use Faerie portals? You can hardly take a half-vampire to France that way. Every wolf in Faerie would be out to kill him. At least here he has a slight chance of survival."

I didn't know what I'd thought, but I hadn't even considered being trapped tens of thousands of feet in the air for hours on end.

"Lia," Adrian began, "do you think we could fly out of Seattle? I…haven't seen my mom in a while. I'd like to see her before leaving the country."

Lia stared at him for a moment, then nodded. "Hmm, I'll have to reach out to Aspen, the alpha of the Puget Sound Pack, to let him know you're coming. I don't expect you'll have to report to him for the few days you'll be in his territory. He's got so much in-fighting that vampires are the least of his concerns. You two can drive to Seattle for the weekend and fly out from there."

"I lived there most my life," Adrian said. "If Seattle is part of his territory, why was Rowan the first werewolf I ever met?"

Lia shrugged. "It could be that Aspen had his hands full. Or perhaps it's the fact that Seattle is a city. Werewolves tend not to be city-dwellers, and hunting in the city is a tricky business."

Adrian paled at her answer, as if he hadn't asked for the information. "Oh…Um, thanks… I'll let my mom know we're coming."

We're. He means him and me. The word struck a dissonant chord, and I adjusted my shoulders to get used to it. So strange that we were a "we" now when I hadn't even been allowed to be alone with him for over a year.

We'd never even had a real conversation.

"Is it cold in France?" I asked Ashwin as he headed out the study door before me.

Ashwin laughed. "You're going to want to pack all of your winter things."

"Damn it," I muttered. But as I turned toward the stairs to head up to my room, I heard my brother call me from the living room.

"Hey, Willow, could you come here for a second?"

My heart skipped a beat, and I smiled. I headed in that direction. "I thought you weren't coming back until—" I stopped in the doorway. "You've got to be kidding me."

Sitting beside Rowan on the couch, his chin resting in his hand as he leaned his elbow on the armrest, was Alasdair.

Alasdair shot to his feet. "Willow." His orange eyes lit with mischief as he moved toward me. "I've got something I want to talk to you about. The minute I stepped through the veil, I felt strange. I—"

I held up my hand to silence him. "I don't want to hear it. I'm not your alpha. If you feel strange, then go back to Faerie." I frowned. "How the hell did you even find me?"

He waved away my question. "That's not important. What matters is that I'm here with you."

"It kind of is important, though," I told him.

He grinned. "Names are very powerful to those who know how to use them. You should be careful whom you tell yours."

My mouth dropped open.

"Uh, Willow," Rowan said from the couch. "Do you want to…fill me in?"

I glanced around Alasdair at my brother, and I sighed. "What did he tell you?"

Just then, Adrian called from the hall. "Rowan, is Yuti out in —" He froze when he entered the room. He'd gotten quite good at not making any sudden movements upon meeting new werewolves.

Alasdair stiffened, his limbs shaking, and I could tell he was going to shift.

"Nope," I told him, grabbing his face and smooshing his cheeks. "Alasdair, look at me. We do *not* attack Adrian."

Alasdair's eyes wavered, clinging to mine. And then he relaxed. "Whatever you say."

I flinched at his sudden obedience and cleared my throat.

With the disaster averted, Adrian's tension eased. "I'm starting to think we should get a sign. *Beware. May encounter vampire. Do not attack*."

I huffed a laugh.

"Well, don't mind me. I'm just passing through." Adrian glanced over at Rowan. "Yuti in her studio?"

Rowan nodded, and Adrian slipped through the back door.

"I know we haven't had a chance to talk in a while," my brother said. "But I think you could have mentioned something about"— Rowan gestured vaguely to Alasdair—"all this."

"There's nothing to tell," I asserted. "He won't be staying." I turned back to Alasdair. "You'll be going back to the monastery as soon as I can get you a ride."

Alasdair pouted. "But I don't belong there."

I threw my hands up. "What do you mean you don't belong there? You're a wolf mystic."

"I belong wherever you are."

My heart jumped—still unused to his unwavering confidence, declared so seriously and with a straight face. "Well, you can't come with me. I have a mission, and I'm leaving on a trip."

"You're leaving?" Rowan asked. "Where are you going?"

"France."

"*France*? Since *when*?"

"I'll tell you about it later," I growled, overwhelmed by everyone wanting my attention at once.

"You." I pointed to Alasdair. "Follow me."

"Yes, my captain," he said with a salute.

"And stop that!" I snapped.

I was relieved to see Lia had remained in her study. "Lia, do you have a minute?"

"Sure, I was just searching the list of alphas to give the French wolves a heads-up." She glanced up from her computer. "Who's this?"

Alasdair followed me into the room, dipping his head at Lia in respect.

I gestured toward him. "This is Alasdair. He's a wolf mystic. I met him while at Louparest Monastery for the alpha gathering. He's convinced himself that I'm his destined alpha or some such nonsense."

Lia's gracefully arched eyebrows scrunched together as she laced her fingers.

"Is that even a thing?" I asked.

Alasdair stared seriously at Lia. "I'm supposed to follow Willow. I know it in my very soul."

Lia frowned, humming as her gaze sharpened. "Well, he certainly believes it to be true in any case... Unclaimed wolves can be quite insistent when they feel pulled toward a specific alpha. Has he made a formal request?"

I pictured him kneeling in the road, his face turned upward for my kiss of acceptance. "He has."

"Well, if you want him to go away, make a formal refusal."

I flinched at her words. I knew that's what I was supposed to do. I just couldn't bring myself to do it. "I can't...I can't deal with this right now."

Alasdair rested his hand on my shoulder, the weight solid and heavy. "Let me help you, Willow. Whatever it is, we can get through it together."

I whipped around to him, pulling away from his grasp. "Don't you get it? I don't want to be an alpha!"

With that, I stomped away like a petulant child. At the threshold, I glanced back at this man who expected so much without knowing anything about me.

"Go home, Alasdair."

18

*M*y last shift at the Rapids Café was busy. It was the second day of spring semester, and students were keen to meet up with friends after winter break. Coral was flustered but hung in there, assisted by Camille and me.

Once my shift ended and I was climbing the stairs to my bedroom, I felt like a weight had been lifted. I didn't work at the café anymore. And I'd never have to work in food service again if I didn't want to. It was a bittersweet feeling. I'd made good friends there, and I didn't know what my next step had in store for me.

Walking along the hall of bedrooms, I froze when I recognized Alasdair's scent. I listened carefully outside the guest room door but only heard the even sound of restful breathing. *I guess they're waiting until tomorrow to send him back.* With everything going on with my and Adrian's impending departure, I imagined that giving Alasdair a ride to the nearest portal wasn't a top priority.

As I opened my door, a folded sheet of paper caught my eye. I bent down and picked it up.

Willow,

We're leaving mid-morning tomorrow for Seattle. I tried to text you, but Rowan warned me that you might not check your phone, so I'm writing this just in case.

Adrian

I thought about what I'd need to pack and remembered that everything I owned would fit into one large suitcase. *Well, that shouldn't take long.*

I was able to pack my bag the next morning while everyone else ate breakfast. But when I returned to my room after a shower, a towel wrapped around me, I found Alasdair sitting on my bed, waiting patiently.

His orange eyes certainly noticed my state of undress, but he dipped his head respectfully and kept his eyes on mine.

"You're still here," I stated coolly.

"Can we talk?" His voice was low and subdued, not at all what I'd learned to expect from him in our short acquaintance.

My lack of reply gave him leave to speak. He sighed. "Look, I know this all sounds crazy to you. And, believe me, I heard what you said yesterday. I understand that you don't want to lead a pack. But I think if you'll just get to know me, you'll feel differently. I might not need any other reason besides that I know deep within me that I'm meant to follow you..." His voice dropped to a murmur. "But you clearly need more."

The coolness with which I regarded him eased a bit. *At least he's listening.*

He rose from my bed and slowly closed the distance between us. "I gather that you've got a lot on your plate right now. But, please." His eyes were solicitous and desperate. "Don't refuse my formal request. I don't want to be forcibly sent from your side in that way. You aren't ready. I get it. But get to know me first before you throw me away. If nothing else, we can be friends, can't we?"

His words stroked something deep within me—something instinctual, something primal. I didn't want to refuse him. I lowered my chin in the slightest of assenting gestures.

He smiled, all hope and joy and gumdrop dreams. "Let's start over." He held out his hand to me. "I'm Alasdair of the Pink Moon Clan."

My mouth dropped open. *He's from one of the thirteen original families? Why would he want to join my pack instead of staying in his family's pack? He's got to have a relative on the Wolf Council. Why wouldn't he follow them?*

He snorted but continued as if he hadn't noticed my shock. "I'm a first-degree wolf mystic. I like spicy food and reading scary stories. I'm the youngest of seven siblings. Not only am I the best practical joker of the bunch, but I always get away with it. I've been told that I'm incorrigible."

I couldn't help but laugh. "That explains a lot actually. If you're from one of the thirteen families, you're used to getting your way."

He gave me a lopsided grin. "That's right. So would you like to just accept me into your pack now?"

I shook my head but clasped his forearm. "It's nice to meet you, Alasdair. I also like spicy food, and you've already met my only brother. I'm obviously not from one of the thirteen."

With his arm firm beneath my palm and fingertips, Alasdair's smile warmed. I couldn't help but return it. "I won't hold it against you."

I could tell he was serious about wanting to join my pack since he was willing to give up everything to follow me to the realm of origin—and he had more to give up than most. *Maybe the ancestors are bringing us together for some unknown purpose. I'm not going to accept him into my pack, but I'll never say no to a friend like that.*

A soft knock sounded on the already-open door. I jumped, gripping Alasdair's arm a little tighter in my surprise since I hadn't heard anyone approach.

Adrian cleared his throat. "Sorry to interrupt."

I looked over at him. His gaze was fixed on the floor.

"Are you almost ready?" he asked.

"Yeah, everything is packed. I just need to get dressed. I'll be down in ten minutes."

"Do you want me to carry your bag down to the car?" Adrian glanced up at me, his eyes traveling over my towel. His pale face flushed, and he dropped his gaze again.

I snorted at his reaction. *I guess he is half-human after all.* "Sure. Thanks."

Stepping into my room, Adrian shifted his weight from one foot to the other, trying to decide how to get past Alasdair and me to where my suitcase was. "Excuse me," he muttered, pointing through us.

I finally released Alasdair's arm, and Adrian walked between us. Then he grabbed my case and wheeled it to the door.

"I'll wait downstairs." He left the door open when he departed.

I looked back up at Alasdair, his attention on the doorway Adrian had just gone through.

"Well, you heard him. I've got to get dressed so we can get on the road."

"You're really going on a field trip with that"—he gestured toward the door—"that *vampire*?"

"I'm really going to protect Adrian while he does some very important research."

His full lips pouted. "I don't like him."

I walked over to where my clothes were folded on the bed. "Well, I don't need to tell you that your opinion on the subject doesn't matter. In any case, you just dropped into a situation you know nothing about. Did anyone even tell you what he's researching?"

"No, but I don't care about any of that. It's...something else. Something about him makes me uneasy."

I huffed a sardonic laugh. "Why wouldn't he? Vampires are our enemies. We've been taught our whole lives to kill them on sight. I didn't react so well to him the first time we met either. But you get used to him."

Alasdair shook his head as if I was reading the situation entirely wrong. "How long will your trip take?"

I shrugged. "Who knows?"

He opened his mouth to answer, but whatever he was going to say was interrupted by Aryn's shout from downstairs.

"Hey, Alasdair! Let's go!"

But Alasdair didn't move to heed her call.

"You better go," I pushed.

Disappointment at having been dismissed shone in his eyes. "We'll meet again," he vowed.

19

*A*s promised, it only took me ten minutes to get dressed and head downstairs. But it took me another fifteen to say goodbye to Rowan, Yuti, and Lia—especially as I'd hardly gotten to see my brother and sister-in-law since their return.

Rowan had nothing but words of warning and apprehension while Yuti urged us to have some fun along the way. Lia gave Adrian our flight information and told me Ashwin would overnight my passport to me at Adrian's mother's house.

We were in Adrian's blue hatchback just before nine.

After putting on our seat belts, we looked at each other tentatively. The atmosphere grew thick and awkward, but at least he didn't smell of fear.

Adrian's hands tightened on the steering wheel. "You ready?"

I nodded and settled into the passenger seat. He put the car into drive, and we were on our way.

The morning sun was bright, making the snow on the side of the road sparkle. The dashboard thermometer told me it was hovering at freezing, and I felt grateful for the steady heat warming my face and feet.

After twenty minutes had passed without a word, I no longer

felt awkward. I surmised that Adrian was the quiet type, like Noire. And that suited me just fine.

He broke that assumption not a moment after I made it. "So…"

I glanced over at him. His eyes remained fixed on the road, and he looked very stiff with his hands at ten and two and his shoulders tight.

"That guy who showed up yesterday…"

"Yeah, what about him?" I stared at him, but he didn't so much as glance back.

"You two seemed…close. Will he be upset you're leaving for an indeterminate amount of time?"

I sucked my teeth and crossed my arms. "How he feels isn't my responsibility or my business."

If Adrian heard the irritation in my voice, he ignored it. "I doubt he would agree. He was pretty handsy for someone who isn't your business."

My eyebrows scrunched. I didn't recall Alasdair touching me inappropriately, but something about Adrian's tone annoyed me. "What's it to you anyway? Why would you care?"

"I've learned a thing or two about werewolves over the last two years—learned the lines you all are willing to bite over. And even if he got past not attacking me for existing, that doesn't mean I'm safe."

"What exactly do you think you know about us?"

"I know that if he sees you as his mate, or his promised, or even as having the potential for either, he'll be very territorial. I've gone through quite a few scrapes with Rowan over being Yuti's friend."

I'd never seen Rowan show any hostility over Adrian being friends with Yuti, but that didn't mean Adrian was incorrect. Werewolves were extremely territorial when it came to their mates, and they did *not* share on that front. Regardless, he had completely misread the situation. Alasdair didn't want me to be his mate; he wanted me to be his alpha. But the whole affair, and my reaction to it, had left me confused and exhausted. I didn't have the patience to explain it all to Adrian at the moment, nor did I think I needed to.

He wasn't a wolf. He wouldn't understand.

"You'll be fine."

But he wasn't about to let it go. He growled in frustration, and I thought that maybe he *was* spending too much time with werewolves. "This is ridiculous. I didn't ask for any of this, you know. I'm tired of having no control over my own life. Why should I even have to care about how some jacked werewolf wants to chase someone who tried to kill me?"

Irritation crawled across my skin. *How many times is he going to bring that up?* "I said you'll be fine!" I snapped. "No one is going to hurt you because it's my job to make sure that doesn't happen. You could be a little more grateful. Like anyone has ever heard of a werewolf protecting a blood-sucking corpse anyway. My parents would die of shame."

He was silent for a while, and I thought I'd effectively ended the conversation.

"I'm not dead." His voice sounded hurt. "A man's heart beats in my chest."

My cheeks burned with shame. I didn't know why I'd said something so unkind. I glanced over at him. His frown was deep and his eyes sad. I turned my gaze out the window, the blaring reflection off the snow burning my eyes.

"How long of a drive is it to your mom's?" I muttered.

"Ten and a half hours."

I winced. That was a long time to be trapped in a car. "Let me know if you need a break, and I'll drive."

Neither of us said another word for the next three hours. And even then, it was only for him to ask me if I needed to use a toilet.

By the time we stopped at a roadside diner for lunch, the silence had become unbearable. It was a strange sensation for me. I was normally comfortable with silence. But I had a strong suspicion that the awkwardness between us was entirely my fault.

After we'd given the waitress our orders, Adrian pulled out his phone and started to text. It was as if I wasn't there at all.

I frowned. "I'm sorry."

He jerked his head up, his violet eyes meeting mine.

I squeezed my laced fingers tight on my lap, but I didn't look away. "I'm sorry I called you a blood-sucking corpse. And…I'm sorry again for trying to attack you the first time we met."

The corner of his mouth twitched. It wasn't what I would call a smile, but it was enough. "I have been told my…aroma can have that effect on certain people."

"Pff, that's one way of putting it."

He leaned his cheek on his hand, the gesture easy and affable. "You know, out of all the…" He glanced around the diner. "People like you I've met, you're the only one to react that violently. Others seem to have a lot more control."

Because I'm an alpha, and I was very untrained at the time.

"In light of that, how is it that you were able to overcome that drive? You got…let's say intimately close to me yesterday, and you've been in a car with me all morning."

I leaned closer, crossing my arms on the table, and he did the same. We were mere inches apart, and I dropped my voice low, my eyes clinging to his. "I concentrate on the human part of your scent. It's not as noticeable as the other part, but it's actually quite pleasant, even in conjunction."

His pale complexion warmed. "What does it smell like?" he whispered.

I took a slow, deep breath through my nose, closing my eyes. "There's the rich earth that you already know about. Then…hay, bergamot, and…something delicately floral. I can't place it." I took another long sniff. "I know I know it." I opened my eyes and stared back into his.

His lips parted, and the slightest little tip of his fangs peeked out. The softest whiff of a new scent mixed into his base normal. It was crisp and sweet like autumn apples.

"Here you are," the waitress said, stepping up to our table with a tray of food.

We both leaned back to give her room to put the plates down.

As we dug in, I thought about what that new note in Adrian's scent might be. I'd never noticed it before. But then again, the scent of his fear usually made him smell doused in vinegar when he was around me.

I glanced up at him as he chewed his corned beef sandwich. His eyes met mine, and he gave me a smile, a dimple appearing on his cheek.

20

The rest of the drive to Seattle proved to be much more comfortable, though we still didn't talk much. We stopped for dinner along the way, and I took the wheel from there.

"Pull in here," Adrian directed, pointing at a parking lot beside an apartment building.

I parked between two faded yellow lines and cut the engine. Then I handed Adrian his keys before we both got out. Stretching my back, I looked around.

It was already dark, the parking lot illuminated by two noisy streetlamps, one of which flickered on and off. There wasn't any snow on the ground, but I saw plenty of trash, mostly wrappers and cigarette butts. The flickering streetlamp kept illuminating the graffitied, concrete wall of the apartment building, different colors of spray paint overlapping each other in chaotic lines that held meaning only to their creators. I'd seen some great street art on the drive in, but this was not among it.

Adrian opened the hatchback and pulled out our cases, offering my suitcase handle to me.

Under the pool of yellow light, he looked up at the building, smiling that tight-lipped smile of his. "Come on."

I followed him toward the front door, the wheels on my suitcase bumping over cracks and breaks in the sidewalk. Up a few steps, we entered a small hall with tons of little cubby mailboxes.

Adrian unlocked a chipped, red door and held it open for me. The hall had a set of stairs on one side and an ancient elevator on the other. The place smelled old and musty, and the elevator smelled of grease and rust.

Adrian pointed at the elevator. "Do you want to—"

"Let's take the stairs." I eyed the grate that was the elevator's door. *I'm not that brave.*

"All right."

We started up the stairs, which were clean of dust and debris, and stopped on the fourth floor.

Adrian picked up his pace, clearly eager to reach his destination. He entered the third door on the right without even knocking. "I'm home!" he called as he opened the door.

The smell that drifted from the doorway was a cross between a slaughterhouse and a Catholic church, the scent of blood and earthy incense weaving together in a strange but somehow complimentary mixture.

He didn't even get a chance to drag his suitcase inside before a human woman launched herself into his arms. "Welcome home, baby."

Adrian returned her embrace. "Thanks, Mom."

I stood in the hallway, looking over my shoulder as I blocked the narrow passage. But there wasn't anyone around.

After some squealing and a few tuts, Adrian's mom pulled back and surveyed her son.

"You've lost weight," she accused him. "And what the heck is going on with your hair? Do you want me to cut it while you're here? I just got these new shears; the owner of the salon gave them to all the stylists as Christmas presents."

Adrian reached up and touched his hair. "I guess it is getting kind of long, but we can talk about that later. Let's get inside, huh?" He pulled his case into the apartment, and I followed, closing the door behind me.

"Mom, this is Willow. Willow, this is my mom, Sydney Hudson."

Adrian's mom was a tall, lean woman with seaweed-green hair and big, blue eyes. She had the same high cheekbones and sharp chin that her son had. If mermaids had been real, I wouldn't have been surprised if she were one. She certainly looked like a siren of death as she glared at me.

I nodded at her, not brave enough to hold out my hand for fear she'd bite it off.

"I never thought I'd see the day when I'd let a werewolf into my house," she said, crossing her arms over her chest.

"Mom, you said you'd behave," Adrian warned.

Sydney turned her head to the side, dismissing me. "Go put your things in the room. I've warmed up some juice for you."

"It's all right," Adrian answered. "I don't want to take your bed. I'll sleep out here on the floor."

Sydney frowned. "I can't have my baby sleeping on the floor. At least take the couch."

"The floor is fine. She can have the couch."

Sydney squinted at me. "What have I told you, Adrian? No animals on the furniture."

My mouth dropped open, and I felt like I'd just been slapped in the face.

"Mom!" Adrian snapped. "Stop it, or we'll stay somewhere else."

Sydney pursed her lips and turned on her heel, heading through the small living room to the kitchen.

Adrian glanced over at me, wincing. "I'm sorry," he murmured. "She's a bit...protective. You know better than anyone that vampires and werewolves are enemies."

I frowned and thought about sleeping in the car. Then I threw that idea right out. There may not be snow out there, but it was still too cold for my liking.

"She'll behave," he said.

I thought he vastly overestimated his influence. I got the impression that if Sydney Hudson didn't want to do something, no one was going to force her.

21

"*H*ere you are, sweetheart." Sydney set a plate of pink-frosted cookies in front of Adrian with a mug of what smelled like hot blood. "98.6 degrees, just like you like it."

My stomach rolled. I knew that Adrian's "juice" was pig's blood rather than human, but something about heating it to human normal was just too much for me.

"Thanks, Mom."

I cleared my throat. "Could I have a glass of water, please?"

Adrian nodded and rose from his seat to get it for me.

Sydney glared across the table at me, but she didn't say anything, not that she needed to. I stared at the wooden bowl at the center of the table. It held an orange and two bananas, browning a little in the middle.

Adrian set a glass of water in front of me and placed the plate of cookies between us.

I drank deep from the glass, then ran my finger up and down its smooth side, the sensation of the repetitive gesture soothing me.

I glanced down at the plate of cookies, and my mouth

watered. They looked so good, and the sight of them was making me hungry. I snaked my hand out, glancing at Sydney to see if she'd snap at me. She frowned but didn't say anything. The pink frosting smeared onto the side of my finger, and I nibbled one end. It was fluffy and soft, and the frosting was creamy and light. "Delicious." My tone didn't carry my sincerity.

"My mom is great at baking," Adrian complimented with a smile in her direction.

Sydney reached out and brushed his hair from his face, her lips turning upward at his praise. Then she asked him how the drive had been and what he'd been up to lately.

Other than the fact that he talked openly about working with werewolves on his research, the conversation was quite mundane. Still, I couldn't help but feel the pressure of her clear dislike for me.

I didn't make it another five minutes before I stood from the table. "Do you mind if I go to sleep early? I'm really tired from the drive."

Adrian nodded at me. "The bathroom is just down the hall, and there are already pillows and blankets on the couch."

"Thanks."

Ten minutes later, I was staring at the pattern on the couch as I lay under a thick but prickly afghan. The couch was blue and had brown dots encircled by white rings. I counted how many dots were in front of my face without turning my head. I wasn't tired at all. Still, I closed my eyes and tried to force myself to go to sleep. We weren't leaving until Monday, and I'd need rest if I was going to deal with this for the next few days.

"I wish you wouldn't be like this," I heard Adrian whisper from the kitchen, my wolf hearing picking it up as if he were right beside me.

There was the soft *snip* from a pair of hair-cutting shears.

"What do you expect from me?" Sydney huffed.

"I expect you to be the kind and loving person I know you are."

Snip. Snip.

"I don't like this situation. I feel like you're being held against your will. What gives them the right to force her on you?"

He hasn't told her the whole truth then. That's probably for the best. Not that it mattered that Sydney didn't know we were effectively holding Adrian against his will; she clearly had a mother's intuition.

Adrian sighed. "You always warned me to be wary of coming across werewolves. You told me they would try to kill me if they got the chance. Willow is going with me to protect me from any other werewolves I might come across."

I frowned at the thought of a young Adrian lying in his bed, terrified that werewolves would get him.

I suppose to him we are the nightmares. And he's still defending me, even though he wanted to go with anyone but me.

I frowned at the memory of his vehement refusal of my protection.

Snip.

Sydney clicked her tongue. "You don't need *her* help. And who's to say she won't turn on you at any second? They're *dangerous*. It's in their nature."

"That's not right, and you know it. Saying that 'it's in their nature,' is the same as them saying all vampires are just out to kill humans. No one has to be controlled by their nature. That's what you've always taught me."

"I don't much like you using my own words and logic against me."

Adrian chuckled, the sound warm and easy.

As if I couldn't feel any worse about losing control and almost killing him.

I closed my eyes against the shame that lingered in my heart.

Snip.

"Your father is coming into town tomorrow," Sydney said in an offhand tone. "He called me this morning. He wants to see you."

I listened harder, curious now that I'd met his mother.

Adrian remained silent for a long time, the only sound the snipping of the shears.

"It has been a while…" She nudged him.

"Why?"

"Why what?"

"Why does he suddenly want to see me? It's been almost seven years since I've seen him, and that was after not seeing him for ten years."

Snip. Snip.

"He didn't say why. Maybe he just wants to have a relationship with you."

"Oh, now he wants to have a relationship with me? He abandoned us when I was only seven years old. He never called me, not even on my birthday. I'm not sure he even knows when my birthday is. He never paid you child support. You had to raise me entirely on your own. It's not like he didn't have money. He started that business. He had enough money to buy his new wife that ridiculously expensive car and to send my half-brother to private schools his whole life."

"He gave you money when you graduated high school."

"Oh yeah, that five hundred dollars didn't even buy me books for my first semester. In any case, it felt dirty by then, like he was trying to buy my love. He could give me every cent he owns, and I wouldn't forgive him for abandoning us. Even if he wanted a divorce, he was still my father."

"That's right. He *is* still your father. And what have I always told you? You can only expect from people what they're capable of giving. I've known him since we were thirteen years old, and he has never been responsible or anything other than selfish."

"Then why is he taking such good care of Cheryl and Charlie?"

Sydney sighed. "Because they don't expect anything from him but money. If we would have been happy with only that, he might have stayed."

"No, he wouldn't have," Adrian muttered darkly. "The minute you were attacked by that vampire, it was over for us. He was never going to accept me for what I am, and he was never going to forgive you for being a victim. I knew it, even as young as I was. I knew it. I think he almost wished that that vampire didn't just drink off you, but also fed you. Then you would have turned and I would have been miscarried, and he could have just mourned the loss of his wife and son rather than having to actually deal with us."

The snipping paused, and I heard a rustle of fabric.

"Oh, honey," Sydney murmured.

"I'm okay." Adrian's voice sounded muffled, as if his face was buried in cloth. "I don't need some superficial relationship. He probably only wants to meet me because he's told himself he's some great father and wants to make himself feel better. I'd rather put my energy into the people who love me. So I'm going to stay home with you. We can do whatever you want."

"Well, I'll never argue with that."

My mind spun with everything I'd overheard. My whole life, I'd been taught that vampires were monsters, that I needed to kill them without question. I'd never even considered that they had families, friends...people who cared about them.

Maybe this was just Adrian. He wasn't like any other vampire I'd ever heard of. He was still alive, still had a heartbeat, still had the wherewithal to lead a semi-normal life.

I frowned as his frustrated words from earlier in the day echoed in my ears. He was right. He hadn't asked for any of this. He hadn't asked to be born the way he was. I knew that feeling only too well. I also knew how frustrating—how confining—it was to not have control over your own life and your own decisions.

We might have been on opposite sides of the void, but we were more alike than I'd ever have thought.

I readjusted to lie on my back and let the sounds of the soft *snip snip snip* of Sydney's hair shears lull me to sleep.

22

I awoke the next morning to the smell of frying bacon. My mouth watered, and my eyes flew open. I sat up on the couch and looked around. Adrian lay on the floor between the couch and the coffee table, his face relaxed as he slept. His mouth was slack, the tips of his fangs peeking out as he breathed slowly.

A sizzle and pop from the kitchen announced that Sydney was cooking. I lay back down. It felt rude not to offer to help, but I imagined that she'd appreciate me staying away more than me helping her.

As I lay on my side, watching the morning sunlight play in Adrian's hair—the warm brown gilded in shimmering light—I tried to ignore the fact that I had to pee. But I didn't last two minutes before sighing and getting up.

When I returned from the bathroom, Adrian was sitting up on the floor, his hair—shorter and cleaner but still long enough to ruffle—stuck up at angles reminiscent of a modern art sculpture. His violet eyes were unfocused and bleary, and I wondered how long he'd stayed up the night before.

"Wake up, kids!" Sydney called from the kitchen. "Breakfast is ready."

I tilted my head at the word. I hadn't been treated like a kid since before I'd been bound with Feather, not that I was offended by the term. *Should I be flattered that she lumped me in with him this way?*

"We're up," Adrian said, though his voice remained thick with sleep.

I shifted my weight from one foot to the other, stalling while Adrian untangled himself from blankets and stood. I wanted him to head into the kitchen first.

Following his lead, I shuffled to the table and sat beside him. Sydney placed a plate of pancakes and bacon before each of us. I glanced up at her in surprise. I hadn't expected her to starve me while I was there, but this was a major shift from the night before. Her eyes met mine, and she gave me a tentative, little half-smile. *She's trying.*

I smiled at her in return. "Thank you. It looks amazing."

She nodded and retrieved her plate from the counter before sitting across from me.

After carefully buttering each side of his pancakes, Adrian poured red syrup over the small stack.

My throat squeezed as I stared at the thick sauce oozing down the sides of his pancakes.

"Relax," Sydney chuckled. "It's only maple raspberry."

Adrian's eyes flicked toward me, and he laughed. His smile, his fangs on full display, told me just how at ease he was while at home. Gone was the careful, tight-lipped smile I was used to— not that he'd smiled at me often since we'd met. His easy demeanor took the sting out of my embarrassment.

I reached for the syrup.

"It's not so strange, though," he said. "I've read about blood pancakes. There are all sorts of cuisines that use blood actually. Blood sausages, blood soup...I've even heard of something called hematogen. They're like candy bars made with cow's blood. I've never been able to get my hands on them to try them though."

I took a bite of the fluffy pancakes drenched in raspberry syrup. They were amazing. "Does that work?" I asked. "I mean, could you eat blood sausages instead of just drinking blood from a glass?"

Adrian chewed thoughtfully. "It'll do in a pinch. There usually isn't enough blood for it to be a real replacement, but I have used blood foods to hold me over."

I hummed my acknowledgment around a bite of chewy bacon.

"Do you want anything special for dinner tonight?" Sydney asked.

Adrian lowered his face and looked up at his mom through his eyelashes. "Grandma's spaghetti and meatballs?"

Sydney scowled. "I should have known that's what you'd ask for. And of course I don't have any of the ingredients. Fine. After breakfast, I'll head to the store. You two can stay here and get ready for the day."

Adrian grinned. "Thanks, Mom."

Sydney pursed her lips. "You better remember this when I'm old and need taking care of."

He chuckled. "Sure, sure."

After we'd eaten, Sydney left to go to the store. Adrian insisted that I shower first. But when I was clean and dressed, I just sort of stood around, drifting about the living room and looking at pictures of Sydney and Adrian taken while he'd been growing up. He seemed like he'd been a happy child, though it was hard to tell since he only wore that small, tight-lipped smile in his photographs. Sydney must have been quite good at taking pictures because there were only a few where the light caught his eyes just right to make them glow with eyeshine.

With nothing else to do, I started washing the dishes. I was elbow-deep in warm, sudsy water when I heard a yelp followed by a thud.

My instincts kicked in as my heart jumped. Racing toward the bathroom, I dripped soapy water on the carpet as I went. I thrust open the bathroom door, my eyes scanning for danger.

Adrian lay butt-ass naked on the floor, everything on display. He winced, his wet hair plastered to his face. He clutched the towel bar in his fist, the brackets broken off in the wall and the towel in a heap beside him.

I looked over his limbs to make sure everything sat at the proper angles, and then I burst out laughing. I gasped for air, heaving with laughter I couldn't stifle. I doubled over. My stomach hurt as the giggles just kept coming.

"Are you okay?" I tried to look at him as tears blurred my vision.

He pursed his lips, quickly pulling a towel across his waist as if I hadn't seen it all already.

"Do you need a hand?"

"I'm fine," he muttered. "Let me just look for my dignity while I'm down here."

I waved my hand. "Pff, oh, that's long gone. You're never finding that."

His cheeks reddened as he covered his face with one hand. "I don't know how many times I've told her to fix that towel rack."

"Well, you shouldn't have leaned on it," I countered.

"I wasn't—it should be properly secured!"

I shook my head, still chuckling. Then I offered him a hand up. He took my hand, and I hauled him to his feet.

"Seriously though, are you all right? Nothing hurts?"

He rolled his shoulders, and I analyzed him. He may have lost weight, but he hadn't lost muscular definition. My gaze traveled over his shoulders, his arms, his chest and abdomen. He was taut, lean but sculpted. There was an angry red mark on his chest near his collarbone, perhaps where the bar had recoiled and hit him as he'd fallen. I lifted my hand and ran my fingers over it. His skin was smooth and surprisingly warm.

I recalled my dream from not two weeks before—his hard warmth pressed to me as he stroked me to completion. Having just seen everything in the broad light of day, I saw that my dream hadn't done him justice.

Right out of the shower, with his nearly naked body inches

from me, his scent was quite strong. Hay, bergamot, floral, and earth. With secret images floating before my eyes and his scent all around me, I could feel my face get hot.

Get out of my head. Everything about this is wrong.

"Does this hurt?" My voice was not as steady as I would've liked it to be. I looked up, meeting his eyes.

His breath hitched, and the crisp sweetness of apples reappeared. "No," he murmured.

"How about this?" I pressed a little harder.

He hissed, wincing.

"I think it's going to bruise," I whispered.

Adrian cleared his throat, but his gaze didn't leave mine. "I should…get dressed."

I nodded. *He definitely should.* "I'll leave you to it then." Removing my hand from his flushed skin, I went to finish the dishes.

23

The rest of the day—and the one after—were fairly peaceful. Adrian hung out with his mom, and I tried to stay in the background. They mostly sat around chatting, and we watched movies in the evening. Adrian's father wasn't mentioned again. The atmosphere was all right overall. In some ways, I was more at ease than I'd been for a long time. I still felt the pressure that came from being in another alpha's territory, but there weren't any werewolves nearby. I felt like I was simply Willow again, even if I wasn't much welcome.

Early Monday morning, after we'd showered and made sure everything was packed, I sat on the couch staring at the clock. We had to be at the airport a few hours before our flight left, but I still didn't have a passport.

"Take this with you." Sydney offered Adrian a small cooler. "It should be enough to hold you over until you can find a butcher in France."

A loud buzzing made me jump.

Adrian went over to the front door and pressed a button. A few minutes later, a knock sounded on the wood. I breathed a sigh of relief when Adrian handed me an envelope after thanking the messenger.

I tore it open to find a piece of paper, my passport, and a flat, plastic case that easily fit in the palm of my hand. I unfolded the letter.

Willow,

Here is your passport and the address for where you'll check in with Jean-Henri, the French pack's alpha. I've also included international SIM cards for your and Adrian's phones.

Stay in touch.
Ashwin

"What's a SIM card?" I asked, offering the note to Adrian.

He read it quickly and held out his hand for the plastic case. "These will allow us to make calls on our cellphones while overseas. I'll put them in once we're on the plane."

My stomach hardened. *Ugh. The plane.*

After another fifteen minutes, Adrian turned to his mom. "Well, I guess that's it. The taxi is downstairs, and the meter is running. We'd better get on the road if we want to make it through security in time."

"I'm sorry I can't take you to the airport. I pushed my appointments back as far as I could, but I need to be at work soon."

"Don't worry. A taxi is fine."

I glanced at them, two people bound by love and family ties. Adrian hadn't been able to visit his mom in nearly two years. She was able to visit him, but she hadn't come often. At that moment, I thought what a shame it was that he'd gotten mixed up with us.

"Why don't I take the suitcases down, huh?" *Then you can have a moment alone.* I moved toward our cases waiting beside the door.

"Adrian will do that," Sydney said.

I tilted my head. *Doesn't she want to be alone with her son?*

Adrian went about his task.

But as soon as the door was shut behind him, I realized that Sydney wanted to be alone with me. Her eyes were hard and serious as she stared straight into my soul.

"I don't need to tell you that I'm wary of your kind when it comes to Adrian."

Yeah, I think I got that.

"I don't like this situation at all." She sighed heavily, her blue eyes boundless as the deepest ocean. "I'm trusting you, Willow. I hope you know how much it takes for me to say that. Keep my son safe."

I nodded slowly. I'd already taken the task for my own, but something in Sydney's request struck deep within me. I hardly knew Adrian, and completing this mission was my only means to achieving my goals. But to this human woman, he was important. He was everything.

"I will," I promised.

She stared at me for a long moment, checking the veracity of my words. Then she gave me a sharp, satisfied nod. "These are for you." She offered me a large, round tin. "I saw how much you liked them. If you put them in the freezer, they'll last longer."

I opened the lid. Pink-frosted cookies were nestled inside, stacked between layers of wax paper. I gave her a small smile. "Thank you."

Adrian returned not long after, and I took my tin into the hallway to give them a moment together. They exchanged the usual goodbyes, I love yous, and be carefuls.

And Adrian and I were buckled into the taxi within five minutes.

I glanced over at him. He frowned at the back of the driver's head, thoughtful lines on his brow.

"Thank you," he whispered. His violet eyes met mine in the

enclosed space. He'd put on a pair of clear-framed glasses. "You took a lot from my mom over the last few days. I know you could have handled it much less gracefully, and I appreciate your effort."

He was right. I could have gotten indignant. I could have thrown a fit and dragged him away over the insults his mother had thrown at me. Maybe I should have. Maybe I should have stood up for myself, for werewolf kind everywhere. But the fact was, she wasn't wrong. Vampires and werewolves were enemies. We'd been killing each other for centuries. Her prejudice was understandable.

In any case, dealing with one human woman was nothing compared to dealing with other werewolves. She was no threat to me.

I dipped my head, acknowledging his gratitude.

That seemed to be enough for him because he turned and stared out the window. The airport wasn't that far away, not nearly as far as I would've liked. As we approached, I saw a huge plane descending from the fog toward the ground. I closed my eyes, my heart hammering in my chest. Then I took a deep breath in through my nose and let it out slowly, forcing my heart to steady.

The cabbie dropped us off in front of the terminal. It was cold and foggy, the chilled humidity seeping into my bones even during the short walk it took to get inside. But I wasn't relieved once we entered the warmth. The closer I got to the end of this walk, the sooner I'd be trapped in a plane.

24

I was sullen, answering only in grunts and nods as I followed Adrian through the process of checking in. I clutched my tin of cookies when we moved to the long line leading through security.

I took off my coat, shoes, and belt as directed and put them — along with my wallet, keys, cellphone, and cookie tin — into the little tubs to be scanned. Adrian went through the scanner before me. And then he was pulled aside by a man in uniform.

After I'd made it through, I moved toward him. The man held Adrian's cooler in his hands.

"Sir, you can't bring bottles of juice onto the plane. You're going to have to trash them."

My eyes widened. *Oh, no. They're going to confiscate his pig's blood.*

But Adrian seemed unperturbed. Lowering his glasses, he looked intently at the man. "There's been a misunderstanding, officer. These are medically necessary."

The man stiffened as he stared back at Adrian.

"Would you please return my cooler to me?" Adrian asked.

A shudder ran through the man, and he held the cooler straight out as if a string were attached to his wrist.

Adrian took the cooler with a small smile. "Thank you, officer. You have a nice day."

The man didn't respond with so much as a nod. But when Adrian turned toward me, pushing his glasses back up his nose, the man blinked, his brow scrunching in confusion.

"You ready?" Adrian asked me, tucking the cooler under his arm.

I nodded, sliding up beside him as he started to walk toward our appointed gate. Of course I'd heard that vampires had their own type of compulsion over humans, but I'd never seen it first-hand. I'd never considered that Adrian would have such an ability.

"I didn't know you could do that," I said softly.

Adrian frowned. "I don't like to, but needs must in cases like this. Better I compel him to let me take my blood onto the plane than I get too thirsty..."

And attack someone, my mind supplied the end of his sentence. "Is that why you wear the glasses?"

Adrian nodded. "Yes, they provide a barrier so I don't do it by accident." He tilted his head. "You know, I hadn't really thought about it, but I haven't had to wear glasses in a while. I've been around you guys so much that I haven't needed them."

"Have you ever tried to compel one of us that you know it doesn't work?"

Adrian's dimple appeared on his cheek as he gave me a tight-lipped smirk. "Let's just say that your brother isn't keen on sharing when he sneaks a late-night meat-lover's pizza."

I burst out laughing.

After finding our gate, Adrian asked if I was hungry. "It's expensive, but the food is decent. What are you in the mood for? Chinese? Fish? Barbecue? We still have a while before we can board, and they won't feed us for a bit once we're up there."

Up there. My stomach rolled, but I nodded. "Whatever you want to eat is fine."

Adrian decided on Chinese. I ordered ginger beef and an egg roll. I don't recall what he ate, but he washed it down with some pig's blood. I kept my attention on my food, the crunch of my egg roll, the warm and spicy sweetness of the meat. I needed to live in this moment, not worry about what would happen once I got on the plane.

And the concentration worked until we were back at our gate and the woman called for us to board.

I hated everything about the plane. I hated how the seats were crammed together. I hated how loud the engines were even while it was resting. I hated how dry the air was—its smell some weird mixture of human scents, recycled air, and machinery. I even hated the tiny little cupboards above the aisles. My chest tightened as I inched closer to my seat, following the slow line of humans in front of me. I'd never been claustrophobic before, but I felt now was a good time to start.

Adrian stowed his cooler and my cookie tin in the overhead compartment, then turned back to me as people started filling the aisle behind me. "Do you want the window seat?" he asked.

"Only if I can close the shade," I said.

He nodded, and I scooted in before him, immediately drawing the shade down.

Now that we'd boarded the plane, I was a bundle of nervous energy. My knees bounced, and I closed my eyes, leaning my head back and forcing myself to breathe slowly.

"Are you all right?" Adrian asked. "You're looking pale."

I didn't open my eyes. "I've never been on a plane, and I don't like the idea of flying."

He kept quiet, and I continued my slow breathing, counting each inhale and exhale.

Then I felt a hand on mine, and my breath hitched as my eyes flew open. Adrian stared at me intently, his violet eyes earnest behind his glasses.

"It's okay. I've done this tons of times. Once you're in the air, you'll hardly notice. Take-off and landing are the worst parts, and I'll distract you, so don't worry."

I breathed out, his hand warm and firm on mine. Nodding, I turned my hand over to lace my fingers with his. He gave me an encouraging smile and squeezed my fingers.

"Oh!" I jumped as the plane started to move, the cabin rattling while we bumped along.

"It's all right," he assured me. "We're just moving onto the runway."

The woman and the front of the plane started talking about seat belts and tray tables, but I blocked her out. I clenched Adrian's hand and focused on his eyes staring into mine. My heartbeat was wild, and I'd stopped trying to control my breathing.

The plane halted, and I glanced around.

"Look at me," Adrian urged me.

I met his eyes.

Then he opened his mouth and let out a high-pitched keen. "Eeeeeeeee-eeeee-eeee-eeee-eeeeEEE—eeeeEEE-oooo-aaah…"

My mouth fell open; he wasn't even trying to keep his voice down.

He continued his song, singing a whole verse as the plane suddenly burst forward.

My stomach clenched, then rolled, but all I could concentrate on was the sound of Adrian's voice as he sang to me.

Once the plane had leveled out and my stomach had stopped dropping, Adrian smiled, squeezing my hand. "See? Nothing to it."

I let out a huffed laugh of disbelief. "What the heck was that?"

His face reddened. "That was 'Werewolf' by Michael Hurley… Sorry, it was the first thing that came to mind." He glanced around, nodding in apology to the people who stared at him from across the aisle.

*a*drian released my hand and dug into his jacket pocket. He pulled out his phone and the SIM cards Ashwin had sent us.

"Hand me your phone." He lowered his tray table and put his phone and a little tool onto it. I pulled out mine and gave it to him.

He made quick work of changing our SIM cards, placing the domestic ones into the little case. Then he opened the packet of headphones the airline provided and stuck one into his left ear. He held the other out to me.

I just stared at him.

"I have music loaded onto my phone. It's a long flight, and this will distract you from the sound of the engines."

I took the earbud he offered and stuck it into my right ear; it was silent and did little to stifle the sounds of the plane.

"Do you like music?" he asked, looking at his phone screen.

I shrugged. "I don't dislike it. But I don't know much music from here."

His violet eyes flicked to mine, and he smirked. "Well then, you're about to get a crash course in the sixties."

"Ugh, don't say crash."

He chuckled. "Sit back and enjoy."

The plucking of an acoustic guitar sounded in my ear before a group of men and women started singing about dreaming of the warm weather in California. This message, I could get behind.

Adrian tapped his finger on his knee along with the music. When the song was over, he paused his phone and turned to me. "What do you think?"

I nodded. "I liked it. I hate cold weather. Is it warm in California then? Maybe I'll go there one day."

"It's warm in LA at least. I don't like the cold either..." His voice trailed off, and he dropped his gaze. "It reminds me of the dead...or the undead."

I frowned. I'd been told all about the incident with Rowan's ex-promised and Rowan feeding Adrian his blood when he'd tried to kill himself by starvation. I knew a little about wishing a part of myself was different than what it was, though I'd never gone that far. I guessed the cold reminded Adrian of that part of himself.

"Do you have anything else about warm weather?" I asked. "Maybe it will make the winter a little less cold."

He glanced over at me and smiled. "Sure. Let's see. Oh, this one is from the eighties, but the band started in the sixties."

The song started with a list of places and painted a scene of a tropical paradise where people could relax and fall in love. The singers' voices harmonized beautifully, accompanied by drums and other percussion sounds. I closed my eyes. I could almost feel the warm sand between my toes as they sang. It was over too soon.

"So...?" Adrian asked, pulling me from the world the music had created and forcing me to open my eyes.

"Got any more?"

He grinned, the tips of his fangs peeking out. "Of course."

We listened to music like that for a while, only taking a short break to eat dinner and use the bathroom—which was a harrowing experience that would never be repeated if I could help it. Then we listened to more, long after they'd turned the lights low and the other passengers had begun cuddling under their thin blankets.

"Can you leave it on?" I whispered to Adrian when we too readied to sleep.

"Sure. But I don't know how long the battery will last."

I frowned. "That's okay. I have my phone if we need it when we land."

He nodded, and we settled in to sleep.

Well, I tried anyway. Despite my eyes drooping and my heavy head, I couldn't manage to really fall asleep while sitting up.

I glanced over at Adrian in the dim cabin light while a band sang in my ear about an umbrella that brought two people together. His eyes were closed, and his breathing was soft and easy.

It was strange to think that I'd learned so much more about him in the last few days than I had in the year and a half since I'd been in the realm of origin. He'd been a threat, then a challenge, then a tool. But looking at him now, I saw he was really just a man—a man who had no problem embarrassing himself in front of a plane full of strangers to make me feel more at ease, who loved sixties music and his grandma's meatballs, whose father had abandoned him, and whose mother loved him with all her might. He was a man who was just as burdened by the threads of fate as I was.

I reached out and adjusted his blanket so that it covered his hand.

I wonder what else I'll learn about him in the future. And, leaning against the window, I closed my eyes and drifted off into a shallow and restless sleep.

A few hours later, the airline served us breakfast. It wasn't great, but what could be expected that high up in the air? Not a lot of options.

Adrian's phone had died in the night, and that was probably a good thing. My ear was sore from the earbud being in it for too long.

"So what happens when we land in Paris?" I asked after drinking orange juice from a tin-covered plastic cup.

Adrian chewed his egg and cheese croissant, then swallowed. "We rent a car and do whatever, I guess. My meeting with the curator at the Château de Chantilly isn't until tomorrow. It's closed on Tuesdays."

I shook my head. "We can't just do whatever." I lowered my voice to a whisper. "We need to meet with the alpha first. We don't know how long we're going to be there, and we can't just enter his territory without making ourselves known to him."

Adrian sighed. "Ugh. Fine. We'll go there first," he grumbled.

Adrian asked if I wanted him to sing to me again when we landed, but I told him that wasn't necessary. I could see our neighbors eyeing us with trepidation. Still, he held my hand through the whole thing while I concentrated on counting my slow breaths.

26

---

*C*harles de Gaulle Airport was a madhouse even in the morning. As glad as I was to be back on the ground, I couldn't believe all the sights, sounds, and smells swirling around me. Though, by comparison, this still wasn't as bad as going to the alpha gathering. I may have been in an unfamiliar place, surrounded by unfamiliar sensory experiences, but at least everyone around me was human. Dealing with humans was easy in most cases.

Still, I could feel the clear pressure within me that said I was in another alpha's territory. I wondered what Jean-Henri was like. But I had faith that Lia paved the way for our visit as best she could.

Adrian seemed completely undisturbed by the commotion of the airport as he guided me past gates and through terminals, following signs I couldn't read. We stood at baggage claim for a while, squeezed together with our fellow passengers as we all watched for our suitcases. Our patience was rewarded when Adrian handed me the case that held all of my worldly possessions.

Customs was a bit nerve-wracking. Why I was more worried

about the French officials figuring out that my passport was fabricated than I'd been when first leaving the States, I didn't know. My heart hammered in my chest with every step I took toward the little booth. I watched Adrian carefully as he went through before me and mimicked exactly what he said and did when my turn came. I stifled my sigh of relief as the man handed my passport back to me.

We next went to the car rental desk, where Ashwin had reserved transportation for us. It took us nearly two hours from landing before we were buckled into a tiny, white car.

I let out a heavy sigh.

Adrian chuckled. "I concur. But I have to say: one good thing about working with the pack is that they take care of all the logistics. Do you have your phone?"

I pulled my phone out and offered it to him, but he was already plugging his into the car with a cord.

"Text your brother and Lia while I put in the address for the pack. I promised him and Yuti that I'd encourage you to check in."

I pursed my lips but complied, sending Rowan and Lia each a text that we'd arrived all right. Then I turned my phone back off.

"All set?" he asked.

I nodded. "How long will it take us to get there?"

"Maybe three-quarters of an hour north if we don't stop. But we should probably get lunch along the way."

"Good idea. We don't know what to expect once we get there."

The weather was the same here as it had been in Seattle — warmer than the mountains, but not warm enough that I'd leave my coat off. There wasn't any snow on the ground, but the sky was gray with clouds that promised no chance of sunshine.

I leaned my head against the window, and the gentle hum of our tires on the road — that solid reminder that I was on the ground — lulled me into a light sleep.

Half an hour later, I awoke to the rich smell of pizza. My

eyes flew open just as Adrian was climbing back into the car with a pizza box.

"Oh, you're awake. I thought this would be easier." He offered me the box, which I took from him. Then he reached into the back seat for his cooler. "Go ahead. I asked them to make the most popular pizza. I hope you like olives."

I opened the box to find a pizza with tomato sauce, mozzarella cheese, ham, mushrooms, and olives. My mouth watered as the scents filled the car.

It tasted even better than it smelled.

"Why is it so much better than at home?"

Adrian put a bottle of blood in the cup holder next to a bottle of water, then returned the cooler to the backseat. "The French are known for their cuisine. They excel at bread, sauces, and cheese. So their pizza is bound to be excellent."

He grabbed a slice from my lap and took a bite.

"You studied abroad, right? Have you ever been here before?" I asked after swallowing the first mouthful of my second slice.

He chewed slowly and shook his head. "No, I stuck to the British Isles mostly, though I did hop over to Spain and Italy a few times—not that I got to do much sightseeing, what with being buried in archives."

"How's the pizza in Italy? Better than here?"

Adrian smirked. "I plead the Fifth." He shoved the rest of his slice into his mouth before washing it down with some pig's blood.

The pizza was gone in less than ten minutes. And, after stepping into the restaurant for a moment to use the restroom, we were back on the road.

I didn't see much of the countryside as we traveled along the wide highway. But once we exited, it was all country roads surrounded by fallow fields and naked forests, interrupted only by idyllic and quiet towns. I remained tired after not having rested well the night prior, but the combination of a short nap, good food, and the ground beneath my feet lifted my spirits beyond that.

I hummed to myself while I watched the landscape drift by, tapping my foot to the melody playing in my head. It was from one of the songs Adrian had played me the night before. I couldn't remember the name of it or the artist, but it was upbeat and about a man who hadn't believed in love until he saw a woman's face.

As the hour mark approached, I sat up straighter in my seat. We were getting closer to our destination; I could feel the pressure within me growing with every mile. The forest around us gave way to stone houses and cobbled garden walls, ivy spilling over the sides.

I wondered how many wolves were in Jean-Henri's pack and frowned at myself for not asking Lia for more details.

"Here we go," Adrian murmured, his voice steady despite the whiff of fear sprinkled into his scent.

I stared at the white sign with a red border. *Bosquet-aux-Loups*, it declared in tall, black letters.

drian continued down the single-lane road, which soon led to the center of a small village. There wasn't much in the way of a downtown area. We were on a main street of some kind, but I could only tell because there was a post office. There wasn't a grocery, a butcher, a pharmacy, or even a café. I wondered how the people of Bosquet-aux-Loups got their necessities and decided they must travel to nearby towns.

At the end of the street, a sign shaped like an arrow declared the direction of the château, and Adrian turned to follow it.

The road holding the château was narrow and unassuming, flanked on both sides by small cottages. I was starting to wonder if the sign had pointed us in the wrong direction. Quite suddenly, a large house appeared beside the road behind a straight line of hedges. It was wide and at least three stories tall with a black roof atop its sandy stones.

Adrian parked close to the hedge on some dirt beside the road. He turned to me, the vinegar in his scent getting steadily stronger.

"Hey." I rested my hand on his arm. "Take a deep breath. You don't want to enter a den of werewolves smelling like fear."

"That's easy for you to say," he muttered, frowning.

"Well, then it's a good thing I'm here to protect you, isn't it? Don't forget: I'm an alpha, too."

He let out a long sigh, but the scent of his fear only eased a little.

"What's worse than a werewolf?" I asked with a smile.

He tilted his head, scrunching his eyebrows.

"A right-there-wolf."

He started to laugh, the tips of his fangs peeking out and the fear in his scent disappearing. "That's an awful joke."

It worked, didn't it?

His laughter sobered quickly, but at least he was more relaxed. "Let's get this over with."

"Right. Stay behind me."

After climbing out of the car, I stretched my arms above my head, twisting my back to loosen the stiffness that had settled in. We walked over to the simple, chain-link gate. I lifted the latch, and we both headed inside.

The brown double-doors were recessed and looked antique, with thick, weathered wood and metal decorations that had long since rusted.

I lifted the knocker and slammed it down three times. Then I glanced back at Adrian. "Stay close."

A few moments later, one of the doors opened to reveal a tall werewolf in human form with long, straight hair. Her sweater-dress left nothing of her lean figure to the imagination. Her blue eyes widened and her nostrils flared, and then she bared her teeth, her thin limbs shaking in her effort not to shift.

"We're expecting you," she said through her clenched jaw. She gave me the slightest of nods in respect to my status, but she didn't look at Adrian at all.

She didn't invite us in. She just turned on her heel and started to walk, leaving the door open for us to follow.

The heels of her boots echoed on the stone floor, its shades of brown and cream laid in a repetitive pattern. The house was much too cold for my liking—all hard floors, stone walls, and exposed rafters. Despite the dark wood of the doors and ceiling, it didn't even look warm.

We followed our guide through the small entrance hall into a large sitting room. Solid, redwood stairs led up to a gallery looking down on the stone floor. A crystal chandelier hung in the center of the room above a heavy coffee table. Dark leather couches and chairs faced a huge fireplace, the blazing fire warming the room surprisingly well.

"Jean-Henri," the woman who'd shown us in called to a broad man with dark hair to his chin.

Jean-Henri glanced up from his phone as if annoyed by the interruption. After setting his device down on the round lamp-table beside him, he rose to his feet with a sigh. Something within me bristled. It wasn't possible that Jean-Henri, as an alpha, didn't know that another alpha had entered his den.

The woman who'd answered the door moved to stand beside him. My eyes flicked upward as four more werewolves appeared in the gallery above us, all of them leaning their elbows on the railing while they looked down at us.

Any nonchalant feeling I'd picked up from Jean-Henri disappeared when he met my eyes. His gray eyes burned into mine, and I stiffened. I could feel his alpha power pressing in on me, trying to crush me. I squinted at him, pushing hard against the feeling.

He curled his upper lip and crossed his arms. "You are in the territory of the Soissons Pack, and you are not welcome."

A tingle ran up my spine, and I stood straighter. I gritted my teeth. I had no idea what to do. "It was my understanding that Lia of the Northern Pack worked everything out with you."

He clicked his tongue. "We have a place where you can stay outside of my territory. *It* is not welcome here, except for when it is doing research at the Château de Chantilly." He growled low, glaring at Adrian, and the woman beside him tensed for action.

The tang of vinegar crept into Adrian's scent, but I didn't turn to look at him.

I dipped my head slightly at Jean-Henri, acknowledging his

authority. "We're grateful for the accommodations you offer." *It's best that we don't stay here anyway.* "I'm assuming you're aware of our special needs?"

Jean-Henri's nose wrinkled in disgust. "I have instructed our butcher to collect what he can. You are permitted to pick it up. Alone."

The longer I stood in this sitting room, the more cornered I felt. I needed to get out of there, but this was too important to run away from, too important to fuck up.

Jean-Henri jerked his head to the woman beside him. She strode forward and held out a folded sheet of paper.

"These are the addresses of where you will stay and that of the butcher."

I took the paper and put it in my coat pocket. "How can I get a hold of you if I need to?"

"You won't. I have given you everything you need. The butcher is already expecting you. *I* expect not to hear anything from you. Do what you must and leave quickly." He squinted at me. "And ensure that *thing* stays under control, or my hospitality will become decidedly less welcome."

An instinctive growl rumbled in my chest at his threat. I was sure he heard it, despite it not leaving my lips.

He waved his hand. "You may go."

I stayed where I was a few moments longer, just to stand my ground, then slowly turned to leave.

But as I took a step forward, a fae woman flitted into the room, her bright eyes smiling and her arms laden with shopping bags.

"Jean-Henri, my darling," she gushed. "You will never believe what I found in Paris."

Everyone froze, and my eyes shot sideways to Adrian.

28

*A*drian's nostrils flared, and his lips quivered. Even from my angle, I could see the black of his pupils slowly engulfing the violet of his irises. His predatory gaze was fixed on the fae woman.

"Adrian," I warned him.

He didn't react...didn't move at all.

And then the fae made the worst mistake she could have. She ran.

Adrian didn't get even a single step. The moment his muscles tensed to chase her, I tackled him to the hard stone floor.

I heard the tearing of clothes as the wolves around us shifted while I wrestled with Adrian. It wasn't a few seconds before I straddled his stomach, pinning his arms to the floor with my hands on his wrists. The tips of my hair brushed over his cheeks. In truth, I didn't think it was my alpha strength that allowed me to subdue him so easily. His face was scrunched with turmoil. He was fighting within himself more than he was fighting me.

I didn't dare look at the werewolves encircling us. I could feel their malice and hear their growls. I just focused on Adrian's black eyes.

"Adrian," I said, my voice laced with alpha power. I knew it didn't work on him, but it would keep the other wolves at bay.

His eyes met mine, and they didn't recognize me. His pulse beneath my palms pumped wildly.

"You don't have to be controlled by your nature." I repeated the words I'd overheard him speak to his mother, the lesson she'd taught him throughout his life. "Adrian, remember who you are. Focus on me. Listen to the sound of my voice. Focus on my scent rather than the fae's. What do I smell like?"

His breathing was heavy and deep. I couldn't tell if he was internalizing my words, but his eyebrows wrinkled as if in concentration.

After a few seconds, his tense muscles eased beneath me. A little more, and the violet started returning to his eyes. Deep sorrow filled his gaze as he looked up at me.

"Are you okay?" I asked, not loosening my grip on his wrists.

He nodded slightly but frowned.

I finally spared a glance around us. The gathered wolves surrounded us, their eyes fixed on Adrian. I looked to Jean-Henri, his alpha power the only thing keeping them in check.

"He's fine now," I told the alpha, whose hackles were still raised. "No harm was done. We will leave your territory immediately."

Jean-Henri let loose a ferocious growl, which echoed off the stone walls and floor. I tensed, wondering if I could shift in those two seconds Lia had insisted on.

My heart pounded as fire gathered in my gut. This was not going to happen. Adrian was under my protection, and we had a job to do.

"I'm taking him out of here in one piece." I laced my voice with power, pushing my will onto the other alpha. I could feel the effect ripple through the wolves surrounding us, but I didn't look away from Jean-Henri. I stared him down, not giving him an inch.

Finally—after what seemed like an eternity—he dipped his head, though his following snarl told me to get out quickly.

Climbing off of Adrian, I pulled him up with me, being sure to keep my hand locked on one of his wrists. The wolves blocking the door parted for us to pass.

We were out of the house in less than thirty seconds.

"Give me the keys," I said once we were on the other side of the gate.

Adrian reached into his jacket pocket and handed me the car keys. Then we both climbed into the car, and I sped away in no particular direction. I drove a few miles before I saw a sign with the name of the town crossed out, telling me that we were at least out of the village's borders.

I pulled to the side of the road and let out a sigh, my hands still gripping the steering wheel. After a heavy minute, I turned to Adrian. Whatever I was going to say died on my lips.

Tears ran down his paler-than-usual face. His shoulders were hunched as he gripped his elbows. "I thought I'd beaten it." His voice was raw as it trembled. "I worked so hard with Ashwin. He exposed me to all kinds of things that smelled of fae. And I made sure to drink way more than usual. I wasn't even thirsty. Then the first time my work is tested…I failed miserably."

"I know the feeling," I said quietly, remembering just how it had felt when I'd gone to the alpha gathering.

Adrian scowled. "Really? You know what it feels like to want to rip someone's throat out?"

Has he forgotten whom he's talking to? I stared right into his eyes. "Yeah, just back there." I jerked my thumb over my shoulder.

His Adam's apple jumped as he swallowed hard. "See? Even you know that the only way to stop me is to kill me."

I scowled at his conclusion. "I wasn't talking about *you*. I told you, didn't I? You're under my protection."

His eyes widened with realization.

"And I don't want to hear any more crap about how the only way to stop you is to kill you. Got it? That's obviously not the case because here you are alive. You stopped on your own."

He cast his gaze toward his knees. "Not on my own. I stopped because of you."

I frowned. "While I appreciate the credit, I don't think you're giving yourself enough. I could see you fighting yourself."

He shook his head. "But it was what you said about concentrating on your scent that pulled me out of it. Ashwin never suggested anything like that."

I shrugged. "We're all bound to get a thing or two right once in a while."

He looked over at me, meeting my eyes with an intensity that begged me to understand. "You saved me. You saved me from the other wolves, and you saved me from myself. When I concentrated on you, it was like nothing else in the world existed, like your presence *demanded* that nothing else but you exist."

I frowned. All wolves could smell their own scent to a certain extent, or at least we could recognize something that we had marked or claimed. But we didn't know what we smelled like to others. "What do I smell like to you?"

His eyes softened, and he smiled the tiniest of crooked smiles. "Autumn. You smell of leaves and harvest and that pleasant warmth you can only find when the weather starts to turn cold."

A tingle traveled over my skin, my hair raising in its wake. My mind skidded to a halt, and I swallowed as my mouth moistened. Just when I'd identified the feeling as pleasant, I pushed any more thoughts away and turned my attention through the windshield. After pulling the folded paper from my pocket, I offered it to Adrian without looking at him. "Type this into the GPS. Let's get out of here."

ver the next hour and a half, we didn't speak outside of Adrian giving me directions and telling me what road signs meant.

The place the Soissons Pack had designated we stay was to the west and much more picturesque than I'd have imagined, given how Jean-Henri had offered it. A narrow dirt road traveled through the winter woods and ended at a small lake house. I wondered what it would be like to run through these trees in wolf form. It seemed like an idyllic place, and I wanted to be a part of it. I wanted to sniff out prey in the snow, to hear the birds that nestled in for the winter.

The lake house at the end of the road was painted dark green and seemed to have more windows than proper walls. A little dock, jutting into a frozen lake, wasn't thirty feet from the house.

I parked the car in the driveway. "How are we supposed to get in?" I wondered aloud, realizing too late that they hadn't given us a key.

Adrian pointed to the paper. "There's a code under the address."

I frowned. "I'd like to take a look around before we bring our stuff in."

He nodded and climbed out of the car with me.

I hadn't known exactly what the hum under my skin while visiting Louparest had been. I'd thought it could've been because I was an alpha in an unclaimed territory. But as I stood before the lake house, the quiet forest around me, I knew that wasn't the case. I felt completely at ease here—more at ease than I'd ever felt in my life. It was as if my instincts were telling me that this was my home. It had everything I could ever want. All I had to do was lay claim to it. I knew that no threat, vampire or were-wolf or otherwise, was anywhere near us. This place was just me and Adrian and the natural things that belonged here.

I guess the hum had more to do with being around other werewolves in an unclaimed territory.

I could feel myself smiling broadly like an idiot, but I didn't even try to stifle it. The path from the drive to the front door was made of stepping stones, browned grass hugging the sides. Upon reaching the front step, Adrian typed in the code and opened the brown-painted door.

The front hall was narrow, as if it were trying not to take space from the rest of the house. A set of stairs to the right led to the second floor, and doorways sat to the left and straight ahead of us. I passed the doorway oo the left, only peeking in to see a sitting room with large windows showcasing the forest. Through the door at the end of the hall was the kitchen. It was large and modern with paned French doors that opened onto a wide porch. There was a clear view of the lake, secluded and surrounded by trees. At one end of the kitchen, there was a small bathroom that also included laundry machines.

"I guess they've thought of everything," I said, looking at the laundry machines.

"Well, not quite everything. We're going to have to buy food." Adrian closed the refrigerator and looked back at me as I left the bathroom.

I waved my hand. That wasn't a big deal.

Heading back to the front hall, we next went up the stairs. There were three doors. The center one led to another bathroom, and the two on either side opened into bedrooms. The large windows of the bedrooms were covered in thick curtains.

It was perfect. Quiet, secluded, and away from all responsibilities—save protecting Adrian. I was instantly in a good mood.

After we'd brought everything in, we got back in the car to go buy food. Luckily, a grocery store was less than ten minutes away.

I froze as we walked in, feeling like I was truly in a foreign country for the first time. Such a mundane place, a grocery store, so familiar and yet so different. I was glad most of the products were either recognizable or had pictures on them because I couldn't read a word.

"Do you know French?" I asked Adrian while he scanned the shelves.

He shook his head. "No, but I know Latin and English. If that doesn't get me through, I have a translator app on my phone." He glanced over at me. "Do you, uh, know how to cook?"

I tilted my head. "Sure, I do. Feather was big into cooking, so I learned a lot from helping her."

"Feather?"

"My bondmate," I clarified.

"Ah." He tugged on his ear. "I'm a little ashamed to say that I don't really cook unless boxed mac 'n' cheese or canned soup counts. You should have seen the sad attempt at vegetable soup I made for Yuti once. Just awful."

I stared at him. "You're a grown man. How have you survived until now? Don't you live alone?"

He shrugged. "There are people who are way better at it than I am. I might as well let them do what they're good at. In any case, I have a bad habit of forgetting to eat real food these days, so when I realize I'm hungry, I need to eat something quick."

I sighed and shook my head.

Likely too buried in his books thanks to us.

"Hey," he said, affronted. "I'm sure it's not that hard if I put my mind to it. I learned how to bake from my mom."

I blinked at his complete misunderstanding of my response. "I feel like baking is a different skill. I can't bake to save my life. How about this then: I'll cook if you clean."

Adrian nodded. "Only if you teach me what you know."

"Deal. Now let's see what we need…"

I didn't know how long we were going to be in France, so we bought enough food to last us a week. I settled on making simple pasta with peas for dinner that night since it was quick and easy.

And I saw the wisdom of that decision as Adrian cleared the dishes from the table. The day had been long and way too eventful for someone who hadn't gotten a good night's sleep. I contemplated the origin of the term jet lag as I climbed the stairs, calling it a night immediately after dinner.

30

"Send us pictures!" I heard my brother call from the background.

Bacon sizzled and popped in the frying pan as I flipped it, my cellphone held to my ear by my shoulder.

"Fine!" I barked.

After being so rudely interrupted by my brother's demands, I finished telling Lia what had transpired with Jean-Henri's pack the day before. She asked that I keep her informed, and I promised I would before saying goodbye.

The cloudy sky outside the kitchen windows was just starting to lighten with dawn. Rain speckled the many panes of glass, but the precipitation wasn't even hard enough to make that pleasant tapping sound. It was a quiet morning—perfect—and I concentrated on the sensations around me. The smell of the sizzling bacon, the feel of the eggshell cracking in my fingers as I tapped it on the counter, the gray haze of dawn light on a rainy morning making everything feel hushed and dull.

The floorboards above my head creaked, and I knew Adrian was awake. He shuffled downstairs a few minutes later, eyes rested but hair a mess.

"Good morning," he said.

I was in such a good mood that I ascribed a cheerfulness to his words that wasn't in his tone.

"Morning. There's coffee in the pot."

"Oh, thank God. You're an angel."

I huffed a laugh. *Well, that's a first.*

Adrian poured himself a cup of black coffee and took it to the round table near the windows.

I portioned eggs, bacon, and toast onto two plates, leaving some bacon between a few paper towels for later. Then I placed one plate before Adrian and sat across from him with the other.

He thanked me and started to dig in.

Realizing I didn't have anything to drink, I got up from the table and poured myself some orange juice, bringing Adrian a bottle of blood while I was at it.

"Is it all right cold?" Every time I witnessed him drinking blood, it got a little easier to see, but I wasn't up for heating it for him.

He waved his hand. "It's fine. My mom is just...well, a mom."

"How long will what you have last you? Should I make a trip back to Bosquet-aux-Loups soon?" Jean-Henri had said I was welcome without Adrian, but the thought of leaving him unprotected for a few hours made me uncomfortable.

"I have some time."

I dipped my head, turning my attention out the window toward the thinly frozen lake. It struck me that this entire situation was very surreal. A week before, I hadn't even been allowed to be alone with Adrian, and his scent had stunk of fear whenever I'd gone anywhere near him. Now I was making him breakfast and talking about going to the butcher for him. I smiled to myself, shaking my head at how unexpected life could be.

"What is it?" Adrian asked.

"Hmm?" I glanced over at him. "Oh, nothing. I was just thinking about how funny life is sometimes. Two weeks ago, all I could think about was completing my training and becoming a lone alpha. It's uncomfortable to live in another alpha's territory with their pack all around you. I never would have expected that this is how I would manage it."

"Can I ask you something?"

I shrugged, giving him leave to ask whatever he wanted.

"Why do you want to be a lone alpha? Don't werewolves like to live in packs?"

I frowned, reaching for my orange juice without picking it up to drink, instead staring into the cheerful brightness of the glass, so dissonant from the gray, rainy morning. "It might be hard for you to understand. I know it's hard for other werewolves to understand—alphas in particular... There are a set of expectations that go along with being an alpha, a level of responsibility that ranges from life and death to the emotional and mental health of the wolves in your pack. And you don't get to choose any of it; fate chooses for you. You're born an alpha, and these expectations are thrust on you. For me... You know about the bondmate system, right?"

I glanced up at him, and he nodded.

"I was bound with Feather when I was only seven. Before that, my entire young life was dedicated to training to prepare for that binding. And once I was bound with her, my entire life became about making sure she was safe. Don't get me wrong; I loved her like a sister, but I was never really able to do what I wanted. Anything I dreamed of had to wait until after. I thought it best to not even dream, to just concentrate on the task and worry about that later. I'd always have time later, right? *Wrong.* Because I was an alpha. The moment I was unbound, another set of shackles were clasped on my ankles."

Adrian stared out the windows, his gaze unfixed as he listened. "I can understand where you're coming from." He smiled, but the expression was sad and bitter. "You can imagine what others expect a vampire to be like. There isn't much room to live the way you want when they stuff you in a box. What's the purpose of life if you're only living it the way others expect you to?"

I tilted my head. "I always found that a curious question:

what's the purpose of life? Why does everyone think life has a purpose? Are we so much more special than everything else in the natural world? Trees serve a purpose in the greater system, but do they know that it's their purpose? Do they work toward that purpose with that goal in mind? I don't think so. I think their very existence is their purpose. Why would it be different for us?"

Adrian rested his chin in his hand. "I suppose it comforts people to think that all this struggle is in service of something greater than themselves."

"Well, I find the idea of a set purpose unsettling." I shrugged. "But then again, I've been told that people find my outlook very bleak. They can't fathom an existence without purpose, as if life has no meaning without it."

"I don't find that bleak at all. It's the ultimate free will. I feel that life, or the purpose of it, is whatever you make it."

I smiled broadly. Finally, someone understood what I'd been saying for years. "I agree. Fuck fate."

Flashing his fangs in a smile, Adrian raised his bottle of blood. "Fuck fate."

I tapped his bottle with my glass of orange juice, and we both drank.

---

31

*B*uckled into the front seat with Adrian's little cooler—packed with our lunch—we started toward the Château de Chantilly. While it was inconvenient to have to stay so far away, I didn't mind the hour-and-a-quarter drive to the château.

The windshield wipers lazily scraped the droplets of rain every minute or so—it was more of a mist at this point—as we traveled through the French countryside.

"So we're going here to look at a special book?" I asked, glancing over at Adrian as he concentrated on the road ahead.

He nodded. "Not a book per se, more a notebook of research notes."

"We came all the way to France to look at someone's research notes?"

Adrian smirked in a way that said he was trying not to laugh at my ridiculous question. "Not just *someone's*. We came all the way to France to look at Wilhelm Grimm's research notes."

I waited for him to continue, but he didn't. "Uh...should I know who that is?"

His eyes widened, and he spared me a shocked glance. "You don't know who the Brothers Grimm were?"

I shrugged. "Are you just now realizing that I grew up in another realm? Do you know who Jaakko Halla is?"

"No."

"Well, everyone in Faerie would be just as shocked by what you just said as you are at me."

He chuckled. "Point taken. The Brothers Grimm were German folklorists, among other things. They collected folktales —mostly oral but some written—and published them in volumes."

I nodded to show I was following.

"Actually, let me back up. A few years ago, I was sifting through sources and found an offhanded reference in an unrelated fairytale. The line was almost a throw-away. It was talking about the fate of a well-intentioned character whose plan backfires and said something like: her cruel fate was worse than that of Lucilla of the Black Wood, the fae who created vampires."

"That's all it said? So you and Ashwin have been looking for references to Lucilla of the Black Wood?"

"Right. But we couldn't find anything in any of the books from Faerie. In any case, I found a discussion on an internet forum where someone mentioned folktales that never made it into the Grimms' fairy tale collections. One of the tales they listed was called 'Lucilla of the Black Wood.' I reached out to the poster and asked them where they'd heard of it, and they said they'd seen it mentioned in Wilhelm Grimm's notebook while it was traveling with some Grimm exhibit. It took a bit to track the notebook down, but I figured out that its permanent home is in the archives at the Château de Chantilly."

I raised an eyebrow. "So the hope is that this notebook will have the full story of Lucilla of the Black Wood, and we won't just have been sent on a wild goose chase by some rando on the internet?"

"That is the hope, yes."

"Then we should know by the end of the day, right?"

"Well…"

"Why not?"

He cringed. "The notebook is probably in German. I don't speak or read German, so it could take me a while to find and translate the story."

I held my breath, rolling my head back, then let out a sound somewhere between a laugh and a sigh.

"Hey, I spent years doing stuff like this. It takes a lot of patience. I never thought I'd be working with werewolves reading over my shoulder," he said defensively.

I raised my hands. "I didn't say anything. Other than this whole business with the Soissons wolves, this is a major improvement for me." His complexion warmed, and my eyebrows scrunched. "Why are you blushing?"

His face reddened further. "What? I'm not. The heater must just be on too high."

I stared at him hard. But then I looked back out the window when I felt my own face flush. *It would've been cute if me saying I'd rather be with him than with the Northern Pack made him blush.*

I flinched at the thought, shoving it away as though it had bitten me.

As we approached the château, the fields and farms and narrow-streeted villages gave way to parkland—trees with paths winding through them. I longed for a nice walk along one of those paths, no idea where it might lead. Thinking about the possibilities, I looked at the car dashboard. I didn't know what one degree Celsius was in Fahrenheit, but I guessed it wasn't as warm as I would've liked.

We parked in a lot hidden by a group of trees quite a distance from the château. After a few minutes spent walking, we crossed a narrow bridge, frozen water on both sides, and made our way toward the castle. The cobbled stones of the path were slightly uneven beneath my feet as I took in my surroundings.

The main building sat up ahead to our left, a moat of frozen water separating it from the trees farther on. Architecturally, it was interesting—gray, round domes melding with more angular roofs, bridges topped with turrets connecting wings of sand-colored stone. I couldn't see much of the grounds from this angle, but I imagined that they were extensive. Anyone who could have afforded to build and live in a place like this could also afford large tracts of land. There was a statue of a man riding a horse high on a pedestal in the center of a roundabout. We followed the cobbled road into a courtyard.

Adrian showed a museum employee our passes, which he must have printed before we'd left the States. We entered almost immediately into a gift shop. To the left, there was a spiral staircase, its railing ornately carved and topped with a handrail that was polished to shine. We climbed it to the second floor and landed in a grand vestibule. Everything was marble—the floors, the walls, and the stairs.

We turned to the left and entered a long room that was rounded at the far end, its lower half holding glass display cases of pottery. The top half of the walls were a dark blue, embellished with gold paint. A buck's head mounted on the wall stared down at me, his glass eyes distracting me from the elaborately decorated ceiling. I'd eat a deer as near as look at one, but I'd never understood the human habit of stuffing dead animals. It just seemed so disrespectful. I'd actually vomited in a restaurant after first arriving in the human realm; for whatever reason, they'd proudly displayed a taxidermied wolf.

I shifted my eyes to something more palatable, focusing on the slouchy knit hat covering Adrian's hair. It had cute little reindeer and snowflakes on it. He went through a doorway on the left, and I followed him into a library, wondering whether he'd bought the hat for himself or if it had been a gift.

32

*T*he curator was a very thin man with thick, round glasses and a wrinkled face that seemed to hide his eyes. He smiled kindly at us as we entered and shook both of our hands when Adrian introduced us. Adrian thanked him for meeting us when he was so busy, and the curator thanked Adrian for understanding and meeting him in the book cabinet while he worked.

I didn't pay much attention to the conversation after that but started to look around the library. As one would expect, the library was full of books. Tall cases filled most of the walls, interrupted only on one side by windows. Above our heads, a second row of shelves ran along an upper gallery. The shelves on the ground floor were glassed in, but the ones above us breathed freely. Warm light filled the space, provided by spherical lamps on the window side, which overtook the dim, overcast light from outside. The ceiling, like all of the ceilings in the place, was sculpted and decorated with gilded paintings. I wondered what the painters and sculptors had been paid for their work. They'd certainly been talented.

The place as a whole was very ostentatious. To my knowledge, this level of decadence was only comparable to the royal palace in Faerie, which glittered atop the mountain of Mysraina. Of course, I'd never been in the royal palace; it was likely even more elaborate than this on the inside. It made me wonder if France was a particularly wealthy nation or if the rich just kept it all for themselves.

"Willow," Adrian called, and I turned my attention away from the dead eyes of a bust above a fireplace. "We're finished."

The wood floor creaked beneath my boots as I hurried to where Adrian waited on the other side of the room; the curator had just moved away from him. "Already?"

He nodded. "Yeah, we can come back tomorrow. There are only ten seats in the reading room, and there's no opening until then. I was just coming to meet the curator and let him know what I will need."

"So what do we do now?"

"Well, what do you want to do? We have passes for the whole grounds. We could look around the museum. Paris isn't that far away if you want to make the trip there, though I'd suggest we park and take the train in."

I frowned. Jean-Henri had permitted us to be at the château in Chantilly, but I doubted that grace extended into Paris. I glanced around the blue room with the deer heads. I didn't have much interest in art. It wasn't that I couldn't appreciate its beauty or the talent and hard work it took to make it. I'd seen Yuti do it enough times to be impressed. I just didn't fancy the idea of wandering around the hushed rooms of an old house that had once been created and owned by people who were now long dead. I preferred the living world.

"Are we allowed to wander around outside? I know it's cold, but could we take a walk? It looked like there might be paths."

Adrian nodded. "Sure. I think there are gardens, not that there will be any flowers or greenery this time of year."

"That's all right. Why don't we go back to the car and grab the cooler? We could eat our lunch out there, too."

"Sounds good."

After retrieving the cooler and making sure I was bundled warmly in my winter things, we made our way to the French garden first. It was very flat—gravel paths led in patterns through winter grass and frozen pools that might have boasted fountains at any other time of year.

We followed the paths for a while, the gravel crunching beneath our feet. The area seemed very tamed to me, and I wondered if there would even be flowers in the summer. It was pleasant in its own way, still and quiet, and I imagined it would be a good place to walk if I were trying to work through a problem.

Following a path toward some trees, I reveled in the moment. It was nice to just enjoy being outside, even in a carefully maintained landscape. I might not ever have believed it in the past, but Adrian was a good companion. He didn't pressure me to speak. And he wasn't a werewolf, so I didn't have to worry about anything on that front. I was starting to not even notice the vampire in his scent, so well-blended with the hay, bergamot, and floral of his human side.

I'd said it over and over again: I didn't like people. But that wasn't strictly true. It wasn't that I disliked being around others. It's more that I'd never found anyone I could just exist beside. Everyone wanted or expected something from me. I didn't get that feeling from Adrian. If anything, he wanted even less than the protection I was giving him. I felt sure he would much rather have been on this research trip alone instead of having a werewolf following him around, monitoring his every move.

But as I glanced sidelong at him, he didn't seem put off by my presence.

His violet eyes met mine, and he gave me a small smile. "Are you hungry? We could sit up against those columns over there." He pointed to a round structure beside a pond, open on all sides with only columns supporting the roof. A marble statue of a woman either dressing or undressing stood in the middle of the little temple.

I turned my steps in that direction.

Entering the space, we each chose a column to lean up against and slid to the ground. While the structure was open, the column at my back did a decent job of blocking the wind. I reached into the cooler and handed Adrian one of the turkey club sandwiches I'd made before we'd left, along with a bottle of water and one of his mom's cookies. Then I stretched my legs out in front of me, crossing my ankles as I tucked into my sandwich.

I stared up at the statue of the woman while I chewed. Her manner of dress and the proportions of her figure spoke of ancient Rome. I'd learned about ancient Greece and Rome and tons of other places in the realm of origin while at school in Faerie. These were times of shared human and werewolf history. There were tons of werewolves to be found in ancient sources. The oldest written story in existence, *The Epic of Gilgamesh*, even had a werewolf in it. Werewolves showed up everywhere, from the female werewolf who had suckled Romulus and Remus to Borte Chino, the werewolf ancestor of Chinggis Khan.

"Do you know who this is a statue of?" I asked Adrian before shoving the last bite of sandwich into my mouth.

He took a drink of water. "Venus. She's the —"

"Goddess of love and beauty," I supplied.

He nodded, taking up his pink-frosted cookie.

I'd thought the cookie would thaw even in the cooler, but it was frozen when I took a bite. Though still good, the texture wasn't as soft and chewy as I'd expected. Adrian bit into his, then wrapped it back up, clearly not as determined to eat a frozen cookie as I was.

I rubbed my hands together, getting any leftover crumbs off before I shoved them back into my warm mittens. Rolling my head to the side, I looked over at Adrian as he gazed at the pond beside us, his elbow resting on his bent knee.

He looked contemplative—comfortable and picturesque. I wondered how different his life would have been if he'd never fallen in with us.

"What are you going to do when all this is over?" I asked.

His violet eyes flicked to mine, and he removed his glasses when they began to fog. "What do you mean *over*?"

"Like after you've answered this big question about vampire origins. What do you want to do?"

He frowned. "Assuming I will be permitted to decide what I do next?"

I flinched. "Yeah."

He turned his attention back toward the pond. "I'm almost afraid to say it out loud. This question, this burning desire, to know who and what I am—how something like me could exist—has driven me for as long as I can remember. Can you imagine what it's like to have to hide who you are from the world? Or worse, have to be afraid of what you might do to the people you care about should you let one part of yourself have too much sway? If I slip up one time, I could go from innocent to murderer."

I couldn't imagine that, no. I may not like the cards fate had dealt me, but I'd never felt afraid of myself.

Lacking control of my instincts, sure. Dissatisfied with how that felt, absolutely. But not afraid. And while I'd had to partially hide my werewolf nature since coming to the human realm, I hadn't had to do it my entire life.

That was the benefit of living under the treaty, of living as a werewolf in Faerie.

"If this is ever over," Adrian continued, "if I get the answers I'm seeking, I'd like to just exist for a while. It doesn't even sound possible. How will I ever be comfortable enough with what I am to let go like that? I'd love it if I could just find a quiet place to be still, to not worry, to watch the sunset without fear of what the darkness will bring. And if I want to dream big, maybe I'll find a way to help others like me. I don't want anyone else to have to struggle the way I have. But I can't help anyone else if I can't even help myself."

He met my eyes again, his sad smile telling me he didn't believe any of this was possible.

"What do you think?" he asked. "I jinxed it, right? There's no way a vampire like me deserves any of that."

I didn't speak for a long moment, the ache in his words seeping into my heart. "You're a good guy, Adrian. A man like you deserves all that and a lot more."

33

His eyes softened as he stared back at me. Then he rose to his feet and held out a hand. "Come on, let's get back. Your nose is starting to turn red."

I placed my mittened hand in his, and he hauled me to my feet.

The view of the château was picture-perfect when we stepped out of the trees, and the thought shook something loose in my mind. "Oh! Hold on."

Adrian halted as I took off my mittens and pulled out my phone.

"Rowan was nagging me about pictures this morning." I turned my phone on and tapped the camera icon. After snapping a picture, I started to put it away.

"Do you want me to take a picture of you?" Adrian asked.

"Uh, sure. Let's both take one." I handed Adrian my phone.

He stepped close to me, holding his arm out so both of us and the château were in the frame. His scent washed over me, his shoulder firm against mine. He smelled of late summer rain. I felt like I was in a rustic place. I was standing in the middle of a field of tall hay, fuzzy seed heads tickling my palms as I

reached out. The field was dotted with bright flowers, something between orange and yellow. The wind blew through some
trees—heavy with green fruit—carrying the scent of bergamot
to me.

I breathed deep. "Poppies!"

Adrian snapped the picture. "An interesting choice. We
always said cheese, but okay."

I reached out and grabbed his jacket, shaking him a bit as if
that would make him understand. "No, poppies—golden
poppies!" I scowled when he raised an eyebrow. "Remember the
floral note I couldn't place at the diner? In your scent. It's golden
poppies." I sighed in satisfaction. I hadn't realized how annoyed
I'd been that I couldn't place that little undertone until I'd
figured it out.

"Oh, okay. I see now. What made you think of it all of a
sudden?"

I scrunched my brow. I'd been immersed in his scent; I'd
fully given myself over to it. "I guess it finally just came to me."
Shrugging, I started to walk back to the car, and he kept pace
with me.

Once buckled in, I opened my phone's photo gallery to send
the two pictures to Rowan. But when I saw our selfie, I decided
to send only the first one. In the second, my eyes were too wide,
alight with my epiphany. My expression was at complete odds
with Adrian's measured and tight-lipped smile. My thumb
hovered over the delete button, but then I just turned off my
phone.

I made cheeseburgers for dinner that night. And as Adrian
washed the dishes, I stared out into the darkness. The clouds
that had shaded the sky all day were just starting to break,
covering the three-quarters moon in wispy tendrils.

"I wish I could be out there," I murmured to myself.

"Then why don't you go out?" Adrian answered, his vampire
hearing picking up my words with ease.

I turned to him. "I mean, I wish I could shift and go sniffing
around."

He didn't look up as he dried a plate with a dishtowel. "What's stopping you? The cold?"

I frowned. "We may not be in Jean-Henri's territory, but he knows exactly where we are. He or any of his wolves could decide to bust in here at any moment, no matter what he said before."

Adrian's hands stilled, halfway to putting the dry plate into the cupboard. "Well, that's comforting."

"It's probably fine. He said we could stay here, but I don't know him. I don't know how trustworthy he is."

"So you don't want to leave me alone in the house," Adrian inferred, stacking the plate neatly.

I lowered my chin in a nod.

"Then I'll just go for a walk with you." He closed the cupboard and hung the towel on the oven door to dry.

"Would you?"

He shrugged. "Why not?"

I stood from the table and smiled. "Okay, I'll just go shift then." Without another word, I climbed the stairs to my room and removed my clothes. Once I'd shifted to wolf form, I headed back down, trotting happily through the hall.

Adrian looked up as I entered, and his breath hitched. He froze, his eyes widening at the wolf walking toward him. A little whiff of vinegar wafted toward me. I stopped my approach, giving him time to gather himself.

He breathed out slowly, and his features seemed to relax. Hesitating, he stepped toward me and lowered himself into a crouch.

I took this as a sign to come closer, but I moved by inches, being sure to keep my tail and ears up. I stopped when he was only a foot from my snout.

Adrian stared into my eyes, a line of concentration between his eyebrows. It was a few minutes before he spoke, and I wondered what he'd been thinking during that time.

"There you are," he whispered finally.

I snorted. *Well, of course I am. Where else would I be?*

I could appreciate that he would be nervous around me when my teeth were out. The last time he'd seen me as a wolf, I'd tried to take a bite out of him. And even though he knew tons of were-wolves by now, it had to be strange for him to reconcile the me he knew in human form with the me in wolf form. It had taken Feather a good six months to recognize me from amongst other wolves when we'd first been bound, though we'd never been a perfect match.

I tilted my head at Adrian, asking him when we would be heading outside.

He bit his lip, his eyes sparkling. "If I say something, will you bite me if it's rude?"

I tilted my head to the other side, asking him to go on.

His words burst forth as if he couldn't hold them in another second. "You're so fucking cute when you make that expression."

I barked a laugh.

"I'm sorry. I just couldn't take it. I don't mean it disre-spectfully."

I didn't know why he thought that was an offensive thing to say. Perhaps it was because it was something one would say about a dog. But dogs were descended from wolves, so why wouldn't they be similar? Werewolves had no problems with dogs—we loved them just as much as humans did. And we likely had a better relationship with them.

Besides, who didn't like to be called cute?

Adrian lowered his gaze to the kitchen floor.

I moved forward and bumped him with my head, the motion knocking him out of his crouch and onto his butt. When he looked up at me, his eyes wide, I let my tongue hang out and wagged my tail.

He gave me a full smile, understanding I wasn't upset.

I lowered my front half and then took off, running in a circle around the kitchen while always returning to the door.

"Yeah, I get it," he said with a chuckle.

He opened the door, and I bounded outside. I was off the

porch in three pounces, sniffing the frosty air. He followed after me at an easy pace.

The night around us was cold and quiet, filled with the frozen smells of a winter about to break. There weren't many woodland creatures around, but I could smell that a fox had passed by not long before. The cold didn't bother me at all when I was in wolf form, my thick fur made for this sort of weather.

I trotted forward, starting a circuit around the lake. I'd catch a scent, follow it a few steps, identify it, then move on. I'd run ahead, enjoying the feel of the frozen grass beneath my paws and the sense of freedom that always came from being in wolf form, and then I'd come back to where Adrian walked at a steady pace. After checking in with him, I'd go ahead again, always returning to receive a gentle smile.

For the last little bit of the walk, I trotted beside him, booping his hand with my nose every few minutes to see how cold it was.

The lake wasn't very big, so we reached the porch again within an hour. But it had been enough for me. I'd wanted to be a part of the night, and it had been everything I'd hoped it would be. I wondered if this was what I had to look forward to once I became a lone alpha—just me in the wilderness—and decided that I would find my own territory once this was over. I wouldn't want to have to constantly move from territory to territory after knowing what this pure bliss had felt like.

Once inside, I went to my room to shift and redress. Then I returned downstairs to the kitchen and put the kettle on.

Ten minutes later, I knocked on Adrian's bedroom door. He called for me to come in.

"I made you some tea." I set the steaming mug on his bedside table. "You looked pretty cold by the time we got back inside."

He was sitting up in bed, his computer in his lap. "Thanks." He shifted his laptop to one side and reached for the cup.

"Holy fuck! What the hell happened to you?" I demanded, grabbing his hand before it even got to the mug. A bruise wrapped around his arm, just above his wrist.

He raised his eyebrows. "Do you not recall pinning me to the floor yesterday?"

My face flushed, and I gasped, sinking down beside him on the bed. "I am *so* sorry. I didn't think I grabbed you that hard." I held out my other hand, and he placed his other wrist in it. The second one was just as marred.

"You held me as hard as you needed to," he murmured.

I scowled. "Some kind of protector I am. I hurt you worse than those who threatened you."

Adrian flipped his hands over to hold mine. I looked up at him, seeing his eyes were earnest.

"You did protect me. You know what would've happened to that fae if I'd reached her. And you know what those wolves would've done to me if you hadn't taken me down. I think I can live with a few bruises. Besides," he added lightly, "I bruise easily."

I heard what he said, but his words didn't seem to matter. All I could feel was sadness as I stared down at the marks I'd put on him. "Is there anything I can get you to make it feel better?"

His mouth widened into a toothy grin. "Well…if you really feel bad about it, I wouldn't mind if you made my grandma's spaghetti and meatballs. I can get the recipe from my mom."

I clicked my tongue. "You're a meatball. I'm being serious here."

He pursed his lips. "Who'd joke about Grandma's spaghetti and meatballs? There's nothing in the world more serious than that."

"It was pretty good." I knew he was trying to make me feel better, so I smiled. But I didn't feel the emotion of the gesture — couldn't feel it while the memory of the pain I'd caused him still showed on his pale skin. I pulled one hand from his and brushed my fingers gently over the bruise.

The hairs on his arm rose, and a shiver ran through him. I looked up to see if I'd pressed too hard, to see if even that soft caress had hurt him.

His violet eyes watched me, a question brewing in his gaze.

His lips parted. And as he let out the softest breath, the scent of crisp apples drifted to my nose.

I blinked and concentrated on the new scent, leaning forward to get a better sniff.

His face reddened, and he cleared his throat, sliding his hands from mine.

And then I saw it, that little hesitation, that little fluster, and something clicked in my mind. I knew exactly what that elusive scent was, knew why it was there sometimes and not others.

The sweet tartness of autumn apples was the scent of Adrian's arousal.

34

In the intimate hush of Adrian's bedroom, the only light the soft glow of the bedside lamp, a thick atmosphere settled between us. Adrian's eyes shifted to the red plaid pattern of the bedspread as I watched him.

He reached for the laptop and pulled it onto his lap. "Thanks for the tea. I better get back to this."

"No problem." I rose from his bed and closed the door on my way out.

As I walked down the short hall to my bedroom, I pushed away the heavy awkwardness that lingered. I concentrated on what I was doing as I removed my sweatshirt and pants, tucking them under my covers so they'd still be warm in the morning.

The sheets were cool and clean against my bare skin. I shivered and curled onto my side—hoping that would warm me faster.

I liked to be woken up by morning light if I didn't wake up earlier on my own, so I'd already pulled open the thick curtains. At the resort, I'd worked the late shift to avoid the pack, but that lifestyle wasn't my preference. I was a sun person, and I didn't like to sleep during daylight hours. I stared out the large windows. I could see a few bright stars peeking between wispy clouds. But as my body relaxed, my mind wandered.

I didn't expect that. It didn't even occur to me that it was the scent of his desire. I thought back to the few times the scent had come up. It was clear that he wasn't going to act on it. In fact, he usually looked uncomfortable and pulled away.

Well, that's no surprise. It's got to be weird for him to be aroused by a werewolf. Wasn't I also uncomfortable with that dream I had of him? We've been taught to hate each other our entire lives. We're mortal enemies.

I frowned.

But you can't control what your body responds to.

Still, there was the issue of compatibility. It was strange enough that we could manage to share a meal and a civil conversation.

I suppose we're both human in our own ways.

Even if he'd been a full vampire, he'd still have had a man's body, as the dream that wouldn't die had so helpfully reminded me. I, of course, had my human form. So it wasn't a question of physical compatibility.

I thought about what I'd told Adrian at the diner, that to control my instinct to kill him, I'd concentrated on his human scent. And I was noticing it more and more as we continued to spend time together. I hardly registered his vampire side after nearly a week of constant exposure; it just sort of seemed part of the whole now.

Do other wolves smell his human side? Or is it just because I'm an alpha that I can pick up on it?

I didn't know the answer. What I did know was that I needed to be more cognizant of the situations I got into with Adrian. No more touching him or invading his personal space. I would watch my words as well. He couldn't control if his body was responding sexually to me, but the idea clearly made him uncomfortable. We were starting to settle into each other's company. And whether this trip was over tomorrow or a month from now, there was no reason why we couldn't spend that time pleasantly.

Even with that resolution in my mind, I slept restlessly, dreaming of autumn orchards heavy with ripe fruit.

As we sat down to breakfast the next morning, I was pleased to see that the awkwardness from the night before was gone. The sun was bright and the sky clear, though it was still cold. The violet of Adrian's eyes seemed more vibrant in the dawn light. I watched him closely, his movements smooth and easy.

He picked up his bottle of blood, his eyes flicking to me as he tilted his head back to drink.

"What does blood taste like to you?" I asked him.

He flinched, then coughed, lowering the bottle from his lips.

I let him catch his breath but continued to stare, my question standing.

"Why do you want to know that?"

I shrugged. "I'm curious. You've only ever had animal blood, right?"

He cleared his throat. "And your brother's," he added, hushed.

I nodded thoughtfully. "Did Rowan's blood taste different than other animal blood?"

His gaze skittered around the kitchen, finally resting on the fork he'd set on his empty plate. "Yes, it was different. It was... sweeter...like salted caramel."

I hummed my acknowledgment.

He looked up at me, his eyes meeting mine. "What about you?"

I tilted my head.

"You've eaten meat before. How does vampire taste in comparison?"

I shrugged. "I don't know. I grew up in the capital of Faerie. It's not near any portals, and it's the most well-protected place by far. I'd never even smelled a vampire until I met you. I've only ever tasted my own blood. To me, blood tastes mostly metallic, though I can understand where you get the salted taste from."

Silence fell between us.

"Is it very hard for you to resist?" I asked gently.

He didn't answer for a long time, and I regretted asking. Even if it was difficult, would he tell me the truth? It was in his best interest to assure me that he was in full control. I was with the wolves after all.

"Sometimes," he admitted, his voice soft and low. "You ever been on a diet and walk by a bakery? You can smell the scent of fresh baked cookies and pies, and you know you shouldn't, but you really want to."

I lowered my chin.

"But as tempting as it is, all I have to do is look into a person's eyes. If you eat a cupcake on a diet, the only person you're potentially harming is you. But if I drank from someone, I'd be harming them more than I could ever know. My mom wasn't even showing yet when she was attacked by a vampire. If she'd been given his blood too, she would have turned and I would have been miscarried as her body died. But even by just drinking from her, he affected and changed me. What would my life have been like if that vampire had had more self-control?"

I didn't have an answer for that. The world would likely be a much better place if people in general showed more self-control.

"It's like you said," he continued. "I remind myself of their humanity. And that worked out for a long time...until I smelled the scent of a fae. Even worse than that. I lost control and nearly attacked Rowan's ex-promised because she carried a half-fae child in her womb." His face drooped in an expression of deep remorse, and he clenched his fists on the table.

I clamped down on my instinct to reach out and loosen those fists. "It all worked out in the end. I was at Eoin's first birthday party, you know. That's what Runa and Konner named their son. He seemed like a very happy baby. He should be about two and a half now."

Adrian smiled softly, though the sadness didn't leave his eyes. "I'm glad."

35

When we entered the château that day, we didn't head in the direction of the library we'd been in the day before. Instead, we walked through the gift shop and a comparatively plain room with a white ceiling and wood-paneled walls. After that, we entered a much larger library.

It had at least three levels of floor-to-ceiling bookshelves. Stairs led to both an upper gallery and a lower level with some cabinets in the center of the floor.

"Bonjour." The curator greeted us with a smile and a friendly nod as we entered. "I have everything you need right through there." He gestured toward another door.

Adrian thanked him and then turned to me, frowning. His eyebrows puckered as if he was about to deliver bad news. "I'm sorry, but you can't come with me."

"What? Why not?"

He shifted his weight. "There aren't enough empty seats."

"I'll stand." I crossed my arms over my chest.

Adrian lifted his hands in a soothing gesture. "Look, this is going to be boring for you. Do you want to watch me struggle through German translation? We won't be able to talk. And anyway"—he lowered his voice, his eyes flicking to the curator, who was examining some folio on the lower floor—"what's the likelihood that I'm going to be attacked in broad daylight in a library? I won't leave this room without texting you first to come meet me."

I pursed my lips. He was right on all counts. "Fine. I'll wait for your text."

"You'll have a lot more fun out here, believe me. Wander around the museum and grounds, get something at the café, go for a drive if you want to. Here." He held the car keys out to me, and I took them even though I had no plans to leave the premises. "I'll see you in a few hours."

I nodded and watched him head toward the reading room. The moment he was out of my sight, I took out my phone and turned it on, glad that eighty percent of the battery remained.

With a sigh, I decided to walk around the museum for a while, not yet ready to face the cold. I wandered through gorgeous galleries and lavish bedrooms. It was all quite beautiful, of course, a magnificent home of a bygone era, and it was all quite beyond me. I'd have enjoyed a hotdog on a park bench while watching ducks swim in a pond just as well, if not more.

I supposed I was too simple for such elegance.

But at least it was warm inside and interesting to watch the people at the museum ooh and aah over the treasures. One woman had a hell of a time keeping her daughter from smearing boogers on everything. The moment the mother's back was turned, that little finger went right back up into that little nose. I managed not to laugh, but I couldn't stifle my smile.

A few hours later, I bundled up in my scarf and mittens to head out onto the garden paths. I thought about how much Yuti would love a place like this. She'd appreciate the art in the way only an artist could.

Pulling out my phone, I looked at the time and did some quick math. Then I swiped my brother's name on my contact list. Yuti picked up on the second ring.

"Hey, Willow, everything all right? Rowan is in the shower right now."

"Oh, that's okay. Yeah, everything is fine. I just had a minute to talk and thought I'd give him a call. I'm at the Château de Chantilly right now. I was just thinking about how much you'd enjoy looking at the art." I smiled. "Though, maybe not. I haven't seen anything featuring aliens."

"I've seen pictures of the gardens there. If that isn't someone signaling extraterrestrials, I don't know what is."

I laughed. "Could be."

"So where's Adrian?"

"Oh, he's in the reading room doing his research. Apparently, there aren't enough chairs or something, so I'm out here."

"You sound pleased," she said sarcastically.

She knew me well. "Thrilled."

"Hey, while I have you a minute. Would you mind doing something for me?"

"Sure, what's up?"

She hesitated a moment, and even when she began speaking, it was clear she chose her words carefully. "I talked to Adrian yesterday…and he's struggling with something."

"What's he struggling with?"

"It's not my place to say. But…I know you're there to protect him and everything, but could you look out for him for me? Not in the way you already are. I know no physical harm will come to him if you're there. In other ways. Do you know what I mean? Adrian is a really sensitive guy, and he tends to push people away when he thinks he's being a burden."

He didn't seem like he was struggling any more than normal to me. I'm sure he's just stressed with all the pressure we're putting on him, not to mention that incident in Bosquet-aux-Loups.

But Yuti is his best friend—if anyone would know what's going on with him, it would be her.

"What do you want me to do?" I asked.

"I don't know. Just little kindnesses, I guess. He likes to watch old TV shows when he gets down. *Star Trek: The Original*

Series is his favorite. If all else fails, give him some marshmallow fluff. That boy will demolish a jar of marshmallow fluff."

"What's that?"

"Oh, um...it's like just the insides of a marshmallow. It comes in a jar. Usually, it's in the baking aisle or the peanut butter aisle."

"Okay. I'll see what I can do."

I could hear the smile in Yuti's voice when she said, "Thanks, Willow. I know he's in safe hands."

36

*A*fter hanging up with Yuti, I looked at the clock on my phone. The château wouldn't close for another hour. I pulled up the maps app and searched for a grocery store. There was a whole cluster of them within a twenty-minute walk, but since I didn't know exactly what I was looking for, I decided to drive.

I had no luck at the first store, so I just went to the next and then the next. Finally, I found a place that seemed to carry marshmallow fluff, but they were out. The English-speaking employee was very helpful and apologetic. I returned to the car in defeat.

I thought this would be easy.

But as I buckled my seat belt to head back to the château, I wondered how hard it would be to make it myself. Maybe it was super simple. Maybe I just needed to buy marshmallows and mash them. So I pulled out my phone and looked up recipes.

It wasn't as easy as mashing marshmallows, but the recipe I found only had a few ingredients. I headed back into the store and collected what I'd need. I couldn't find corn syrup, so I got honey instead. The same employee as before was instrumental in my finding the cream of tartar. I didn't even know what kind of container it would come in.

I pulled into the château's parking lot just as Adrian texted me to meet him back in the large library. The tense lines on his face told me that he hadn't found what he was looking for.

My shoulders tightened. "Was it not the right book? Did we get played by someone on the internet?"

He shook his head. "I don't know. The thing is all over the place. In some sections, there are full tales written out. In others, it's more like bibliographic citations. And sometimes it reads like a thought journal or sticky notes. And, of course, the whole thing is in German, and it's written in cursive. Normally, I can read cursive just fine, and Grimm had neat handwriting, but it's a lot harder when it's in a language I don't know." He blew out a heavy sigh.

This must be what Yuti was talking about. He's carrying all of this on his shoulders.

"I'll get through it," he assured me. "I've taken a few pictures of pages to try and translate on the computer tonight, too."

"I know you'll get there." I reached out and touched his arm, and that seemed to relax him a bit.

After dinner that night, while Adrian worked on his translations upstairs, I collected the things I'd purchased at the grocery and pulled up the recipe on my phone. Then I went about step one.

Fifteen minutes later, I was stringing all manner of curses together as my sugar syrup started to form hard clumps. I turned off the stove and slammed the pan onto a cool burner.

"What's that burning smell?" Adrian asked, entering the kitchen.

I didn't look up at him. I just leaned my butt against the counter with my arms crossed and my head down. "I fucked it all up. I obviously don't know as much about cooking as I thought."

Adrian looked into the ruined pan. "What were you trying to make?"

I thrust my phone into his face. "It shouldn't be that hard. What did I do wrong?"

He took the phone from me gently and began to read. "You stirred the syrup, didn't you?"

"What do you mean? Of course I stirred the syrup. You don't stir stuff, it burns."

He shook his head. "Not with sugar syrup. If you stir it, it burns."

I threw my hands up in the air. "Well, how the hell was I supposed to know that? Why didn't it say that?"

"It does. See how there's an asterisk next to step two? If you go down to the notes section, it tells you not to stir the syrup."

I groaned, covering my face with my hands.

"What made you decide to make marshmallow fluff anyway?"

I spread my fingers and peeked at him. "Yuti told me you liked it, and you seemed stressed about the research. I tried to buy some at the store, but they were out, so I thought I could make some instead."

He stared at me for a heavy moment, but then he smiled, his dimple appearing as his eyes warmed.

A butterfly took flight in my stomach.

Adrian grabbed the handle of the saucepan and took it to the sink.

"You don't have to clean that. I messed it up, and you didn't even get to eat it."

He glanced over his shoulder at me. "Well, it needs to be cleaned if I'm going to teach you how to make it."

"I thought you didn't know how to cook?"

"True. I'm not great at cooking. But this is more of a baking technique. I've used it for certain buttercreams and caramel sauces. While I do this, why don't you read all of the instructions to the end?"

My face flushed. I should have done that before I'd even bought the ingredients. I picked up my phone and started to read.

After washing and drying the pan, Adrian measured out the honey, sugar, and water and put the mixture back on the stove.

"Did you take the eggs out already?" he asked.

I nodded. "It said 'room temperature' on the ingredients list."

"Okay, good. Separate the yolks and put the whites in the mixing bowl."

I did as he told me, cracking the eggs and gently pulling the yolks out with my hands. I put the yolks in a little container to use for breakfast the next morning. Holding the bowl of egg whites, I pursed my lips as I stared at the standing mixer. I'd never used one before. It wasn't like we had them in Faerie. I gritted my teeth while I tried to put the bowl in the base. It wasn't sitting flat.

Adrian came up behind me, placing his hands over mine.

My heart jumped. His hands were warm, and I could feel the solid heat of his chest so close to my back, so close but not touching. He twisted the bowl until it lay flush in the cradle, then locked it in place with another twist.

He didn't linger. His warmth was gone as fast as it had come, leaving only my pounding heart and the drifting scent of apples in its place.

37

*U*nder Adrian's experienced guidance, we finished the recipe to perfection—not that I did much of anything. The standing mixer stiffened the egg whites and cream of tartar, and Adrian poured in the syrup and vanilla. Even if I'd known what I was doing, I wouldn't have been much help.

Our little exchange, our simple physical contact, had left my mind whirling. It was different this time. Before, I had taken the active role. I had leaned in closer; I had touched his bare chest or his bruised wrists—and he had always retreated. But this time, he had initiated the contact. And while he'd still pulled away, it hadn't felt like a retreat.

It hadn't felt like he was trying to get away from me.

My eyes flicked to his face across the small kitchen table as he brought another spoonful of fluff from the mixing bowl to his mouth. *What could have changed since last night? Why is it different now? Is it even different, or am I looking too much into it? If I reached out and touched him now, would he pull away again?*

Despite my curiosity, I wasn't going to do that. If I made him uncomfortable and he pulled away again, then I would have just sacrificed whatever familiarity we'd found. If something was different and he didn't pull away, then I'd just have encouraged whatever desire he had for me.

I took a bit of fluff onto my spoon and put it in my mouth. It was sweet and creamy, though I couldn't imagine eating a whole jar of it. I watched Adrian as the fluff melted on my tongue. His face was clear of the worry he'd had since we'd left the château. His eyes were warm and bright with simple pleasure. He must not have shaved since we'd left the States because his facial hair was starting to turn from a shadowy stubble to a short scruff. His hair looked as if he'd been ruffling it in frustration while working on translations in his bedroom.

I thought of the first time I'd seen him and the eagerness with which I'd wanted to meet him. *He really is an attractive man.* As his scent of hay, bergamot, and golden poppies after a summer drizzle filled my nose, I couldn't think of a more pleasant smell.

He met my eyes, and the sweetness of crisp apples drifted toward me. "So what do you think?"

The wheels of my mind spun without gaining traction. "What?"

He huffed a laugh through his nose, and the dimple in his cheek appeared as he flashed his fangs. "It's good, right? The marshmallow fluff? To be honest, it's much better than store-bought."

My eyebrows scrunched. *What did I think he was asking about?* "Oh, right, the fluff. Yeah, no, I like it."

He tilted his head. "You're a hard woman to read. Do you know that?"

"Am I?" My head felt foggy, and my words sounded confused and distant. What was I even saying right now?

"Well." He frowned, shoving another spoonful of fluff into his mouth. "Unless you're trying to kill someone. Then you're pretty easy to read."

Any warmth I'd felt from him cooled as the echo of that memory, and the reminder of who and what we were in relation to each other, resurfaced. I'd apologized for the unfortunate incident, and it didn't feel like he held a grudge. But forgiving wasn't the same as forgetting, and we would both be foolish to forget the real danger that came along with our instincts taking control.

Adrian stood from the table, his smile much more subdued than only a few minutes before. "Thanks for the gesture. I really do appreciate the thought." He grabbed the bowl of fluff. "Do you want any more?"

I shook my head.

"I'll put it away then."

I didn't watch Adrian as he stored the fluff and went about cleaning the few dishes. I just stared out at the cold winter night. The moon had dwindled slightly from the night before. In a few days, it would be the dark moon. This night was just as beautiful as when we had taken our walk, but I wanted no part of it. I felt heavy at the moment, and I didn't even want to move from my chair.

I didn't analyze why I felt that way. I didn't try to distract myself or make myself feel better. I just leaned into the feeling, letting it weigh me down, press in on me like so many stones.

I knew it would pass, as every feeling—pleasant or otherwise —passed eventually. And, in a strange way, the weight was comforting. If I would've fought it, it might have crushed me. If I would've pushed it away, it might have gotten even heavier in the back of my mind. But as it was, it just settled atop me, and that was okay.

Adrian wished me a good night, and I murmured my response.

Eventually, I picked up the weight and headed upstairs to bed. I fell asleep to the tap-tapping of Adrian's fingers on the keyboard of his laptop.

The next morning, the heaviness had lifted. I didn't feel like singing or dancing around the room, but I was open to whatever joys the day would bring.

That day, and the few days that followed, passed in much the same way. I made breakfast, I packed lunch, and we went to the château. While Adrian was doing his research, I wandered around the grounds. The weekend was particularly nice, the temperature climbing to fifty. I spent quite a few hours researching recipes for meals. I knew how to cook a handful of dishes, but I wasn't an expert, and I liked variety and trying new things. In the evenings, Adrian and I would go for a walk before he retreated upstairs to his room to translate whatever pages he'd photographed before leaving that day.

By the following Monday, we'd gotten into a proper rhythm of things, and I couldn't have been happier. It was a nice little picture of domesticity. My days were full of simple pleasures, and I didn't have to worry about being an alpha or any of the problems that came with it.

But as we started toward the château that morning, Adrian ruined that particular aspect with a request. "I'm running out of blood. While I'm in the reading room today, would you head out to the butcher? I'd go with you…but Jean-Henri made it clear I'm not welcome anywhere near there."

38

Bosquet-aux-Loups was about a half hour's drive from the château, and the butcher was on the outskirts of town. As I approached the address on the GPS, I took in the fields where cows stood around doing whatever cows did, unbothered by the cold.

I turned onto a long driveway that led toward a cluster of buildings. The cobbled stones of the farmhouse walls varied in color, and the tiles appeared a bit bowed in the center of the roof. As I drove closer, I saw a few chickens braving the cold, their talons scratching at the muddy ground.

There was no one in sight when I got out of the car. I closed the door louder than necessary to announce my arrival to anyone around.

A werewolf in human form exited a barn, the sleeves of his thick sweater rolled up to his elbows. His yellow eyes widened as he met mine, and he dipped his head at me in respect, not that he looked happy about it.

"Are you the butcher? Is this where I get the blood?" I asked him.

He curled his lips. "Yes, I was told to expect you. Follow me."

As I stepped into the barn, I was overwhelmed by the scents and sounds within. Pigs grunted in their pens, jostling each other to get at their troughs. The foul scent of them made me reconsider ever eating bacon again.

I followed the man to a pen filled with straw.

"Are you serious?" My eyes slid to the farmer where he stood, arms crossed, beside me.

"You ask for blood; I give you blood."

The blood he had collected was in large white buckets stuffed to one side of the pen. He must have added something to stop it from coagulating because it remained in liquid form.

"You couldn't have put it in gallon jugs or something? How am I supposed to transport it?"

He shrugged as if none of that was his problem at all.

I sighed. "Can I at least get some lids for the buckets? It will spill all over if I try to drive with them uncovered."

The farmer squinted, clearly annoyed, but nodded. He didn't even lend a hand as I hauled them to the trunk.

I was glad to see the farm in my rearview mirror, and I wondered how long I could avoid coming back. I decided to buy some gallon jugs at the store before heading back to the château. It would be more manageable to ladle blood into gallon jugs with a funnel than individual water bottles.

That night, Adrian and I spent the evening pouring pig's blood through cheesecloth into the jugs. It seemed the butcher hadn't much cared if debris—mostly bits of straw and bugs—had found its way into the buckets.

"How long do you think this will last you?" I asked Adrian as I took in the fruits of our labor sitting neatly on the counter.

"Hmm, like a month? We might want to freeze some of these so it doesn't go bad."

His calculations would prove to be about right.

The next month was just as perfect as the first week had been.

We spent most of our days at the château, and I was pleased that the daytime temperatures were consistently in the fifties. We still had a while before spring, but winter's bitterness seemed to be over. On Tuesdays, when the château was closed, Adrian would work from photographs he'd taken of the notebook's pages.

I tried to make a point of calling my brother at least once a week, but I wasn't great at remembering to take pictures for him. In any case, what would he want to see? My life with Adrian in the little lake house in the woods was calm and quiet, all orange-juice mornings and sunset walks, the gentle lapping of the no-longer frozen lake the rhythm to our footsteps.

The only disturbance to our otherwise-tranquil existence was the occasional scent of autumn apples. I thought I had identified the instances in which it arose. I was careful not to carelessly touch Adrian, not to lean in too close. I even tried not to stare too long. But sometimes I would catch the scent at the most unexpected times—when I was getting laundry from the dryer, when I pulled my hair up to start dinner, when I enjoyed a cup of tea while gazing out the window. I tried not to let it distract me, tried to remind myself that he didn't mean anything by it. But the more it appeared, the more I found myself aggravated when it disappeared.

It was the end of February when I had to go back to the butcher for more blood, and I both hoped this would be the last time and that I could stay in this routine forever. Adrian's progress through the notebook was slow, but he'd warned me it could be. I wondered how long it would be before the other alphas lost their patience. Jean-Henri had made it apparent that he wanted us gone as quickly as possible. I couldn't imagine he was pleased with our current pace.

As I approached the butcher's long driveway, my view of the still-distant farm was obscured by a line of motor homes parked on the side of the road. At the very end of the line, a cluster of people hovered around the last trailer. Just past the group, I turned into the long driveway.

The butcher stomped past my car in his rubber boots,

heading toward the caravan with his yellow eyes blazing with anger. Turning off the car, I climbed out. The stench of farm animals almost covered the scent of the gathering werewolves.

A jumble of emotions not my own slammed into me. *Worry. Stress. Shame.* And, as the butcher approached the cluster of werewolves in human form, *fury.*

39

The butcher jerked his arm, clearly telling those gathered to leave while he shouted at them in French.

A woman stepped out of the group. "We'll be out of here as soon as we can fix this flat tire. You want us out quicker? Lend a hand."

"Jean-Henri has made it clear you are not welcome here! You weren't last time, and you aren't now. Either join the pack or get out!" the butcher roared.

The woman's rage flared, and I realized that she was unclaimed. In fact, all five of the werewolves present except the butcher were.

"We wouldn't join your precious pack if our lives depended on it," she growled.

"Then get off our land, you fucking gypsies." The butcher spat on the ground.

The woman lunged at him, pride and pain boiling her anger. But before she could reach him, a younger man caught her around the waist.

"Don't, Mama. This won't help Lolly. Let's just fix the tire and move on," he murmured in her ear.

The woman snorted and stomped farther up the road, away from the butcher.

The butcher turned and stalked back toward me. He dipped his head. "Meet me at the barn." Without another word, he started down the muddy drive.

With the farmer gone, the emotions of the unclaimed wolves were even more a-jumble, but a gut-wrenching worry was by far the most prominent feeling among them.

I frowned and started to walk toward them.

Before I was even within twenty feet, they all froze, their eyes snapping to me. I was a little surprised to feel fear join the emotional cocktail. My brow furrowed, and I tilted my head when no one so much as lowered their gaze.

The woman who'd argued with the butcher stepped forward again. She was not old but not young either, likely in her early to mid-fifties. Her face was creased with lines that spoke more of hardship than age. "We have no interest in joining your pack," she declared.

I blinked at her and shoved my hands into my coat pockets. "Well, that's good because I have no interest in gathering one."

Her face looked as surprised as I felt over her greeting. "You're a lone alpha?"

I nodded. *Well, I will be when I finish this mission.*

The fear of those gathered lessened but didn't disappear.

"What seems to be the problem?" I asked.

"My wife," replied the man who'd stopped the fight.

His mother shot him a warning glance.

"Please, Mama. Lolly needs a safe place right now. You put your pride aside to ask Jean-Henri for help."

She pursed her lips, looking back to me. "My daughter is pregnant, and it's not going well. We asked the alpha here to let us stay in his territory for a little while, but he refused. It's not good for my daughter to be on the move right now."

I frowned. "Do you have any fae amongst you?"

The woman shook her head. "No, we are just werewolves and a few humans."

I stifled a sigh, a bitter taste rolling over my tongue. "I'm staying in an unclaimed territory near here. You can park there, but...I need your word that no one among you will attack my charge. If there's even the slightest hint of danger directed toward him, you will have to leave. And I don't have to tell you what I'll do to anyone who harms him."

"Why would we attack him?"

"Because he's a vampire, sort of."

Everyone tensed, and a murmur ran through the group.

"Mama, please." The man, his worried eyes far more concerned about his wife than some random vampire, squeezed his mother-in-law's shoulder.

After a heavy moment, the woman looked around at the others gathered and then nodded my way. "For my daughter's sake, we won't attack him unprovoked."

"Good." I told them the address and said they could park around the lake. Then I walked away and climbed back into the car.

With a heavy sigh, I grabbed the steering wheel and leaned my forehead against my hands. Their emotions still swirled within me, pulling me in so many directions that I felt I would be torn apart.

I closed my eyes and breathed slowly in through my nose, counting the seconds until my lungs were full. I held it for a few seconds, then breathed out in a controlled breath through my mouth. I did it again and again until my mind was clear enough to push their emotions to the side.

I was left only with my own anxiety. The perfect, almost carefree days I'd experienced over the last weeks were over. My blissful little lake house in the woods was about to be overrun by unclaimed wolves. And not only would I have to be constantly bombarded by their emotions, but I needed to be vigilant that no harm would come to Adrian.

As I turned on the engine and started toward the barn, I wondered how Adrian would react to all this.

Will he understand?

40

When I met up with Adrian at the end of the day, it was clear he still hadn't found his answer.

"I took more pictures today since tomorrow is Tuesday," he told me as he started driving back to the lake house. "So I'll be working upstairs again."

I was barely listening while I tried to think of how to break the news to him. "Um, Adrian, something happened while I was getting the blood."

He immediately tensed, and I clenched my jaw. I'd chosen the wrong way to start.

I went on quickly, "Since I've been around you this last month and then some, you seem like a kind and considerate person."

His violet eyes flicked toward me before returning to the road.

"So I know that if someone needed help, even someone you didn't necessarily like or want around, you would help them, right? I mean, you've helped me a few times…"

"I don't dislike you, nor do I mind having you around," he said, his voice low.

My heart jumped. *Good to know.* "Well, thank you. So…when getting the blood, I ran into some people who needed help, and I offered it to them."

"Okay…"

"It seems a young woman, who is pregnant, is having a really hard time, and she needs a place to stay."

He nodded slowly. "So you offered for her to stay with us?"

"Right…Well, I offered for the group she's with to park their campers around the lake."

He frowned. "We're going to have to be careful not to expose who we are, I guess. But it's no different than what we're used to."

I laced my fingers together in my lap, squeezing my hands tightly. "It wouldn't be…except that they're a group of unclaimed werewolves." I stared at his face as anxiety made my heart race.

His jaw tightened, and he looked straight ahead, tension around his eyes and mouth. "Are there any fae?" he asked, the words ground out of him.

I shook my head quickly. "No, that was the first thing I asked. Just werewolves and humans."

"*Just* werewolves," he huffed.

I grimaced.

After a few heavy moments, he sighed. "I don't think you would have offered if you thought you couldn't protect me, right? I trust that you made this decision believing it was the best option."

My heart swelled at his words. He understood. Even though it would go against all his instincts, he understood my intentions, trusted my choices, and had faith I would protect him. I smiled, shaking my head in disbelief. "You really are something—do you know that?"

"Something…spectacular? Handsome? All-around awesome-sauce? If you're going to compliment me, use your adjectives."

I chuckled. "Seems like you have enough adjectives to go around. How about all of the above?"

But his joking tone left just as he pulled up to a red light. He looked over at me, his violet eyes clinging to mine in the small car. My breath rushed out of me as the scent of apples reached my nose.

Time stopped in that moment. There was only him and me and the scent of his arousal, promising taboo caresses and forbidden kisses in the darkest night. My heart pounded, and I couldn't remember how to swallow.

The car behind us honked loud and long, and Adrian looked away, heeding the green light to drive ahead.

My breath was uneven, and it took me a minute to get my heartbeat under control as I watched the French countryside out the window.

That was intense.

I'd lost myself for a moment there. It wasn't as if I'd forgotten what he was, what I was. I couldn't even say that I'd pushed that awareness aside or that it hadn't mattered as much in that moment. In a way, it had been the very thing that made the whole idea so tantalizing. He wasn't a wolf; he wasn't governed by the same instincts and conventions as a wolf. What would it look like to see the moon shine off those violet eyes of his? What would it feel like for his fangs to brush my skin?

I shivered, and warmth pooled in my core.

But my mind wasn't allowed to explore that feeling. I knew the moment we'd entered the unclaimed territory, and I knew that the unclaimed wolves were already there. The same hum that had nagged and tugged at me while in Louparest surfaced the moment we crossed the invisible border.

I sighed as we entered the lake house and made our way to the kitchen, a bucket of blood in each hand. Looking out the window, I could see the caravan parked around the lake. There would be no pleasant night strolls for a while.

I turned to head back to the car to get more blood, but Adrian blocked my way, his arms stretched out across the space of the hallway.

"What's wrong?" His voice was gentle but firm, and his eyes scanned my face for answers. "You seem off somehow."

I cringed and lowered my gaze. "I'm not great at being an alpha, okay?" I said softly. "All of those wolves are unclaimed. And I can...feel them. My instincts are poking at me. 'Claim the territory. Make these wolves part of your pack.' It's...really uncomfortable and unnerving. I hate everything about it."

Now that I'd said all that aloud, I realized how whiny it sounded.

Adrian's hands were warm and firm as he lowered them to my shoulders. He stared straight into my eyes. "You just need practice, like Lia said. I'm impressed that you invited them here even while knowing how it would affect you. You're strong enough to do this, and I'll help you however I can. You just let me know, okay?"

I pressed my lips together when my eyes started to burn; his words were so soft and encouraging. I reached up and grabbed one of his hands where it rested on my shoulder. "Thank you. I—"

My words were cut off by a hard knock sounding on the front door.

I sighed and dropped my hand. "That's probably one of the unclaimed. I don't even know their names yet. Stay behind me, okay?"

Adrian nodded and stepped aside. He stayed a few paces behind as I moved toward the door.

With a deep intake of breath, I opened it. And then my mouth dropped open. "Are you serious right now?"

Alasdair bowed his head to me from the doorstep.

41

"Willow." Alasdair grinned at me. "Did you miss me?" He boldly stepped into the house and wrapped me in a tight hug like we'd been friends all our lives. "Oof, you've been spending too much time with the vampire." He pulled back, scrunching his nose. "Your scent is off."

I glanced over at Adrian. His face was flushed, and his lips were pressed into a hard line.

"Is it?" I wasn't even paying attention to his words, so off-balance was I by his sudden appearance.

He gave me that lopsided smile. "Don't worry. I wouldn't even have noticed if I didn't know your scent so well."

I crossed my arms. "What are you doing here? How do you keep finding me?"

"Fate is on my side."

I clicked my tongue. "Will you just answer the question?"

He smiled, unhindered by my irritation. "Of course. Would you like me to stand in the front hall with the cold air coming in? My story isn't a short one."

I frowned and glanced back at Adrian. He glowered, but he didn't smell of fear. "No, come in. I'll put the kettle on." I spun on my heel to head back toward the kitchen, and Adrian turned to go before me.

As I went about boiling the water and gathering cups for tea, Adrian stood by the paned doors, staring out at the caravan with his arms crossed. Alasdair sat at the kitchen table, his eyes analyzing Adrian.

A few minutes later, I placed three cups of hot water down on the table, tea bags floating as they steeped. I sat, and Alasdair scooted his chair closer to mine. The sound of the legs scraping against the floor drew Adrian's attention, and he came to sit on my other side.

I stared at Alasdair. "Start with how you found me again."

Alasdair reached for the tea and took his sweet time taking a sip. "You told me where you were going to be."

I squinted at him. "I *did not*. I didn't even know where I was going to be when I last saw you."

"You said you were coming to France. Once I knew that, it wasn't hard to find out where the human realm packs are in the area. I was lucky there's only one in France. I knew you'd have to introduce yourself to the alpha here. So I would only have to do the same and ask him where you were."

"And he told you?"

Alasdair shook his head. "This is where fate stepped in. Jean-Henri wanted me to stay with them. It seems the packs in this realm don't have many wolf mystics — plus, my name carries a lot of weight, as you know. He promised he would tell me where you were if I did. But then, Amelie and her group of unclaimed came in asking for refuge. After I saw how Jean-Henri treated them, I couldn't stay with him in good conscience. So I asked Amelie if I could travel with them. It seemed things weren't going very well for the troupe when one of the motor homes got a flat tire. But then Amelie came back to where I was waiting with Lolly and told us a lone alpha had offered for us to stay with her. I knew that lone alpha had to be you."

I sighed and reached for my tea. I pulled the bag from the

water and added four teaspoons of sugar before stirring it in. "But why did you come at all? Why did you leave Faerie?"

"I suppose if I said I missed you, that wouldn't be enough of a reason?"

"Is it the reason?"

He frowned, and my inner alpha didn't like the expression on him. "Not the only one. Remember when I told you back in the States that I felt strange? The moment I stepped into this realm, I felt...different. I mean, completely different, like I hadn't been fully alive until that moment. At the time, I thought it was just my excitement at finding you. But when I stepped back into Faerie after Aryn dropped me off at the portal, the feeling faded. I was still excited about having found you. And, even though I had to wait until your task was finished, I was so happy that you said you'd give me a chance."

Did I say that? I guess I did sort of nod when he asked me not to turn him away without getting to know him.

"I went back to the monastery to wait for you, but I couldn't get rid of this nagging feeling. And then I remembered something from very early on in my training. A wolf mystic's power comes from two sources: our ancestors and the land. That made me think. Werewolves originated in the human realm. Perhaps by leaving, we cut ourselves off from the land. They say that when the treaty was forged, the fae magicked werewolf territory into Faerie. But what does that mean? Did they really magic the actual land, take it from one realm to the other? If that's how they did it, maybe they didn't capture what connects us to the land on a spiritual level. So I thought I'd come back to this realm and explore the idea." He grinned.

I found Alasdair's thoughts very interesting. Were the wolves of Faerie, cut off as they were from the land of their ancestors, sacrificing some spiritual connection and power? Could that be a reason why the wolves in this realm were so much better at being wolves? We'd thought it was because they were raised by the pack their whole lives. But maybe there was more to it.

In the time I'd been in the realm of origin, I'd never met a wolf mystic. I'd never heard anyone talk about one either.

Do we have mystics in this realm? Did they all go to Faerie? Alasdair's exploration of this idea could have a major impact on the wolves here.

"So you're staying with the werewolves in the caravan then?" Adrian asked in that deceptively easy tone of his.

Alasdair didn't even look at him, meeting my gaze instead. "Well, I thought I could stay in here. Willow did agree to get to know me better. What better time than the present?"

My inner wolf's ears perked, her full attention on this potential pack member.

"We don't exactly have the room," Adrian said. "And who knows what you'll do to me in my sleep."

I shook my head. "Adrian's right. It's not a good idea. There are too many unknown variables hanging around. I can't be distracted when there are so many unclaimed wolves near Adrian. That includes you."

Alasdair pursed his lips. "You told me not to attack him, so I won't."

I sighed. "Even so, there's still the bed situation. I suppose I could share a bed with Adrian. That way I'd know the moment something happened to him."

Adrian's face flushed, and the scent of apples wafted toward me. I gritted my teeth.

I probably shouldn't have suggested that, even if it was a practical solution.

A growl emanated from Alasdair's human throat. "I'd rather sleep on the couch."

42

In the end, we agreed that Alasdair would sleep on the couch downstairs, and Adrian and I would sleep in our respective rooms. The whole situation left me confused and conflicted. I knew I didn't want Alasdair in my pack—not that the feeling was personal—but I couldn't make myself refuse him. And, of course, if I refused him at this point, I would be going back on my word.

There wasn't really any harm in him staying. He'd said he wouldn't attack Adrian, and I had said we could be friends.

On the other hand, I'd been so happy with just Adrian and me in our peaceful little lake house—no other wolves around to muck it up, no alpha instincts to muddle whom I thought of as Willow. But it was obvious that something was going on with Alasdair. My response to him whenever he came near was very real. And no matter how much I wanted to brush it off, I couldn't let go of the feeling that there was something to his assertions. Was it really as he claimed? Were the strings of fate pulling us together?

I hated that idea. But I was either too curious—or not in control enough—to push him away.

One practical benefit of Alasdair staying with us was that he could act as a go-between with us and the unclaimed wolves. It wasn't a good idea for them to come to the house with Adrian there, nor did I want to leave him alone to go to them if I could avoid it. Plus, the less interaction I had with them, the less their emotions would assault me.

I watched Alasdair walk across the grass toward the caravan to collect whatever things he had brought with him. I glanced over at Adrian, who stood beside me, following Alasdair's progress. "Are you okay with this?"

Adrian's eyes met mine, and I couldn't help but feel there was something sad in his gaze. "If this is what you want, Willow."

The way he whispered my name, low and intimate, tugged at my heart. Too many things had changed in too short a time. I'd left that morning in a state of peaceful joy, a state so easily shattered.

A tingle ran up my arm when Adrian brushed my hand with his fingers. "*Is* this what you want?"

I trembled as warmth spread through me, my nerves keying in to Adrian's fingertips stroking my palm. And suddenly the world outside didn't exist. I didn't feel the hum of the other wolves' emotions, nor did I even feel the tug of being with them in an unclaimed territory. How could I, with my every nerve ending tingling at Adrian's touch?

Werewolves? Vampires? What did any of it mean to Willow and Adrian?

And then he stopped; he pulled away. And I scrunched my eyebrows, confused and desperate to understand. My chest tightened, and I snatched his hand to stop his retreat.

His violet eyes widened as his breath hitched. I could feel his pulse pumping in his fingertips. The points of his fangs peeked out when his full lips parted.

I swallowed and blew a resolved breath through my nose. Lacing my fingers with his, I turned fully toward him. His face flushed, and I wondered what expression I was making.

One step, one small step, and I could press my lips to his. I could feel his heat against me. The scent of apples told me his body wanted it. But what of the rest of him? He'd drawn the line pretty well, making it clear that we were too different; I'd tried to kill him after all.

I could revel in him. I knew that he could make me forget the outside world, if only for a while. But what would that do to him? I doubted he would thank me for it.

I frowned, and my eyes started to burn. I was overwhelmed. Too many things pulled at me, and I couldn't decipher what was me and what came from everyone else. It was stupid to cry. It wouldn't help. But as I doubted my own desire—as I wondered whether I actually wanted Adrian or if I just wanted to use him as a shield to deflect my alpha instincts, my reaction to Alasdair, and my own desperate need to hold onto what made me me— tears blurred my vision.

I turned away, releasing Adrian's hand and closing my eyes to stop the tears from spilling over. "There are leftovers in the fridge for dinner. I'm going to bed early." Then I left the kitchen without looking at him again.

Even while lying in my bed, staring up at the ceiling, I could hear when Alasdair returned to the house. He asked where I was, and Adrian answered as shortly as possible. As the microwave beeped with Adrian's dinner, I heard someone climb the stairs. And I knew that it was Alasdair who listened outside my door. I kept my breathing slow and even, not at all ashamed that I feigned sleep to avoid this conversation. After a minute or so, Alasdair retreated downstairs.

I could hear a fork clinking against a bowl as Adrian carried his leftovers up to his room.

After a few minutes, I heard a voice coming from his bedroom. It spoke of space being the final frontier and the mission of a starship.

I wasn't familiar with whatever he was watching on his laptop, but I concentrated on the sound of it, a lifeline in the tumultuous sea of the churning emotions inside me—both mine and others. As I focused on what was happening in Adrian's room, I stared at the picture we'd taken together at the château.

Eventually, I fell asleep.

It was well past dusk when I awoke. I didn't look at my phone to check, but I guessed it was still the wee hours of a new day. The delicious scent of something sweet baking made me breathe deeply, and my stomach grumbled. I hadn't eaten dinner. Getting out of bed as quietly as I could, I sneaked downstairs.

I tiptoed past the sitting room, where Alasdair slept soundly, his leg hanging off the side of the couch.

"What's that smell?" I whispered to Adrian.

He started, chocolate sprinkles jumping from the bowl he held onto the sheet full of frosted cookies on the counter in front of him. He blew out a breath.

"Sorry. I didn't think I could surprise you. What are you doing?" I glanced at the clock on the microwave. It was one in the morning.

"When we first arrived, you used to come down here in the middle of the night and eat a frozen cookie from the tin my mom gave you. I know you ran out a while ago, so I thought I'd make more."

I tilted my head. I hadn't known he'd paid such close attention to my cookie habit. The truth was, I'd said I wasn't going to eat in the middle of the night, so I wouldn't take a cookie out of the freezer to thaw. But then I'd inevitably come down and eat one frozen. My heart warmed at the sweet gesture.

"Try one." He held out a cookie to me, topped with cream-colored frosting and chocolate sprinkles.

I accepted it and took a bite. These weren't the soft sugar cookies his mom had made. He'd frosted gooey chocolate chip cookies. They were warm and sweet and everything I needed in that moment. I smiled at him. "Thank you. It's very good."

"Are you…feeling better?" he murmured.

I frowned. "I'm sorry about earlier."

His eyes searched mine. "Are you?"

"Yes." *It wasn't right for me to want to use him in that way. It must have been uncomfortable for him.*

He dropped his gaze back to the cookies, nodding slightly as his expression wilted. "I'll just...put these in the freezer when I'm done."

"Can I have one more?"

He held out another to me, and I took it. He didn't so much as look at me as our fingers brushed. "Goodnight," he whispered when I turned to leave the kitchen.

The sweetness of my next bite seemed bitter somehow.

43

I awoke the next morning to the sound of raised voices.

"This is ridiculous," Adrian scoffed.

"Don't lie to me, vampire. I can smell her all over you, and there are only two ways that could've happened," Alasdair growled.

"Oh, yeah? So you jump straight into the idea that I've fed on her? And you think Willow would allow that, do you? Did you happen to miss the buckets of pig's blood everywhere?"

The snarl that rumbled through the lower floor had me jumping out of bed. I didn't even bother to put on my pants. I just ran downstairs, pulling a sweatshirt on over my underwear as I went.

"That better be what it is," Alasdair said darkly. "Because the only other way her scent could almost cover yours is if you've had sex."

My bare feet thumped on the hard floor as I ran into the kitchen. Alasdair had Adrian backed up against the refrigerator, their faces mere inches from each other. Alasdair's body was tense with menace. But Adrian stood firm—no fear in his scent—

glaring back at Alasdair in a challenge I'd never seen from him when facing down a werewolf.

"That's enough!" I snapped. "Alasdair, back off." Alpha power surged in my voice, though I didn't know how much effect it would have on a mystic compared to any other werewolf.

Alasdair stiffened but didn't move away.

"You said you wouldn't attack him. He's under my protection. Do you really want to square off with me?"

Alasdair blew an angry breath through his nose and stepped back.

Adrian clicked his tongue, his eyes sliding to mine. "See? What was the first thing I said to you when we got in the car? I knew some shit like this would happen." He stormed from the room, muttering to himself. "Fucking werewolves, Jesus Christ."

I turned to Alasdair, crossing my arms. "Do you want to explain yourself, or should I just guess?"

Alasdair raised his chin. "Something is off about him. I've known it since he came into your bedroom at the resort. I told you yesterday that your scent smells a little like his—not enough to make you smell like vampire, but enough that I noticed the change. And his scent...it smells so much like you that I might not even have thought he was a vampire if I came upon it by chance."

Huh, I didn't know that.

But that wasn't the case when he spent all that time with the Rowan and Ashwin. Is it because I'm an alpha?

"Every time I see his stupid vampire face, I want to rip the life out of him. And I don't think I have to defend my instincts on that front."

He's right. He doesn't need to explain. By the standards we were raised with, he's completely in the right.

I frowned. "I think you should leave. At the very least, I think you should go stay with the unclaimed in the caravan."

Alasdair's face crumbled—his orange eyes wavering—and his deep sorrow slammed into me.

Something within me cried out at the pain in his face. "Listen. I understand that vampires have been our enemies since they've existed. And I get that you'd be protective of your friend and potential alpha. But, the fact is, that those totally under-standable instincts are getting in the way right now. This is an unprecedented situation. Adrian needs to do his research, and it's my job to protect him from other wolves."

Alasdair shook his head. "I can't leave your side again. Everything in me is saying that something terrible will happen if I leave you again."

I closed my eyes against his pain, against the deep ache that pulsed within me. My inner wolf whined. "What am I supposed to do, Alasdair? You just said you want to kill him every time you see him. Can't you see that having you around him only creates more unnecessary work for me and will make it harder to protect him if someone else tries to attack? Do you think I can get to know you better while constantly worried about whether you're going to ruin the one task I have to perform before I'm free? Is that the atmosphere you want for me to get to know you in?"

"I'm sorry," he whispered.

No sooner had the words left his mouth than a faint new scent came from him. It was stale and disgusting, like gym socks that had been worn for a week straight. But then it was gone.

"I'll try harder to keep my instincts under control."

I frowned, resting my hand on his shoulder. He stared down at me. "I don't want that, Alasdair. Your instincts are part of who you are. You shouldn't have to suppress them. You shouldn't have to be half of who you are just to be friends with me. You say we're fated to be connected, but even an alpha has no right to ask so much of you."

"I'd do anything for you," he declared with that unflinching loyalty.

My heart ached at his words, and I swallowed around the lump in my throat. "Then you'll leave, as I'm asking you to."

His agony seeped into me, but I didn't push it away. I took it in, letting it wash over me in waves, soaking my very soul. And as I did, the line between his emotions and mine became clear. He was in pain, conflicted and confused. He wanted to do what I asked of him, but he was certain something bad would happen if he did. And I was just sad—sad to see him hurting and, to be completely honest, sad that he had to leave.

"Today," Alasdair whispered. "Can I just have this one day?"

Staring up at him, his heart swimming in his eyes, I couldn't refuse him this one request. I nodded.

44

The day before, Adrian had told me that he planned to spend the day translating the pictures he'd taken of Wilhelm Grimm's notebook. But as Alasdair and I moved to the sitting room after breakfast, Adrian followed, sitting in the armchair facing the couch we settled on.

My eyes flicked toward him, but Alasdair's full attention was on me.

"How should we spend our day together?" he asked.

I adjusted my shoulders, uncomfortable with Adrian's violet eyes watching me so intently. I cleared my throat. "Well, I suppose we have to go to the grocery store. But...I didn't really have anything planned." I glanced over at Adrian. "Adrian was going to do some research, I guess. So I was just going to hang around. Nothing special."

Alasdair smiled. "Every day with me is special, I promise. We could play a game, or..." He leaned in close to me and dropped his voice. "I could tell you a scary story."

"Do you have a list of things we need to get from the supermarket?" Adrian asked, his voice dry and even, pulling my attention from Alasdair's eyes glinting only inches from mine.

I dipped my head. "Yeah, I looked up some new recipes and wrote down all the ingredients."

Alasdair quirked an eyebrow at Adrian. Then he grinned a mischievous grin that made me freeze.

Oh no. What's that look?

When he spoke, his tone took on a sultry little undertone that hadn't been there before. "Cooking it is then. I look forward to tasting it. What are you making this evening?"

I blinked at him. *What is he up to?* "I was thinking roast beef and vegetables. Since I'll be here the whole day, I can roast it slow."

"Slow is the best way to get meat hot and juicy. I'll help you." Alasdair reached out and stroked my hair, and I tilted my head at him, squinting at his sudden change.

Adrian shot to his feet. "If you're planning on cooking it slow, then we'd better get going to the store."

My eyes followed him while he stomped from the room. Alasdair chuckled under his breath beside me.

I frowned, looking over at his too-innocent expression. "He's right. We'd better get going."

Our trip to the grocery store took much longer than it should have. I could hardly concentrate on completing my list with Alasdair and Adrian sniping at each other, not to mention vying for my attention. The whole thing was exhausting. I couldn't see why Alasdair was provoking Adrian in this way. I knew he didn't like him, but he was starting to act more like a jealous lover than a protective friend. Even stranger was how Adrian played into it.

Perhaps it was just a pride thing. Alasdair had accused Adrian of things that Adrian hadn't done. Still, I was surprised. Adrian hadn't seemed like a petty person before.

Once we'd returned to the lake house and had put the groceries away, I felt sure I would get a break. Adrian had taken all those pictures of the notebook, and he'd been so keen on working even though the château was closed. But he didn't head upstairs to his translations. He stood in the kitchen, watching as I unwrapped the meat.

"Don't you have work to do?" Alasdair sneered at him.

Adrian crossed his arms. "Willow promised to teach me how to cook. I love roast beef."

I stifled a sigh. "All right. Alasdair, peel the carrots, and wash and quarter the potatoes and mushrooms. Come here, Adrian, and I'll show you how to season the meat."

After placing the meat in the roasting pan, I grabbed the herbs and spices I would need. Alasdair started washing vegetables in the sink, and Adrian came to stand near me—very near me. I could feel his body heat as he leaned over my shoulder to watch what I was doing. I tried to ignore the tingle that ran over my skin every time his breath brushed my neck.

"Excuse me," Alasdair growled, forcing his way between us as he reached for the largest kitchen knife in the block. "Need a knife if I'm going to chop anything."

The two men exchanged a glare, and Alasdair returned to his task.

"And that's pretty much it," I told Adrian. "We put it in the oven for a few hours, and then we add the vegetables toward the end. Not so hard."

"I think you underestimate how *very hard* it is for me."

A loud clang reverberated through the kitchen as Alasdair dropped his knife on the counter, and I raised my eyebrows at Adrian's suggestive tone.

Is he trying to get himself killed?

Alasdair surged toward him, stopping only when I held out my arm.

"Don't even think about it," Alasdair growled, glaring at Adrian across the two feet that separated them.

Adrian smirked. "Think about what?"

Alasdair's fury slammed into me.

"Okay, all right. Alasdair, why don't you take those vitamins you got for Lolly out to the caravan, huh? Adrian, you said you have work to do. I'll put the roast in and finish chopping the vegetables. Okay?"

Neither man even flinched.

"*Go!*" I snapped.

They reluctantly retreated, and I sighed in relief once I stood alone in the kitchen. But my quiet respite—where I concentrated on the feel of the vegetables as my knife sliced through them, at the gentle sound of the blade meeting the cutting board—was short-lived.

Adrian, in all his wisdom, brought his laptop down to the kitchen table, where Alasdair sat watching me make tea. I shook my head, grabbing another mug from the cupboard.

"How much longer is this research going to take?" Alasdair demanded of Adrian. "Aren't you supposed to be a professional or something?"

Adrian clicked his tongue. "How many languages do you read?"

Alasdair raised an eyebrow. "Eight if you count the dead ones."

Adrian scowled, and I had a hard time not laughing aloud as I sat at the table.

"Wow, eight, that's pretty impressive," I said. "But I suppose mystics do a lot of reading."

Alasdair nodded. "We do a lot of research, too."

"Really? What do you research?" I asked.

Alasdair leaned forward, and I could feel his delight that I was interested in something about him. "All kinds of things. Some mystics ask big questions, like where werewolves come from. But mostly we study the bonds that connect wolves, how they work and how to make them stronger. We spend a lot of time learning rituals to honor our ancestors and the land. Some concentrate on spiritual medicine to help the community, and others are on a more personal journey."

"What about you?" I asked.

"I've always heard the call of the ancestors. I knew I would be a mystic even before I was bound. I haven't yet reached the level of individual research within the ranks of mystics, though."

I frowned. "You shouldn't have left the monastery."

Alasdair shook his head. "Don't say that. The ancestors have always spoken loudly within me; they have always pointed me in the direction of fate. They told me to follow you, and so I did."

As I stared into Alasdair's bright, orange eyes, I knew he was successfully nudging his way into my heart.

There were many kinds of bonds wolves formed in our lives: family, friends, pack, mates. All of them were important, and none of them were easily broken. And as peculiar as this mystic was, he was growing on me. He'd bared his soul to me that day when he'd knelt before me on the road. He was loyal, honest, and kind. He would make the perfect addition to any pack.

Would it be so bad to form a bond with him?

Adrian's breath hitched. "I think I found something."

45

I shot from my seat and moved to hover over Adrian's shoulder. "What did you find?"

On his computer screen, he had the photo of a notebook page on one side and a translator app on the other.

"Right here, see?" Adrian pointed to the last line of the page. And there it was in neat script: *Lucilla aus dem schwarzen Walde.*

I gripped Adrian's shoulders, grinning. "You found it! What does it say?"

Adrian sighed. "Just her name. Everything else must be on the next page."

"Well, pull it up then."

"I can't. This was the last picture I took. We'll have to wait until tomorrow."

I groaned. *So close.*

"But that's great news," Alasdair said to me. "If you've found the reference, the research is almost finished. Your task will be over soon, and you'll have fully completed your training."

Adrian harrumphed. "I thought you knew about research. *I* might have found the reference, but we don't know what it even is yet. It could be nothing."

I nodded slowly, patting his back. "Or it could be what you've worked so hard for, Adrian. We'll just have to wait until tomorrow. I'm going to call Lia."

I went to do just that. Lia was pleased with our progress and told me to call her as soon as we knew more, no matter what time it was.

When I returned from my call, the atmosphere was charged with excitement and anxiety. I wished there was an easy way to blow off some steam. A run would be nice, though not a good idea with the unclaimed hanging around.

So the charged atmosphere stood, mounting with every hour that passed, with no reasonable way to ease it. After dinner, Alasdair lingered. It was clear he didn't want to leave, and I didn't force the issue.

I stared out the kitchen window. The unclaimed had built a fire, and the flames danced below the sliver of crescent moon. It was getting late; I would need to turn in soon if I wanted to be ready for our important day tomorrow.

Adrian stood from the kitchen table and went to the fridge.

"Step outside with me for a moment. I'd like to say good-night," Alasdair requested.

I frowned, my gaze flicking to Adrian as he pulled out a bottle of pig's blood.

"No harm will come to your vampire. I'll be out there with you, and you'll be in between him and the unclaimed."

I lowered my chin and stood to follow him onto the back porch.

The night was cold without my coat, and I wrapped my arms around myself. Still, it was beautiful. The stars were bright overhead, and all was quiet.

Alasdair turned to me, his orange eyes glimmering softly in the light that filtered out through the kitchen windows. "You know that leaving you is the last thing I want to do—that the only thing that could make me do it is your request."

I nodded.

"My heart quakes at the thought of you being packless, with no backup if you should need it."

I knew he spoke the truth. I could feel his anxiety, and I silently accepted it into myself.

Alasdair rested his hands on my shoulders, sharing his warmth against the winter chill. "I don't want to push you beyond where you're comfortable, but I feel I must ask. May I bless you? I don't know how much protection it will provide, but it will make me feel more at ease."

"Why would I be uncomfortable with that?"

He looked straight at me without even blinking. "Because I need to kiss you for this blessing."

I quirked my mouth. There were many kinds of blessings wolf mystics could provide, but very few of them involved kisses. Still, kisses held a powerful place in werewolf bonds. The promise between mates was sealed and broken with a kiss on the lips. Alphas kissed the forehead of wolves to claim them as pack members. Hands were sometimes kissed in signs of fealty, though that wasn't as common these days.

What could one kiss hurt?

"Where?" I asked.

He didn't look away. "With your permission, I'd like to bless you with the protection of a true friend."

The protection of a true friend was not a blessing given by mystics but by faithful friends with open hearts. It formed a bond of true friendship. It was not the empathetic bond of a bondmate or the symbiotic bond of an alpha and her pack. It was not the golden thread of one mate to another.

It was more of a vow from one wolf to another. A vow that one would always be a true friend and would always be there when needed.

My heart swelled. It was such a sweet thing for him to offer me, and I nodded—trying to hold back tears at the gesture.

Sliding his hands down my arms, he took my hands in his. He dipped his head, kissing each one. "When you fall, I will be there to pull you up. When you need a claw or a fist, I will be there to protect you," he vowed.

Letting go of my hands, he stepped closer to me and kissed my forehead. A pleasant warmth spread through me.

"When you are sick, I will be there to care for you."

I looked up into Alasdair's eyes, warm and sincere. He leaned his face down to mine, stopping before our lips met. "When you speak, I will be there to listen." His whispered words tickled my lips, and I held my breath in anticipation.

He pressed a delicate, fleeting kiss to my mouth.

I smiled up at him. "A vow for a vow, I give to you what you have promised to me." Then, raising myself on my toes, I kissed his lips a second time.

He sighed contentedly. "I feel better."

I patted his shoulder. "Good. I'm glad. Now that we're true friends, would you mind telling me why you've been acting like that all day?"

"Like what?"

"Don't 'like what' me. You've been poking at Adrian all day in the weirdest ways."

He shrugged. "I just figured out what would get under his skin most and did that."

"But *why*?"

He grinned at me. "Because it's fun."

"Gods, you're annoying. Maybe I should have thought this through more before making this bond with you."

"It's too late. No take-backsies."

I huffed and turned on my heel. "Yeah, whatever. Goodnight, Alasdair. Let me know if the unclaimed wolves need anything."

"You'll love me more and more every day!" he called after me.

When I re-entered the house, Adrian was still standing in the kitchen. I gave him a nod and wished him a goodnight. Then I passed through and headed up to my room.

46

I didn't sleep well that night. My mind couldn't rest, worrying about what Adrian's research would uncover the next day.

Listening for the quiet sounds of Adrian in his room, I tried to put my mind at ease. Surely, concentrating on his even breathing would eventually lull me to sleep. But that soft, steady breathing never came. It seemed Adrian was just as unsettled as I was. He paced his room most of the night, his feet shuffling gently on the carpet in a rhythmic rate.

I did drift off as dawn approached, but I didn't sleep more than an hour.

Adrian looked as worn out as I felt the next morning at breakfast. There were dark circles under his eyes, and his complexion was paler than usual. The look on his face didn't encourage conversation, and I was too tired to attempt it anyway.

I managed to have a little doze on the way to the château, but I wouldn't say I was rested. I followed Adrian to the reading room. And though I was forced to stay in the larger library due to lack of space, I didn't wander around the grounds that day.

I didn't know whether the curator was annoyed with me as I drifted around the bookshelves, but I wasn't going to move from that room unless I was dragged out. He mostly ignored my presence though, so it never came to that.

Time passed slowly, and I took that as a good sign, despite my impatience. There had to be something there, or Adrian would have told me otherwise. Or at least I hoped he wouldn't have left me in suspense for no good reason.

After two hours, Adrian appeared at the door connecting the two rooms.

I scanned his expression. He frowned, his face stiff, as he clutched his bag to his chest.

I rushed to meet him. "Well? Did you find anything?"

He nodded once. "Yes, it was a bibliographic reference."

"What does that mean?"

He sighed loudly. "It's just a line telling us where he got the information. It means that if we want the full story, we have to find the book he's referring to."

"So the whole story isn't in the notebook? Then what the heck took you two hours?" My outburst earned me a censuring glance from the curator.

"I was trying to find where this other book is," Adrian defended.

"And did you find it?"

"Yes, it's in Munich."

"Is that far?"

Adrian shook his head. "If we get back to the lake house and pack quickly, we can be there by tonight."

I smiled, slapping him on the shoulder. "That's what I'm talking about! Let's go."

Adrian had a quick conversation with the curator, and we were driving away from the château not a quarter of an hour later.

I called Lia as Adrian drove, shoving my lunch into my mouth while the phone rang in my ear. It was still a little early for them to be up at the resort, but not so early that I felt bad about calling.

"Hello?" Lia's voice was alert.

"Hey, so I guess the book had a... What did you call it, Adrian?"

"Bibliographic reference," Adrian supplied.

"Right. The thing he found yesterday was a bibliographic reference to another book. But I guess he found that book, and we can be there by tonight."

"Where is it?" Lia asked.

"Munich. We're heading back to the lake house now. I don't want to take my leave of Jean-Henri, and I'm sure he'll appreciate us staying away as well. But I have no way of getting a hold of him. Could you reach out to him and let him know we're leaving?"

Lia remained silent for too long, and I looked down at my phone to make sure the call was still connected. "Hello?"

"This isn't a good idea. We should send someone else."

"What? Why?"

"It has nothing to do with whether I think you're ready or not. The fact is that Günter Kraus—the alpha of the Bavarian Pack—is very intolerant. He doesn't care what our reasons for allowing Adrian to live are. He would've killed him without a second thought had he shown up in his territory like he did mine. It's too risky to send Adrian there. I'm not sure what he'll do now."

My chest tightened at the thought of Adrian entering a territory even more inhospitable than Jean-Henri's.

"There's no fucking way I'm handing this over to someone else!" Adrian snapped, his vampire hearing picking up Lia's words even without speakerphone. "I've worked my whole life for this. You're not taking it away from me!"

Lia was silent for a long moment, then sighed. "Fine. But I'm sending Noire with you. If you're going to bring Adrian into the Bavarian Pack's territory, you're going to need backup."

I suppose this is the downside of being a lone alpha. Maybe I should bring Alasdair.

But the moment I thought of that solution, I threw it right out. I knew Alasdair would have my back, but would he protect Adrian?

Noire should be enough help, or Lia wouldn't have given in so easily. "Do you want us to wait for Noire to get here before we leave?"

"No, let us know what train you catch, and I'll have Noire get on at the station closest a portal before it gets to Bavaria."

"Okay. I'll text you the info."

We said our goodbyes and hung up.

Once we reached the lake house, I thought about just how much we had to do. We had buckets of blood we couldn't take with us, a fridge full of food, and a whole troupe of unclaimed wolves camping in the backyard. I packed my suitcase and told Adrian to fill his little cooler with as much blood as he could.

"I'll make some sandwiches to take with us, but we might as well let the unclaimed have the food we bought."

Adrian nodded as he put a funnel into an empty water bottle.

I frowned. Without me on the property, I didn't know how long the unclaimed would be welcome to stay. This area might not be in Jean-Henri's territory, but he did own the lake house and the land.

"Stay here," I instructed Adrian. "Don't let anyone inside, and lock the door behind me. I'll only be five minutes."

I stepped out onto the back porch, the cold wind blowing my hair from my face. The lock clicked as Adrian slid it into place behind me.

47

The hum beneath my skin increased with every step I took toward the gathered campers, and the emotions of those inside prodded me harder. I took a deep breath and knocked on the door of the first motor home I reached.

The man with the pregnant wife answered a moment later. Again, he didn't dip his head at me.

"We never introduced ourselves," I said. "I'm Willow. Who's the leader of your group?"

"Come in, Willow." He stepped back, and I climbed into the cozy space. "I'm Russett. This is my wife, Lolly, and my mother-in-law, Amelie. And you already know Alasdair, I believe." He gestured toward the others gathered.

His wife, large with child, sat beside her mother on a wrap-around seat that took up the end of the space. Alasdair leaned against a small kitchen counter. The family had tensed at my appearance, their emotions flying like sparks. Alasdair, of course, was happy to see me.

As all of the emotions crashed into me, I didn't push them away. I accepted them, analyzed them, then let them go. I had done this a few times now with Alasdair, and it seemed easier than wrestling with them for control. It seemed easier to work *with* my alpha instincts rather than fight against them. I knew now that I'd been trying too hard to control my inner wolf and her alpha nature, when all I needed to do was accept and integrate those instincts to maintain my sense of self. After a tense moment, my own emotions dominated my mind again. I was still aware of theirs, but they didn't push at me. They simply hummed in the background—a white noise easily ignored but there if I should want to listen.

Alasdair eyed me seriously. "Are you all right? You look tired."

"I'm fine." I turned to the other wolves. "Who's in charge here?"

Russett and Lolly looked at Amelie, who frowned. "This might seem strange to you since you're an alpha and all, but no one is in charge. We make our decisions together. We reject the idea that we need to be ruled, obedient to someone who was simply born with more power than us."

I tilted my head. I'd never heard of such a thing. But then I grinned at the older woman. *I love everything about this.* "Well, then I'll just tell you since I'm here, and you can discuss what to do with everyone else. Adrian and I are leaving shortly, hopefully within the hour. This is unclaimed territory, but the land is owned by Jean-Henri and his pack. It's my understanding he isn't very friendly toward you?"

Lolly lowered her eyes, gently rubbing her belly. Her mother shook her head.

I nodded. "I don't know when they'll come out here again after we leave."

Amelie's frown seemed more an expression of thought than feeling. She dipped her head, then stood. "As this is unclaimed territory, it shouldn't be difficult for us to find a place nearby to settle until the baby is born." Amelie held out her hand to me, and I grasped her forearm. I had the sense that this gesture was not just a simple exchange between werewolves to her. She wasn't one who offered her respect lightly. "Thank you for allowing us to stay as long as you have. Even a few days rest has been helpful."

"I wish I could have helped more."

Amelie smiled. "I believe that."

"Oh, and we just bought tons of food that we can't take with us if you all want it. It would be a shame if it went to waste."

Amelie nodded her acknowledgment.

I glanced around the group again. "Good luck to you." My eyes landed on Lolly. "I hope all goes well for you and your child."

Lolly smiled gently. "I'm not worried." Her voice was soft and delicate.

That awful scent of old gym socks hung in the air, and I blinked at its sudden reappearance. I glanced over at Alasdair, but the smell wasn't coming from him. It was coming from Lolly.

I said my goodbyes and took my leave, but the scent nagged at me.

"Willow!" Alasdair called after me.

I halted, not even five paces from the camper.

"Is it all over then? Are you heading back to the Northern Pack?"

I shook my head. "No, the thing Adrian found was a reference to another book, apparently. We're on our way to Munich."

Alasdair sighed, his full lips pouting. "So no end in sight just yet."

I shrugged.

His worry bubbled up inside me. "Can I come with you?"

Everything in me told me to say yes, but I shook my head. "I don't think so. Not this time. I'd like you to stay here with them." I gestured toward the caravan. "I don't know how long Jean-Henri is going to let them stay here, and I'd like you to smooth things over...should something happen."

He frowned. "What would you like me to do?"

"Just say that they're under my protection until Lolly has her baby. Can you do that for me?"

He nodded once. "Yes, captain."

I laughed. "You're not going to stop that, are you?"

He gave me that lopsided smile. "You've already accepted my undying vow of friendship. I'll get you to be my alpha one of these days. Mark my words."

My inner alpha pricked up her ears, but I shook the urge to accept him from my head. "Don't hold your breath." I started to walk back to the house.

"I will hold my breath! I'll hold my breath until I pass out, and then who will have to take care of me? My true friend, that's who!"

I rolled my eyes, chuckling.

"Hey, Willow!" he shouted.

I looked back at him. All trace of his silliness was gone.

"Take care of yourself, okay?"

"I'll do my best," I promised.

I stared at my reflection once I'd reached the glass door. And then I glanced back at Alasdair. He smiled and gave me a full-armed wave. I raised my hand in farewell.

The door clicked when Adrian unlocked it, and I turned to him, his face becoming clear as I gazed past my reflection. He opened the door for me.

"Are you ready?" he asked.

"Yes. Let's go."

48

Our hour-long drive into Paris was silent while I thought about everything that had transpired with the caravan and Alasdair. I'd figured out how to reconcile my alpha nature picking up on unclaimed wolves' emotions, but it seemed I still didn't have a handle on my desire to accept Alasdair as part of my pack. Conflict churned within me. I'd never wanted to form a pack, so how could I get rid of this urge?

Eventually, the country roads turned into city streets, as picturesque as they were crowded.

After dropping our car off with the rental people, we headed into the train station—or at least I thought we were going to the train station. But when I walked in, it looked more like a mall, with stores and restaurants lining the halls. I followed Adrian through the bustling place to a ticket booth, dragging my suitcase behind me.

He asked when the next train to Munich was, and the man answered that the 15:55 to Munich had been delayed, so it was still accepting passengers. Once we had our tickets, we rushed to the platform as fast as we could without drawing attention to our inhuman speed; our train was running late but could leave at any moment. We had no trouble finding our platform, numbered as they were with large, blue signs.

But we needn't have run. After we'd stowed our bags at the end of the car and settled into our facing seats on either side of the thinnest table I'd ever seen, we still had to wait another ten minutes before the train made any move to start its journey. I sent Lia a picture of my train ticket. Fifteen minutes later, she told me Noire would be joining us on the train in Ulm.

I looked at Adrian as he stared out the window. I couldn't feel his emotions the way I had with the unclaimed wolves. I didn't know if it was because of the far-off look in his violet eyes or the hard lines of his mouth, but he seemed deep in very serious thoughts—thoughts that he didn't necessarily want to be thinking.

I glanced around us at the packed train. Across the aisle sat a couple facing each other. Scooting forward in my seat, I rested my elbows on the table. I hissed at Adrian when he didn't look over at me. His eyes slid to mine, and I waved my hand for him to move closer.

He mimicked my posture, leaning in so I could whisper to him. I could feel the warmth coming off his cheek, an inch from mine. His hair brushed my forehead, and his scent washed over me.

"Will you do something for me?" I whispered.

"What?" His breath tickled my ear.

"Will you lie to me?"

He pulled back a little so that he could look at my face.

"What do you want me to say?" He didn't even ask why.

I shrugged. "Whatever comes to your mind."

After a tense moment, he stared straight into my eyes. "I think I've fallen in love with you."

I froze, my heart jumping into my throat. His face was totally serious, gaze steady and mouth set. *He lies with such a straight face.* And as I took a shallow breath, I didn't smell anything out of the ordinary coming from him.

I frowned.

Jeez, I asked him to lie. What am I getting so flustered about? But was I wrong? I was so sure I was starting to smell lies. Isn't that what that gross sock smell was?

I leaned back in my seat, gnawing my lower lip in thought. Adrian watched me carefully. My eyes flicked to his.

It is a lie, right?

I scolded myself. *Of course it's a lie. I've seen how uncomfortable his desire for me makes him. Haven't I?*

"You're a convincing liar," I muttered, crossing my arms. My chest tightened, and I could tell I was slipping into a bad mood.

But as I glanced up at him again, all hot and unattainable and gazing out the window, I shot to my feet. The scenery outside the train wasn't enough to distract me.

"Where are you going?" he asked.

"I just need to get something from my bag," I lied.

I walked to the end of the car, sighing at myself. *How stupid. Stop it.* Then opening my suitcase, I grabbed the first thing I touched: my sketchbook of pressed flowers. After zipping the case and returning it to its place among the others, I went back to my seat.

I was acutely aware of Adrian's presence as I opened the book. The first page held the perfectly pressed petals of a few vibrantly pink bitterroot. I gently stroked the petals with my fingertip. The wildflowers on the mountains had been so beautiful. I loved to see how they changed throughout the growing seasons. When I'd first moved in with the Northern Pack, I'd had a hard time adjusting. It hadn't taken me long to realize that retreating into the wilderness was the quickest way for me to find my balance. It had been Ashwin who'd shown me the wildflowers. As the trail guide for the resort, he knew all the best places. I smiled to myself.

"Wow, that's gorgeous. Did you press them yourself?" the woman across the aisle from me asked, her tone friendly and decidedly from the southern United States.

I smiled over at her. "A friend of mine did this one for me to show me how to do it. He knew all the local flowers. I did the rest."

"Beautiful. Do you mind if I have a look?"

I shook my head and passed my book to the lady. She oohed and ahhed as she flipped the pages. Telling me all about her and her husband, she explained how they'd been saving for so long to take this trip across Europe. She told me of the places they'd visited, the nice people they had met, and where they were going next. Eventually, she reached the end of the flowers I'd pressed thus far. "You're quite good at this," she complimented me.

I thanked her when she handed me the book. As nice as the lady was, I was glad when she turned her attention back to her husband. Still, I felt grateful to her. Our little chat had been the distraction I'd needed.

As I settled into my seat, the sway of the train started to relax me. It wasn't long before I fell asleep.

49

"*Excuse* me, hon," the woman across the aisle said as she tapped me awake. "You might want to call your friend or something. The train will be leaving soon."

My face scrunched, looking across the thin table to Adrian's empty seat. I shot to my feet with my heart racing in my chest. "What happened? Where did he go?"

The woman shrugged. "Once we arrived at the Stuttgart station, he got off the train. I thought he was only getting down to stretch his legs since we were stopping for a bit, but it's been a good ten minutes, and he hasn't come back. We'll be leaving soon."

I dug my phone from my pocket, running down the aisle toward the doors while I turned it on.

Where the fuck could he have gone? Why would he get off without telling me?

As I stepped onto the platform, my throat started to close. The whole place smelled like vampires.

I scanned the space, but I couldn't see him. I pressed his name on my phone, my fingers trembling in panic.

"Come on, come on," I muttered to myself as the call tried to connect.

The other line didn't even ring. "We're sorry. The number you are trying to reach is —"

I hung up and called again but got the same result. Sighing heavily, I tried to steady my heart and focus my mind. I closed my eyes and took a good, deep sniff.

Wet earth, sweet decay. The scent of vampires bogged everything down, so strong that there had to be more than one. I breathed out and sniffed deeply again. My eyes flew open. *There.* Hay, bergamot, and golden poppies.

He went that way.

I didn't bother to slow my supernatural speed as I ran through the train station, dodging passengers and display signs. The humans could come to their own conclusions.

But as I followed Adrian's scent, the smell of vampires only intensified. A growl rumbled in my chest, and I skidded to a halt in front of a cart selling flowers. I sniffed the area. The two scents seemed most concentrated here, as if this is where they'd met. My eyes fell on a red rose wrapped in tissue paper that lay on the ground. I picked it up. It smelled of Adrian's touch.

I turned to the woman at the cart. "Excuse me. Have you seen a man about this tall"—I held my hand above my head—"with brown hair and clear glasses?"

A line of concentration formed between her eyebrows. Then she nodded. "Ja." She pointed, and I took off in that direction not a second later.

As I tried to go through a narrow gate, someone started screaming at me. I didn't understand a word of what he said, but I eventually grasped that I couldn't go through without buying a ticket.

I don't have time for this.

I glared at the man, an alpha's snarl climbing up my throat. His eyes widened, and the blood drained from his face. He let me through, trembling from head to toe.

The human part of Adrian's scent, mingled with that of the

vampires', ended at the edge of a train platform. I sniffed around the area, but it was clear that wherever this train had gone, Adrian had been on it. I paced the platform, my shoes squeaking on the smooth, polished floor.

I tried to call him again but received the same result.

Why does this place smell so much like vampires? What would vampires want with Adrian? I thought he'd never met a vampire before. How could they have known he was here?

Was this all planned ahead of time?

But as my mind went to that dark place, I threw it right out. I remembered Adrian's eyes as he smiled at me, how the brush of his skin sent tingles through me. I didn't know what was going on, but I knew that Adrian hadn't deceived me so thoroughly. There was no way he'd planned to run away and meet up with a group of vampires.

I stopped trying to call Adrian and instead called Noire. Her phone also went right to voicemail.

"Noire, it's Willow. Listen, something went wrong. Adrian got off the train in Stuttgart, and I'm trying to find him. We aren't going to be there to meet you on the train in Ulm. I'll call you when I know more."

A few minutes later, a train pulled up to the platform. I didn't even wait for the passengers to get off before I climbed aboard.

I tapped my foot, standing near the entrance as the train moved forward. At every stop, I stuck my head out and took a deep sniff of the station air.

A man sitting near the door raised an eyebrow at me. I glared at him, and he dropped his gaze to his phone. After ten minutes and three stops, I bit my lip.

Maybe Adrian didn't get on this train. Maybe he went in the opposite direction. Or maybe I was confused and they didn't get on a train at all.

But when the train stopped at the fourth station, the scent of vampires reappeared. I hopped off, sniffing deeply, and followed it out of the train station.

The sun was just setting on the western horizon as I stepped into the cold, damp air. It was clear from the wet pavement that it had rained all day, though it wasn't raining at the moment. The trees that lined the streets were naked and uniform, standing every few feet like soldiers presenting themselves for inspection.

The feel of the place, secluded even amid a larger city, seemed familiar to me. And, even though I couldn't read German, I soon realized that I was on a university campus — *universität* was close enough that I figured it out.

The scent was fresher now, easier to follow as it traveled through campus and into the woods. Once under the cover of the trees, I let loose my alpha power, running as fast as my legs could take me. I was closing in now. Every step took me closer to Adrian.

I crashed through the underbrush, tree limbs snagging my coat as I ran. I wasn't trying to be quiet. They could hear me coming all they wanted. The advance notice wouldn't help them survive my wrath.

I was well off campus now, deep in the forest. Finally, I came upon a wide lake with a land bridge leading to a huge house atop a hill. Lights glimmered in the small windows trimmed in green shutters. It looked warm and cozy, a place to go for a pleasant retreat.

I rushed up the stone steps and kicked the front door in.

50

"*A*drian!" I shouted, my voice echoing off the high, bare-raftered ceiling of the front hall. "Where the fuck are you?" My stomach wrenched. The whole place reeked of vampires. I listened hard to the cavernous silence.

"Go ahead, my friend. Call out to her," I heard someone say.

I followed the sound.

"Willow, get out of here!" Adrian called. "There are too—" His voice was cut off, replaced by a choked gasp.

I rushed into a cozy sitting room papered in lavender, with a plush, wrap-around couch and a warm fire at the far end. A vampire, pulsing with fae magic, held Adrian by the throat up against the cheery wallpaper. The vampire's face was young, younger than us by a few years, the creature likely having been in his late teens or early twenties when he'd been turned.

"Drop him!" I snarled, surging toward him.

"Ah-ah," the vampire tsked, his dark eyes meeting mine. He set Adrian back on his feet—coughing as he sucked in air—and dusted off his coat. "It wasn't my intention to hurt him. I just didn't want him to make you feel unwelcome." The vampire smiled, baring his full fangs.

He waved his hand toward Adrian, and I ran to him, seeing a bruise already beginning to form on his throat. Two more vampires joined us, appearing as if they'd stepped out of the wallpaper. Each blocked a doorway.

"You should have left," Adrian wheezed. "There are too many of them for you alone."

The vampire who'd choked Adrian tilted his head, his eyes analyzing me. "So this is the little wolf who so marred your scent. How very interesting. Are you an alpha, little wolf?"

I snarled, my voice pulsing with alpha power.

The vampire didn't even flinch. "Oh, you are. I see you are. Well, that explains it then."

"What do you want with us?" I asked, stepping between Adrian and the vampires.

He can't want our blood.

He quirked an eyebrow. "With you? You're nothing to me. But him?" He nodded toward Adrian. "He's another story. What a curiosity. You know, I've never seen a half-vampire before. I guess he's not so strange compared to me." He chuckled. And as he tilted his head, the tip of one pointed ear peeked out from his hair. "It's funny, don't you think, Adrian? My boys were on the hunt. They think they're doing something good. A vampire who smelled of wolf? They think you're in trouble. They want to help you get away from our enemy. Yet here she is protecting you. Little wolf, you must be quite the exception to your species." He stroked his lip with his thumb. "Maybe we won't kill you after all."

A shiver ran down my spine. My eyes flicked between the three vampires.

I can take them. I'm an alpha.

"Oh, are you calculating how exactly you will kill all three of us?" He giggled, true delight in his voice. "You *are* an alpha after all. Why shouldn't you think so?" He sobered, staring me down. "But you've never met a vampire like me, little wolf."

With a twist of his hand, I started to rise, my feet leaving the ground. My stomach dropped as panic squeezed my throat. He smiled a wicked grin, then flicked his wrist. I grunted as I was slammed against the wall, pain blooming in the back of my head.

"Willow!" Adrian rushed to me, but I was out of his reach.

"How?" I groaned. This wasn't vampire power. This was fae magic. *How many faelings did he have to feed on to be able to do something like this?*

"You're surprised, little wolf." He nodded. "I understand. All of the werewolves I've met were surprised before I killed them. I'll tell you a secret. You see, I'm the fae who started it all."

A fae?

"You're Lucilla of the Black Wood?" Adrian asked.

He clicked his tongue. "Of course not. I didn't create vampires. I *saved* them. And I can save you, too, Adrian. You're stuck, in-between, and therefore belonging nowhere. It would be very easy for me to turn you into a full vampire."

My heart screamed in my chest. I had to protect him, but I couldn't even move.

Adrian scrunched his nose. "I don't want to be a full vampire. I don't even want to be a half-vampire."

The vampire frowned. "How sad. You don't accept your nature. But that won't be a problem if you make the transition. Being a vampire is so freeing. Won't you reconsider?"

Adrian glanced toward me. "Let Willow go, and I'll hear you out at least."

The vampire rolled his eyes and sighed. With another flick of his wrist, I crashed to the floor. I hissed as I landed on my ankle wrong and pain shot up my leg. Adrian helped me to my feet.

"Are you all right?" he murmured, stroking my hair as he squeezed my hand.

I nodded. It wasn't true, but my supernatural healing would make it true soon.

"Ah!" the vampire said as he watched us. "I see now. You love her."

My chest tightened, and I met Adrian's eyes. He dropped his gaze to the floor.

Is that true? Is that why he didn't smell of lies before?

"Yes," he declared, facing the vampire. "Yes, I love her. You said you were trying to save me, right? But as you can see, I'm fine. She won't hurt me. So you can let us go."

Oh. It's a bluff.

The vampire stared at us, analyzing us seriously. "Let me tell you something about love. It isn't real. You think that you love her? That she won't hurt you? I'll admit, I find it amazing that she hasn't ripped your throat out just for being what you are."

I flinched.

"But that doesn't mean she won't hurt you. She *will* hurt you. She'll tear out your heart and leave you *wishing* you were dead."

I moved even closer to Adrian, lacing my fingers with his and resting my other hand on his arm. He looked over at me, and I shook my head.

"Is that what happened to you?" I asked. *The more I can keep him talking, the more time I'll have to heal enough to get us both out of here.*

"You're a smart little wolf." He hadn't said it like it was a compliment. "I promised you a secret, didn't I?" He nodded. "And my story is a cautionary one. Perhaps once you've heard it, you'll see the wisdom of making the transition, of freeing yourself."

51

I glanced over at the vampires who still blocked the exits. Their dark eyes glinted with eyeshine from the firelight. They had yet to speak, and that coupled with their tense stances—as if they were ready to pounce at any wrong move from us—made them feel that much more dangerous. Our captor turned his back to us. He looked deep into the fire as if searching for answers. His pale skin, devoid of the blush of life, did not pick up any of the fire's warm glow.

"I used to be a fae," he started.

My eyes widened.

He smirked. "I know what you're thinking. How can a fae turn into a vampire? Well, I assure you, it can happen. It just isn't common. As far as I know, I'm the only one like me. I suppose most vampires don't have enough control when they taste fae blood to turn them, but...here I am."

He turned toward us and spread his hands.

"As you might imagine, I was raised in Faerie. I even had a bondmate, as most faelings do." He stopped, frowning. "She was...beautiful, with raven hair and yellow eyes that shined like the harvest moon. I loved her more than life itself." He smiled bitterly. "And she said she loved me. So much the fool was I.

"But that's the thing about forbidden romance, isn't it? Everything is working against you. I was willing to sacrifice it all. She was not. We set a time and place to meet. We would elope as soon as we got to the human realm. We'd even entered into the promised bond. But she never came."

His eyes snapped in our direction.

"She left me waiting, alone and unprotected. And that's where the vampire found me. Not only had she betrayed my love, but she didn't even fulfill her duty as my bondmate."

I squinted in thought. Something about his story didn't make sense. "Wait a second. If she was your bondmate, why would you have to set a time and place to meet? Why wouldn't you just leave together? A guardian is never separated from their bond-mate like that."

The vampire snorted. "You were raised in Faerie, I see. Yes, normally that is the case. But my family works for the royal family of Faerie. And werewolves aren't allowed in the royal archives. I went there to say goodbye to my sister. She knew about us and was sympathetic." He shook his head. "I never should have gone to say goodbye. While I was there, I saw something I was never meant to see, something that the royal family would protect at all costs. And it all would have died with me, had my sire not tried her little experiment to see if I could turn."

He met Adrian's eyes curiously.

"You mentioned Lucilla of the Black Wood. How is it you know that name?"

Adrian tensed beside me. "I've been doing research into vampire origins, and I found a reference to Lucilla of the Black Wood as the name of the fae who created vampires."

The vampire smirked. "So they weren't so thorough as they thought. *Good.* While I was in the archives, I saw the records on Lucilla, what she did, and how it led to the treaty."

I gasped. "You're saying that the fae knew one of their own

created vampires, and they still forged the treaty with the werewolves?"

"That's exactly what I'm saying, and that knowledge is something they'd kill to keep quiet."

"That's why you were attacked. You knew too much," I murmured.

"Yes, but that didn't matter. That wasn't the betrayal I'm talking about. If my bondmate had been there, it wouldn't have mattered that the fae had told my sire where to find me."

He grinned, his expression dark and menacing as his teeth flashed in the flickering firelight.

"But she didn't kill me. And once I was turned, I discovered that I still had my fae magic, just as much as if I'd gone through my awakening. I suppose exchanging blood with my sire was one way to connect on a deep level with another—to become one—as the awakening ceremony requires. And so, I saved us. After Lucilla's spell backfired so brilliantly, the fae cast another spell. The vampires were too powerful, too hungry for fae blood—so much so that they'd even killed their maker. So what did the fae do? They made us even hungrier, so thirsty that we couldn't even think straight and couldn't stand each other's company. Well, it was easy enough to put an end to that with my fae magic; the spell was weakening anyway."

I was starting not to be able to follow what he was saying. I didn't know the spell he spoke of, but I gathered that he was the reason the vampires' behavior had changed so drastically. He was the reason they now hunted in groups. He had done something to override their natural tendency to hunt alone.

All the pups who'd been attacked had died as the result of something this vampire had done.

A growl rumbled through me, and I started to shake all over. My ankle still hurt; my head still throbbed. But I didn't care. I would shift and take this vampire out if it was the last thing I did. So many families had been destroyed because of this creature who stood before me, telling me his story as if I was supposed to have some kind of sympathy for the fact that his bondmate hadn't protected him.

Two seconds. If I can shift in two seconds, I can end him before anyone else can reach me.

I slid my hand from Adrian's and took a slow breath in through my nose. But as I did, I picked up a familiar scent. My eyes widened in surprise. *Noire?*

Not a moment later, a black wolf, snarling in rage, knocked one of the vampires blocking the door to the ground. The vampire rolled away and sprang to its feet.

Noire scanned the room, then froze. Her eyes were fixed on the vampire who had caused so much chaos.

Her lips, just curled in vampire-hunting fury, pressed together in a whine. Her whimper turned into a wail of agony as she shifted to human form. Tears streamed down her face, and she shook as she stood naked in the cozy sitting room.

Her voice broke when she whispered, "Heiden."

52

With all eyes on Noire, this was my chance. I shifted, the tearing of my clothes hardly heard over the volume of Noire's scream. "No!"

She sounded as though her soul were being ripped out of her. She threw herself at the vampire, wrapping her arms around him.

I skidded to a halt. If I wanted to kill him, it was clear I'd have to go through her.

What's wrong with her? Why would she protect him?

Noire pulled back only enough to look up into his wide eyes. "You're alive," she whispered.

His surprised expression darkened. "No, I'm dead." Then he closed his hand around her throat.

I glanced at Adrian and the other two vampires. They were as still as gravestones, their eyes fixed on the unfolding drama. I took a step to the side, trying to get a better angle to reach him without hurting her.

Lia will never forgive me if I let anything happen to her.

"Do it," Noire whispered. "If that will make you feel better, I'm ready to die in your arms, even if it's by your own hand."

Not if I have anything to say about it.

I tightened my muscles, getting ready to spring.

His anger flared, and he curled his lip. "Why?" he shouted in her face. "Why didn't you protect me? Why didn't you meet me that night?"

I froze. *Noire was his bondmate?*

Noire trembled, her voice uneven. "I don't understand your question. I *was* there. I waited all night by our special tree. And when you didn't come, I thought you'd changed your mind. I returned to your house, and that's where I heard the news. Weren't you attacked on your way to meet me?"

The anger in his eyes flickered. "The tree?" He blinked. "We'd planned to meet at the portal."

Noire shook her head as if confused. "Yes, but then your sister said it was safer for us to travel to the portal together. She said to meet you at the tree."

His expression went blank, and he dropped his arms.

I relaxed only a little when his hand no longer clutched her throat.

"You never sent word to change the place. Did you?" Noire asked hollowly. "Your sister lied to me."

"And then she threw me to my death," he murmured.

Noire's face crumbled, and tears streamed down her cheeks. Her pain and sorrow slammed into me—so much stronger than before, as if she'd saved it up over years to unleash it all at once.

"But why?" she cried. "Why would she do that? Was our love so wrong that she would sacrifice her only brother?"

He shook his head. "It wasn't because of that. It's because I knew the truth about how vampires were created. I knew the fae had covered it up. I saw it when I went to the archives to say goodbye."

Noire blinked rapidly, her confusion a small respite for the agony pulsing into me like a heartbeat. I used the moment to let go of her feelings. I couldn't be distracted by them if I had any hope of taking this vampire down.

"But she worked at the archives," Noire said. "If you saw it there, then she had to know the truth, too. Your whole family probably knew. Why would you knowing make a difference?"

He smiled bitterly. "You have forgotten me."

Noire grabbed him by the shirt. "Never."

"You've forgotten who I was. Do you think I would've covered something like that up? Do you think I would've let an injustice like that stand?"

Noire lowered her head. "No, you never would have. And your sister would've known that."

The room fell into a tense silence.

"I hated you," the vampire said. "Every moment of my undead life, I hated you. I thought you'd betrayed me."

Noire's eyes filled with tears. "I hated myself for not protecting you. It was my love that killed you. If it wasn't for Ashwin, I don't know if I would've survived. Then again, death was too good for me." Noire stared up into his face, her fingertips hovering just above his skin as if she were afraid to touch him. "You're exactly the same as the last day I saw you. If I die now, I die happy. Do what you will."

Her gaze never left his face. She stood resolute and ready to accept whatever his judgment might be. She didn't even flinch when he wrapped his hand around her neck.

All of my instincts were telling me to stop him, to end him before he could hurt her. But I didn't move. I would end him for what he'd done. But Noire's words—Noire's sorrow—tugged on something deep within me. This was Noire's choice, and she had the right to make it.

A little squeak escaped Noire's lips as the vampire jerked her toward him. I winced in sympathy for the pain she would soon endure.

My eyes bulged when, instead of sinking his teeth into her throat, the vampire pressed his lips to hers.

Noire sucked in a breath as if she had been slowly drowning for years. They wrapped their arms around each other, not at all deterred by their past and the fact that they were the bitterest of enemies.

Tears streamed down their faces as they made up for the many kisses they'd missed.

The sorrow Noire had carried around with her—the sorrow so strong that even an alpha not her own felt it—eased, and I had to admit that my heart warmed at the exchange, not that it changed my mind.

I shifted back to human form.

"Willow." Adrian rushed to cover my nakedness with his winter coat.

And I was grateful for the barrier against the cold, even though I knew his human sensibilities had more issue with my nudity than concern for my comfort.

"I'm happy for you, Noire," I told her. "I'm glad you're finally finding peace. But you don't know what he's done. He just told us that he's the reason vampires hunt in groups now. He's the reason why so many pups and faelings are dying."

Noire looked at him, frowning. "Heiden, is that true?"

Heiden winced. "It's true that I broke the spell that drove the vampires apart, but I didn't kill any pups or faelings."

"But you broke the spell that made vampires solitary," I said. "Because they've started gathering in groups, they're stronger. And as a result, they started attacking pups."

"Hey!" Heiden snapped. "We're just as much victims here as everyone else. I gave the vampires their reason back. They were so blinded by their hunger; they were no better than monsters. And I gave them families. Why should we have to wander around alone, driven only by thirst? We can *think* now. If some of the vampires I freed decided to gather together and attack pups, that isn't my fault. How many of us has your kind killed? You aren't so innocent."

I frowned. He wasn't wrong.

"This is what war looks like," Noire whispered.

"If you're looking for someone to blame, blame the fae," Heiden said. "They started this whole thing, and they've made it worse every step of the way."

"What did the records say?" Adrian asked. "How were we created? And what happened afterward?"

Heiden, still holding Noire in his arms, sighed. "Lucilla of the Black Wood was a fae who lived in the human realm. This wasn't that uncommon then. Most fae lived in Faerie, but some liked to live amongst the humans. She lived out in the woods, and people would go to see her to bless their babies or cure their ailments. At the time, humans were terrified of werewolves. Maybe some werewolves were attacking people, or maybe the people were just scared of what would happen if they did. The fact is that the humans started to actually hunt them. They held trials and everything. But the werewolves were too strong. Some lone wolves were caught and killed. But even a crowd of humans is no real match for a werewolf pack."

I'd learned most of this from school. This human behavior was what had convinced the wolves to make a treaty with the fae to begin with.

"One human got an idea. He went out to the woods to see Lucilla to ask for her help in defending humanity from the werewolves. So she did. She cast a spell, using her own blood, and turned him into something new—she turned him into a vampire. It had unforeseen consequences. Oh, the vampires he spawned after him certainly were enough to take on the wolf packs. But in using her own blood in the spell, she made them crave that magic. The vampires soon forgot their intended target and started going after fae. The royal family found out, of course. So they cast their spell to drive us apart. And though it worked, it also meant that vampires would do almost anything to get that faeling blood. And that's when the fae hatched their scheme. The werewolves were strong enough to take on vampires; even young wolves could do it one on one. Why not offer the wolves a trade? The humans wouldn't be able to persecute the wolves if they were in Faerie, and the faelings would be protected. The werewolves never suspected the truth."

53

This is fucking crazy. The wolves never would have agreed to this if they'd known.

We've sacrificed so much for this treaty.

I was stunned. Sure, I'd thought about what we would discover once we got to the end of Adrian's research, but I hadn't imagined the fae's treachery would be so thorough.

"We have to tell everyone," I murmured.

Heiden snorted. "Yeah, good luck with that. What are you going to do? Scream it from a mountaintop? No one will believe you without proof."

I looked up at him. *He's right. I can barely believe it, and I was prepared.* "Okay. So let's get proof. We can go to Munich." I turned to Adrian. "That book you were looking for should have something about this, right? Then we just have to figure out how to let everyone know about it."

Adrian quirked his mouth. "I doubt a book of fairy tales is going to detail all of this. I mean, it might've been good enough for my personal answers, and *maybe* for the wolves in the realm of origin. But will it be enough for the wolves of Faerie or for the fae? It would be better if we could get our hands on those royal records."

Heiden laughed. "Haven't you two been listening? My own sister literally killed me to keep those records safe. How do you think you're going to get a hold of them?"

I frowned. *The fae certainly aren't going to make it easy. A place like the royal archives is probably well guarded.* "We need to come up with a plan."

"Hello?" someone called from the front hall, effectively ending our discussion. "Anyone there? Something happened to your door!"

Heiden tilted his head. "Oh, I nearly forgot. We have guests coming for dinner. Would you like to join us, Adrian?"

My mouth dropped open. *He wouldn't... Would he?*

"Heiden...are you really going to attack humans right in front of us? We're being very tolerant of what we've heard so far," Noire said.

Heiden waved his hand. "No, no, you misunderstand. My family doesn't take unwilling victims."

"You mean there are people who *want* to be fed on?" I asked.

"We don't kink-shame here. I've been told that it's quite a pleasant experience if you don't fight it. And we never take too much. We even feed them human food before they go, which you're more than welcome to take part in," Heiden said to Noire and me. "Oh, and I'll send Kota to take care of you while we eat." Heiden pressed a kiss to Noire's head.

"Adrian?" He raised an eyebrow at him.

Adrian shook his head. Heiden shrugged and strode from the room, followed by the two vampires who'd blocked our exits.

I just stood there, shocked. "Are we just going to let them feed on humans?"

Noire wrapped her arms around herself. "I don't know...I guess? I mean, if it's consensual, should we stop it?"

"*Can* it be consensual, though? Can't they just compel the humans into thinking it is?" I looked to Adrian.

He shrugged. "I suppose they could. But on the other hand, Rowan offered me his blood consensually. So it's possible."

Yeah, but that wasn't because he got off on the idea. It was because he was worried you would hurt Yuti.

But Heiden said it felt good if you didn't fight it.

I wondered what it would feel like for Adrian's tongue to lick the blood from my skin, and a shiver ran through me.

A moment later, a human walked into the room. He was short and lean and very pretty. "I'm Kota. Heiden asked me to make you comfortable. Follow me."

We hesitated as he left the room, looking at each other for guidance. *We're house guests now?* Heiden had adapted so quickly to the changing situation that it left me off-balance.

"Out here," Kota called from the other room.

I guess there's no reason not to. We need to figure out a plan, and Heiden has the most information to help us.

Even though I felt weird about it, I answered Kota's beckon. Noire and Adrian followed my lead.

I quickened my stride, ignoring the pain that throbbed in my ankle, to walk beside Kota as he led us back to the main hall, turning toward the wide stairs. "You're a human, and you live with vampires?"

Kota lowered his chin in a nod.

"Why?"

His dark eyes glanced over at me. "Because they're my friends."

"Do they feed on you?"

Kota frowned. "That's a very personal question. No."

"Do they pay you? Have they promised to turn you?" I couldn't figure out why this human would stay here.

"This isn't a job, and, no, they haven't promised to turn me. I don't want to be turned. I stay here because *they are my friends.*"

I blinked. It was as if everything I'd known my entire life was wrong. Was there nothing left in this world that I could understand?

Kota opened a door and looked at Noire. "This is Heiden's

room. He said you can use whatever you like. You can come down to the dining room when you're hungry."

"Thanks." Noire stepped inside and closed the door behind her.

Kota glanced at Adrian and me. "Heiden said you two would be sharing a room." His eyes traveled over my frame, and I raised an eyebrow at his blatant stare. "I'll try to find some clothes that fit you." Then he guided us to a door farther down the hall.

Once Adrian had shut the door behind us, I let out a huge sigh. The room we were in was a simple bedroom with an attached bath. It was almost too mundane and normal. There were even window scarves above the drapes.

This was so bizarre that I didn't know exactly how to act.

Adrian approached me. He lifted his hand to touch me but dropped it in favor of just looking me over. "Are you all right?"

Perhaps it was everything that we'd been through over the last few hours, but my mind wasn't quite understanding what he was asking. "What?"

He gestured toward my head. "You were hurt before." His voice was low and shook slightly as he continued. "He slammed you pretty hard against the wall, and you were limping as we walked upstairs."

I tried to play it off. The memory clearly upset him. "Was I?"

He reached out and took my hand gently, as if I were bruised all over and he didn't want to hurt me. "Will you sit down?"

His soft warmth ran up my arm and through my body. *Was I even in pain before?*

"Does it hurt to walk? I can carry you."

My face flushed at the thought of him lifting me into his arms. *I'm embarrassed just thinking about it.* "I'm okay," I assured him.

Still, he led me slowly to the bed, letting me limp along at my own pace.

The bed squeaked when he sat beside me. "Let me have a look."

I tilted my head toward him so he could examine it. He prodded me gently—much more gently than I had poked his bruise after the towel-rack incident. But he wouldn't find anything except maybe a small lump. My healing had progressed so far that even his soft poking didn't hurt.

Crouching beside the bed, he carefully lifted my ankle to his knee. The feel of his fingers sent shivers up my leg and spine as they stroked my ankle. "It's a little swollen," he murmured, looking up at me again.

"It'll be fine," I breathed. "I heal fast."

With his violet eyes on mine and his fingertips touching my skin, I couldn't help but think of his earlier words. My heart sank, and I looked at my hands in my lap. I cleared my throat. I was glad when my voice came out clear and conversational, even as I started to babble. "It was a good idea to lie to Heiden earlier. You think fast on your feet. I appreciate your trying to help me. He wanted to convince you to fully turn, so telling him you loved me might have saved my life."

I could feel Adrian staring at me, but he didn't speak until I met his gaze. "I wasn't lying."

54

"I'm sorry." Adrian dropped his gaze and gently released my ankle. "I shouldn't have said that. I'm sure it makes you uncomfortable."

I closed my eyes. Echoes of his declarations played in my head. His serious violet eyes. *I think I've fallen in love with you.* His shoulders squared as he stood up to a vampire far stronger than him. *Yes, I love her.* His cool fingers stroking my skin. *I wasn't lying.*

Every smile, every sweet gesture, every tingle when we touched, slid together into a picture of something so obvious that I blushed at how foolish I'd been.

My heart hammered in my chest, and I swallowed, trying to get enough moisture to speak. "Do you know what I thought the first time I saw you through my bedroom window?" I murmured, opening my eyes to look at him still kneeling before me.

His face sagged, and I knew what he was thinking of.

"I thought that the human realm couldn't be so bad if you were in it. I thought that leaving everything I'd ever known behind wasn't such a big deal if I could just get to know you.

That's what I was thinking when I came bounding down the stairs that first day."

His eyes flicked to mine before skittering away. "And then you wanted to kill me."

I nodded slowly. "True, and then I didn't. You were created to be my enemy. But I've never been happier in my life than when it was just you and me in that little lake house in the woods. You were my refuge. I didn't have to fight my instincts with you."

He looked up at me, a sliver of hope glinting in his eyes. "But...Alasdair. What about him?"

"What about him?"

He averted his gaze. "Didn't he say fate brought you two together or some such thing? He's obviously interested in you."

"Pfft. I assure you he isn't. He's just a friend—a very annoying friend who can't get it through his head that I don't want to be his alpha."

"Do you...always kiss your friends? I saw you..."

I slid off the bed, kneeling at his level. "I only kiss my friends when I'm exchanging a vow of true friendship. It's...a wolf thing. Can you understand that?"

My breath hitched as he closed the distance between us with unnatural speed. His lips were warm and firm as they pressed against mine. I shut my eyes, all the better to feel him against me, all the better to drift away in the crisp sweetness of his autumn apple scent.

He trailed kisses down my throat, speaking snippets between each one. "I thought you'd be disgusted by the idea of being with a vampire."

I ran my fingers through his hair, soft and smooth, encouraging him to continue. "I thought you were uncomfortable with wanting a werewolf. I did try to kill you."

He pulled away, and I opened my eyes to look at him. He flashed me a full smile. "I guess I like to live dangerously."

I eyed his fangs. "I guess we both do."

Pushing him to the floor, I straddled his waist. He was fully clothed beneath me, but I only had his coat around my shoulders. I wiggled my ass, and his stiff cock ground against me through his pants.

I smirked when he groaned, the violet in his eyes shrinking as his pupils dilated. I leaned forward and kissed him, pressing my nakedness against him. Slipping my hand down his taut body, I swiftly undid his pants.

Cold air slammed into me when he threw his coat off me. But the heat from his hands stroking my back spread warmth through me, raising goose bumps for an entirely different reason.

I could feel myself getting ready for him. I breathed hard against his feverish kisses, and I knew I was as hot and wet as his tongue was in my mouth.

Sighing out a breath, I sat up and gazed down at him. His dark eyes followed me, his chest heaving and his heart beating wildly beneath my palm, his mouth open and his face slack.

"I'm going to make you mine," I declared.

His eyes never left mine. He trailed one hand up my thigh before rubbing his thumb over my clit.

I gasped and trembled.

His tongue ran over the tip of one fang. "Do what you gotta do."

I gritted my teeth, fighting not to just collapse under his attention. This needed to happen right now. As my whole body flushed at his touch, urgency welled within me. I lifted myself on my knees and freed his cock from the very convenient flap in his boxers.

We both let out a moan as I slid him deep inside me. I rolled my hips, pulling him out and thrusting him back in.

He watched me, his black eyes glazed over, and raised his hand to my face. He gasped and smiled when I turned my head and sucked on his warm, salty finger.

Gathering his shirt in my fists, I pulled him up and wrapped my shaking legs around him. I stroked his face with my thumb. "I love you, too."

He clutched me to him, surrounding me in his embrace as he

continued to slowly slide in and out. His breath brushed over my neck in hot bursts, and a shiver ran down my spine.

"Go ahead," I whispered, gently guiding his mouth to my neck with my hand in his hair. "Make me yours."

He pressed his lips to my sensitive skin in the softest of kisses. My heart pounded, and I held my breath.

"Willow," he breathed.

A tingle ran through me as his teeth touched my throat, more gentle than even his kisses had been.

"Ah!" I cried out, the sound a mixture of pain and pleasure. But the pain of his bite was soon overtaken by the stroking of his tongue. He didn't suck the wound; he just licked at my blood while my heart welled it up for him.

"Adrian," I moaned, my voice breathy and lewd. My body was hot, and I shook beneath his appetites.

I clung to him, receiving his life as I gave him mine.

55

Wrapped in Adrian's embrace, I trailed my fingers over his stomach beneath his shirt. We had moved to the bed and snuggled under the warm blankets. His heartbeat was slow and steady beneath my ear.

Despite my mind whirling with implications, I was happy with this decision. I didn't know what would happen from here. But then, did anyone ever know what the future would bring? This wasn't the time or place I would have chosen for this to occur, but that didn't stop the moment from being any less perfect.

"What do you think happens now?" Adrian murmured, his hand petting my hair.

"Now? We lay in each other's arms and enjoy this moment."

I could hear the smile in his voice. "And after that?"

I cuddled in closer to him. "That's a later problem."

After some time of quiet breathing and gentle touches, Adrian whispered. "I never would've believed this would happen with you."

I thought of all the times I'd smelled fear on him. Had the

scent of vinegar ever covered something more? "When did you first think of it?"

"Well...I mean, you were always pretty, even when I thought you might kill me."

For once, I didn't feel the sting that memory usually elicited. "That's not an answer."

"I know I said I like to live dangerously, but I didn't feel any real attraction to you until you threatened to kiss me in Lia's study, and even then it was mixed with fear. Once I'd let go of the fear, that attraction only grew stronger. And the stronger it got, the more I tried to resist. I even talked to Yuti about it that night you brought me tea in my room. I couldn't deny it by then, but I was so sure it would disgust you. I guess she was right when she said you weren't like that."

Oh, that's what Yuti was talking about when she said he was struggling with something. I pursed my lips. *Should I be annoyed that she was over there playing matchmaker by asking me to take care of him?*

I propped my head up on my elbow to look down at him. "That early, huh? I would've guessed it wasn't until you saw me in a towel the day we left for Seattle." I giggled. "You were so adorable, all surprised and blushing."

He flushed, frowning. "If I'm being honest, Alasdair bothered me even then." He clicked his tongue. "He was so smug about it, too. Ugh, that was annoying, like he knew exactly what would get to me." His eyes flicked to mine. "I would've bet that you'd choose him in the end. We're...from very different worlds, you and I."

I stretched out and kissed Adrian on the cheek, then brushed the hair from his face. "You understand me. The whole world, nature itself, sees us as enemies. If I can want you even despite that, it's more real than anything I've ever known."

"You two would be good together, even I could see that. It's probably why he bothers me so much."

"Are you wanting me to choose him? Am I not making myself clear?" I scooted upward, pressing our foreheads together. "I want *you*. I want you because you're smart, kind, considerate. I want you because of all you've endured. I want you because you aren't afraid to challenge me. I want you because you make the best of every situation. And I want you because you didn't back down even when you thought you were facing a werewolf who wanted to be my mate. You're guided by your inner voice. You walk your own path. You didn't let the world tell you we couldn't be together. Right?"

I pulled back a little. His eyes had warmed, no doubt left in his gaze.

I smirked. "Also, you're hot, so you have that going for you."

He huffed a laugh. "Well, at least that's cleared up."

I guided his lips to mine, stopping only when I thought my point had been made. "You don't have to worry about Alasdair or anyone else. You were never competing with him. Besides, we've already agreed: fuck fate. Fuck her and the fact that she made us enemies. I've already made you mine. Every wolf from here to Faerie will know about it the moment they smell you."

He burrowed in deeper, wrapping his arms around me as I cradled his head against my chest. "Won't my scent be on you then? Won't it bother you to smell like vampire?"

"I won't smell like vampire. I'll smell like the man I love."

I didn't know how long we lay like that. I wasn't keeping track of time. I was just enjoying the quiet moments we shared. But eventually, my stomach started to growl.

Adrian met my eyes. "I think you should eat something. I'll go see about getting you some clothes."

Even with me wrapped in blankets, the bed felt cold when Adrian climbed out of it. I wondered what would happen to the suitcases we'd left on the train. *How upset will the humans be when they find a cooler full of blood?*

When Adrian opened the bedroom door, he didn't even step into the hall; he knelt, picked something up, and returned.

"I guess Kota just left them outside for us," he said, placing a stack of clothes on the bed beside where I lay.

"Must have heard we were busy."

His face flushed, and I laughed.

I didn't know where the jeans and sweater Kota had left for me had come from, but I was pleased they didn't smell of vampire. Perhaps Heiden had clothes set aside for guests in case they got blood on them. In any case, the clothes were warm and comfortable. Even the shoes fit.

Adrian laced his fingers with mine, smiling at me as we left the bedroom, all trace of his earlier insecurity gone. I stopped at the room Noire had entered and knocked on the door, but there was no answer.

It wasn't hard to find where everyone was gathered. They weren't exactly being quiet. We walked down the stairs and through a hall until we reached a large dining room. A buffet had been laid out along one wall, complete with stacks of plates at the end and lids to keep the serving dishes warm. There was a long table at the center of the room with tall-backed chairs filled with vampires and humans, talking as if this were a completely normal dinner party.

There were six vampires total: Heiden and the two we had seen earlier plus two females and an additional male. The humans outnumbered the vampires if I included Kota.

At the far end of the table, Noire sat beside Heiden with a plate full of food in front of her. But she wasn't eating. She couldn't take her eyes off of him long enough to fill her fork.

Heiden smiled broadly as we entered. "You're finally here. Grab some food and sit with us."

I blinked at the change in him.

Is this the same vampire who magically threw me against the wall and pressured Adrian to turn into a full vampire?

s I sat between Adrian and a human male who talked with his neighbor, the whole scene felt very surreal. I took in the gathering. This had to be the first of its kind in all of history. Werewolves and humans ate at a table while vampires chatted happily with them.

"Eat," Heiden urged Noire, picking up her fork and stacking it with scalloped potatoes. "I'm not going anywhere. Please." He coaxed the food into her mouth, and she chewed.

He offered her the fork and took her other hand, pressing his lips to her fingers.

I'd never seen Noire this way. Her yellow eyes—bright and unobscured by the blue contacts she usually wore to appear more human—watched Heiden as if she were staring hard at a puzzle. Her sun-kissed skin was pale, and her straight eyebrows were a hard line across her brow. But all the sorrow she'd carried around was gone. She seemed dumbfounded and confused, but hesitantly happy like she was afraid it could all disappear if she looked away.

As strange as it was for Adrian and me to be together, it was that much stranger for Noire and Heiden. I wondered how her

brother would take it, how the whole pack would. One thing was
clear. She would never give Heiden up now that she'd found him
again.

"How very interesting," Heiden said, tilting his head at
Adrian. "Why is it that you no longer smell like a vampire? Your
human scent is there—and the little wolf's—but not the vampire.
What do you think?"

Now that I wasn't thinking about killing him—and he wasn't
in the middle of a villain-speech—it was really strange to hear
him refer to me as "little wolf." I knew he was the same age as
Noire in actuality, but he looked younger than me.

He turned to Noire, who swallowed the large bite she'd just
taken. She nodded. "I don't smell it anymore. Maybe because
Willow is an alpha? I can't smell Adrian on her either."

Heiden smiled. "Oh, I do. His human scent is on her, but not
his vampire scent."

Adrian cleared his throat beside me. "Could we stop talking
about how we smell?"

I shoved a bite of marinated chicken into my mouth.

*That is interesting. Maybe my alpha scent is strong enough to cover
Adrian's vampire half. Alasdair mentioned something similar before. That
could go a long way in protecting him from other wolves.*

"So how are we going to break into the royal archives?" I
asked without preamble.

Heiden snorted. "You're not. Only fae can open the doors,
and even then, you have to be part of the royal family or one of
the two families that maintain the archives."

"What is it, a secret spell or something that you have to
know?"

If he tells it to me, I might be able to ask Feather for help.

He shook his head. "No, you literally have to have the blood
of that family running through your veins or the door won't open
for you."

I frowned. "Would it still recognize you even though you're a
vampire now?"

"I doubt it. My heart doesn't beat. My blood doesn't flow.

But even if it did, how would you manage to sneak a vampire into the royal palace? It's the most guarded place in Faerie."

I clicked my tongue. *Are the fae really going to get away with this? There has to be something we can do.* I thought about all the pups taken from their parents, forced to sacrifice their childhoods to protect fae from their own creation. I thought about the mating system and how it was little more than a breeding program for guard dogs. I thought about how unjust it all was, how they'd lied to everyone for so long, how they were pressuring the alphas for even worse terms while knowing this whole situation had been their making.

"What about Alessandra?" Noire asked.

Heiden's head snapped in her direction. "What about her?"

"Who's Alessandra?" Adrian inquired.

Heiden looked away. "Alessandra was the fae I was betrothed to… She's part of the other family who manages the archives."

Noire's voice was quiet but even. "She never joined the family business. You know it never interested her. After you… disappeared, she retreated to the family cottage in Walpurwood. She was devastated."

Heiden winced at this news, then sighed. "Even if you could convince Alessandra to sneak you in, the archives are massive. You'd never know where to look."

"You can tell me what to look for," Adrian said. "Finding books is what I'm good at. I've been in libraries all over the world. Just explain the coding system and what it looks like, and I can find it."

My throat squeezed in panic. "You're not going. Sneaking you in would be just as bad as trying to sneak Heiden in. Any wolf or fae we ran into would kill you on sight."

Adrian smiled. "Didn't you just hear what they said? I don't even smell like vampire anymore."

"I hate this plan," I declared.

I turned to Heiden for backup, but he was pursing his lips in thought. "It could work."

"What? No, it couldn't," I argued. It was one thing for me to try to break into the royal archives to steal proof of the fae's treachery. It was entirely different for me to bring along my vampire lover. "What about your bloodlust?" I asked Adrian. "What are you going to do when you smell fae?"

Adrian's eyes met mine. "You'll be with me. I can do like last time and concentrate on your scent."

"It's too risky."

He chewed on his lower lip. "Okay. How about this? The second I look out of control, we can leave. I won't argue. Please, Willow. This has been my whole life's pursuit. I have to try. I can't just give up now."

I clenched my jaw.

Heiden leaned forward in his chair. "If you can convince Alessandra to get you in—and that's a big *if*—and if you go at night when there isn't likely to be anyone else there, it's possible, barely."

"Then I find the records, and we disseminate the information however we can," Adrian added.

"If you can get the records to Alessandra," Heiden mused. "There is a handy little spell that the royal family uses for royal announcements. It can put a note on every messages table in Faerie. Even though she didn't join the family business, she should know that spell, or at least know where to find it."

"This entire plan relies on a fae not only believing our story, but risking a lot to help," I pointed out. "I want everyone to know the truth. But what if we can't trust her? She's part of this same family secret. She could already know about it and not care. She could set us up and betray us."

"She doesn't know," Noire said with confidence. "As much as I didn't like Alessandra at the time, she was an honorable woman. I think I disliked her so much *because* she was so perfect. I never thought I could compete with her."

Heiden pressed a kiss to Noire's hand. "I never loved her."

Noire stared into his eyes. "I know."

"Still…it has been a long time. She could've changed," I pointed out.

Heiden nodded. "But this is the best plan."

Adrian's fingers closed around mine. "Isn't this worth taking the risk for?" he asked me.

I didn't like what he was saying. My mind pushed against his words, his reasoning.

Will we ever be able to convince anyone without solid proof?

I thought about everything I'd been taught, the indoctrination that I and thousands of werewolves had lived through — what we'd sacrificed and what we would continue to sacrifice if we didn't do something.

The thought of letting this farce continue unchallenged just wasn't something my conscience could live with. I sighed and nodded.

57

I didn't have a chance to worry about our plan that night. Adrian ensured that I was well and thoroughly distracted by his attentions. I even slept, so worn out by his repeated calls for me to cover his scent with mine.

It was near afternoon the next day when we finally woke, showered, and headed downstairs. The house was quiet, the vampires sleeping.

We found Kota at the stove in the kitchen. I didn't know what he was cooking, but it smelled good. He looked over at us as we entered.

"Good morning," I said.

He inclined his head in greeting. "Help yourself to whatever you can find. Everyone usually sleeps during the day, but Heiden might be up early since you're his guests."

I watched as he pulled an egg from a boiling pot. He wore black pants and a white sweatshirt with a thick red stripe across the chest. The shirt had a shield-shaped, embroidered patch above the heart. "If you don't mind me asking, how did you fall in with the vampires? Where did you meet?"

Kota glanced over at me, but he would find no accusations on my end. "Heiden is a football fan. I play for VfB Stuttgart. He bought me a drink after a game once, and we became friends after that."

"Football? Oh, soccer," Adrian said.

Kota shrugged at the distinction.

I couldn't picture a vampire cheering in a crowded soccer stadium. Then again, Heiden was full of surprises.

I should probably stop making assumptions about what vampires do and don't do.

Kota cracked and peeled his egg, cut it in half, and placed it in a bowl of soupy noodles, which he took to a seat at the counter.

"Have you been here long?" I asked him, opening the fridge to see what I could scrounge up for breakfast.

"Nearly a year." He slurped his noodles.

I took eggs and butter from the fridge and placed them on the counter. *I wonder when Noire will be down. Should I make her some, too?* But as I was pulling bread from the cupboard, Noire and Heiden came into the kitchen.

"How was your workout?" Heiden asked Kota.

Kota shook his head. "I need to ramp it up before the pre-season starts in a few weeks."

Heiden squeezed the man's shoulder and smiled. "You'll get there."

"Noire, do you want some eggs on toast?" I asked.

She nodded and thanked me.

After making a quick breakfast, we took our plates into the dining room since there wasn't enough space for all of us at the counter where Kota was finishing his meal. I was surprised when Noire sat beside me and across from Heiden. She didn't even smell of him.

She's being careful so as not to give us away to the werewolves of Faerie.

I hoped her reunion hadn't been too impacted in service of that cause.

"Do you think we'll be able to get this done tonight?" I asked.

"That depends on how easy Alessandra is to convince." Noire didn't look happy about having to have that conversation.

"Have you talked to Lia?" I inquired.

Noire lowered her chin. "It was all I could do to convince her not to tell my brother."

I blinked.

Noire shook her head. "Ashwin would've wanted to help. I've cost him too much already. He doesn't need to be involved."

Ashwin wouldn't be pleased when he found out. He'd been helping Adrian with his research for a while, and he would do anything to protect his sister.

After breakfast, Adrian and I stood near the door as Noire and Heiden stared into each other's eyes. They didn't so much as embrace.

"Come back to me," he told her.

"They'll have to kill me to keep me from you," she declared.

But as we stepped out into that March afternoon, Noire left behind all the tenderness, all the sentimentality that Heiden had brought out in her. Her face was firm, her eyes fixed. "Follow me."

Rather than heading back into the city, Noire led us deeper into the woods. We followed a cut path, the ground beneath our shoes softened with spring's approach.

I wanted to ask Noire how she was doing, how she was coping with everything that had happened to her. But we didn't have such a close relationship that I felt comfortable doing it. I could have reached out with my alpha power and explored her feelings, but that seemed intrusive.

"Thank you for busting in to help us last night, Noire," I said.

She didn't speak for a long time, the only sound the shuffling of our shoes on the wet leaves.

"Fate is mysterious," she murmured. "I never would've believed that I could love a vampire. If I hadn't experienced losing him, if I hadn't lived in agony for so long, I doubt I could have. Am I fighting fate by loving him despite our opposing natures? Or is this what was meant to be all along?"

I frowned, and my eyes slid to Adrian.

"Here it is," Noire said, stopping before a hollow log. "It's a tight squeeze." She got down on her belly and used her forearms to wiggle her way into the tube.

"Noire?" Adrian called when her huffing silenced.

I turned to him, covering his mouth with his scarf and pulling up his hood. "She's already through the veil. Now, listen. Don't draw attention to yourself. Don't speak if you can help it, and keep your mouth and ears covered. If anyone sees your fangs, we're done for. We want the wolves to think you're either human or a wolf, and we want to keep the fae guessing."

He leaned toward me, pulling his scarf down to press a kiss to my lips. "We're going to be okay."

I willed myself to feel the confidence he offered me, but I just couldn't do it. I smiled, and I wondered how it looked to him. "I'll go first."

58

The moment Adrian came through the portal, I tensed. We were in Faerie, and everything would smell like fae to him. I watched him closely.

He froze, his nostrils flaring.

My heart raced, and I prepared to pounce.

But then he breathed out slowly. His eyes smiled between his hood and scarf. "I'm okay," he assured me. Still, the violet in his eyes shrank as his pupils swallowed it.

I took his hand, more as a security measure than a sign of affection.

"The depot is this way," Noire said, pointing away from the den we'd just crawled out of.

The snow on the ground was fresh and barely covered the grass. It swirled, kicked up by our feet as we followed Noire through the trees. But I didn't pay it much attention—couldn't with my senses on high alert.

Will my scent be enough to cover Adrian's? Will he lunge at the first fae he sees?

It was still early afternoon when we reached the edge of the border town. The sky was gray, and snow drifted lazily to the ground in barely noticeable flakes. The wind howled between the simple buildings on the main street, and I was glad no one was out and about on this cold winter's day.

As we entered the country depot, I tightened my grip on Adrian's hand. This was his first test, the first fae he would come face to face with in Faerie. He stiffened beside me.

"Adrian," I whispered. "Look at me, love."

His black eyes shifted to mine.

In the background, I heard the fae conductor greet us and ask where we were headed. Noire answered him, but I wasn't really paying attention.

I grabbed the front of Adrian's coat with my free hand and pulled him toward me, resting my forehead on his. "What do I smell like to you?"

"L-leaves."

"Yes, and what else? Can you smell yourself on me? Do you smell the poppies?"

"Poppies…" He closed his eyes, and when he opened them again, some of the violet had returned, if only a sliver.

I tried to give him a smile of encouragement as I pulled back, but it probably looked more like a grimace. I led him into the transportation circle. The fae conductor seemed surprised at our intimate exchange. But as he spoke his spell to send us on, I knew he didn't suspect Adrian's true nature.

Adrian swayed a little when we arrived in the Walpurwood depot. It had been so long since my first transport that I'd forgotten that it could be disorienting. I rushed him out, pulling him to the side of the depot where no one would see him.

"Sit down," I urged him.

He slid to the ground with his back to the wall. His breathing was uneven, and he tugged at his scarf.

I knelt between his legs. "No, no." I stilled his hands before he could rip it from his neck. "Focus. You aren't going to be sick. You just need a second. Breathe in through your nose slowly and out through your mouth."

He did as I instructed, and a minute later, I hauled him to his feet. He muttered his apologies to Noire and me, but we waved them away.

"How far is it to the cottage?" I asked Noire once we'd started walking again.

"Not far."

Walpurwood was bigger than the border town we'd arrived in. Row houses lined the road with streets breaking off here and there. It was much warmer in this part of Faerie, so warm that it felt like early spring. A few of the trees even had buds on them, and I wondered if they would survive if there was another frost.

I glanced over at Adrian, still buried in the hood and scarf he couldn't remove.

I breathed a little easier as Noire led us farther out of town. The houses became less frequent, and the forest crowded in around us. I could believe that spring was well on its way as birds chittered and went about their industrious business.

We turned down a narrow road, one that I likely wouldn't even have noticed if I'd just been passing by. The road wound deeper into the woods and ended at a small cottage surrounded by a short, white fence. It was the place of fairy tales, with stone walls and blue shutters. Flower boxes hung beneath every window, and mulched beds lined the stepping-stone path, which led to the door. I could imagine them bursting with flowers in high summer.

Noire hesitated at the gate, just staring at the little cottage. Then, taking a deep breath, she unlatched the gate and marched right up to the front door. Her knock was muffled by the door's thick wood.

I looked over at Adrian to make sure his disguise was firmly in place, and I readjusted my grip on his hand. I didn't want him attacking any fae while we were here, but this particular fae was even more important than the rest.

A few moments later, a fae woman opened the door. Her long, blond hair was braided in a tidy plait over one shoulder. Her green eyes were large and her cheeks dusted with freckles.

She stared at us a moment with an open gaze before her eyes

narrowed in recognition—squinting at Noire. "You've got some nerve showing your face here. Don't think I've forgiven you even after all these years. Was I not clear that I never wanted to lay eyes on you again?"

Noire lowered her head. "You were."

"Then there's nothing else to say." Alessandra started to shut the door, but Noire stopped it with her hand.

"They killed him, Alessandra."

"No, Noire, *you* killed him," Alessandra spat. "It was your job to protect him, and you failed."

"Listen to me. Yes, I shouldn't have left his side, but that's not the whole story. His family betrayed him. They sent him to be attacked on purpose."

Alessandra's eyes widened. "What do you mean?"

"Please, hear me out. I'll explain everything. And if you want us to go after that, we will."

Alessandra snorted but stepped aside for us to enter.

59

*A*s Alessandra stood by her fire, arms crossed over her chest, it was clear she wasn't going to offer us any hospitality.

I stood holding Adrian's hand, as far away from her as possible while still being in the room. His fingers trembled in mine, but he didn't make a move toward her.

"Make this quick," Alessandra ordered. "I'm busy."

I glanced around the little cottage. It was rustic but neat. The walls were stone, the floor packed dirt, and something delicious-smelling bubbled over the fire.

Noire sighed. "Heiden was betrayed by his family. He found out something about the fae, and they killed him for it."

Alessandra pursed her lips. "Yeah, okay. That must have been one hell of a secret."

"It was. That's why we're here. We need you to sneak us into the archives so we can expose the secret he died for."

Alessandra raised an eyebrow. "You ruined my life, and you have the audacity to ask for my help? Look at me. Look around you." Alessandra swept her hand out, indicating her home. "This is the only place I can stay that doesn't remind me of him. Even now, I still dream of the life we might have had together."

"You think it was any easier for me?" Noire snapped. "I loved him, too!"

Alessandra stepped in close to Noire, and I tensed at the threat.

Should I separate them? What will happen if I let go of Adrian's hand?

"Not enough. If you'd loved him more, then this never would've happened."

I could see Noire's limbs shaking under the accusations. "I wouldn't be here if I didn't still care for him. He was murdered to keep their secret quiet—a secret that has hurt many people. You can hate me; the only person who could hate me more is myself. But I *know* you're an honorable woman, and I know you loved him more than anything in the world. He deserves justice. Don't you want to help me get it for him?"

Alessandra turned her head to the side and sighed angrily through her nose. "What is this big secret then? What would make even his family turn on him?"

Noire told her what we knew. She told her about Lucilla of the Black Wood and the royal cover-up. She told her about the spell the fae had cast that made vampires even hungrier than they were. But she left out any mention of Heiden being turned and the hand he'd had in breaking that spell. It may have been dishonest, but it was likely for the best. Heiden was dead in Alessandra's mind, and we probably needed to keep it that way unless we had no other choice.

By the time Noire was finished, Alessandra had gone pale. "How do you know all this?" Alessandra asked, her voice hardly above a whisper. "You've never been in the archives. How will you even know what to look for?"

I bit my lip, watching Noire carefully as she weighed her answer.

"My friend here"—she gestured to Adrian—"is a researcher. He's been researching all this for a long time."

Adrian stiffened beside me as Alessandra's green eyes fell on us. Her gaze lingered, and goose bumps rose on my skin.

"But we need absolute proof," Noire said, drawing Alessandra's attention back to her.

I let out a breath, and Adrian relaxed.

Alessandra frowned, her eyes staring into the fire of her hearth. "If this is true, we're about to topple the entire bondmate system. All those faelings will be unprotected."

"No, we're about to give people the knowledge they need to decide for themselves. I don't want the faelings to die either. They're innocent children. But should it not be a parent's responsibility to protect their own children, whether those children be fae or werewolves? Think about it. Would you have wanted to be given away to another family at only the age of seven?"

Alessandra sighed once again, shaking her head. "You're right. The people should be able to decide for themselves." She looked up at us, her green eyes steady and clear. "We can go tonight. It's the best chance we have of the archives being empty."

I felt no relief over Alessandra having agreed to help us. Yes, we were one step closer to accomplishing our goal, but we were also one step closer to danger. I may have been able to cover Adrian's scent enough to fool the few fae we'd come into contact with so far. But fae didn't have a keen enough sense of smell to pick up on vampire scent anyway.

We were about to travel to the biggest and most well-protected city in Faerie, and that was even before we got to the royal archives.

After Noire and Alessandra had gone over the plan, I excused myself and pulled Adrian outside with me.

I led him through the woods to a secluded place, sniffing to be sure that no werewolves or fae were nearby. Finally, I released his hand. "There's no one around here. Are you all right?"

He yanked the scarf from his face. "This thing is stifling."

"I know. I didn't expect it to be so warm here." Approaching him, I looked up into his eyes. They were still dilated but not as much as before. "Are you adjusting to the scent?"

He frowned but nodded.

"Just concentrate on me."

He gave me a tight-lipped smile. "I don't need encouragement to do that."

I raised my hand to his cheek, touching his smooth face. "You're doing well."

He turned his head and pressed a kiss to my palm. The smell of apples swirled into his scent. "I'm doing amazing. I deserve a reward."

A tingle ran through me as he gave my hand a tentative lick. "You have the worst timing," I told him.

He raised an eyebrow. "Do I? We're about to head to a place where everyone wants to kill me, and I might want to kill a few myself. I feel like now is the *perfect* time to reinforce your scent."

I glanced around us, seeing nothing but trees and smelling nothing but the two of us. He leaned down and kissed my cheek, then trailed his lips along my throat.

"Come on, Willow," he whispered, his breath hot on my skin. "Make me yours."

I closed my eyes, giving in to the sensations he stoked within me.

His hands were warm and firm, and I trembled beneath them as they traveled down my body. I welcomed the solid steadiness against me when he backed me up against a nearby tree.

He dropped to his knees, his hair soft on my fingers, and unfastened my pants.

With little warning, he ran his tongue over my clit. I gasped and bit my lip so I wouldn't cry out. The naked limbs of the trees far above me swirled as my vision blurred. My knees wobbled, and my legs shook. But still, his mouth did its work.

"Adrian." My voice was weak, barely a whisper, and my head spun. "I want you inside me."

Even the few seconds it took him to comply with my request

felt far too long. But I was rewarded for my patience when he thrust deep within me.

His eyes were the blackest night, never leaving mine. The birds, the blanket of last autumn's leaves on the ground, and the silent trees were the only witnesses to the expression of our shared desires.

60

It was late when the four of us entered the Walpurwood depot. The conductor jolted awake, clearly not expecting anyone at this time of night. I was just grateful we weren't in a border town where depots closed after certain hours.

Alessandra quietly named the depot number in Mysraina, and we arrived in a flash of yellow light.

My eyes immediately went to Adrian to make sure he wasn't sick this time and to make sure the overwhelming scent of fae didn't cause him to lose his reason.

His eyes were shaded by his hood.

Alessandra and Noire stepped out of the circle, but I kept Adrian and myself inside. If he was about to freak out, then we'd need to be transported anywhere but here.

"Adrian?" I murmured.

He made no move, no indication that he'd heard me.

My heart skipped a beat. "Adrian?" I shifted to stand in front of him, to get a better look at his face.

His eyes were completely black, and they held no recognition.

I wrapped my arms around him, squeezing his middle, and then I let out a high-pitched keen—the same as he had done for me when I'd been nervous about flying. I could feel everyone's gaze on me, and drawing attention to us wasn't the best plan. But this was all I could think of to try to snap him out of it, to give him one last chance to overcome his bloodlust before we retreated in failure.

Adrian shook in my arms, and his soft chuckle reached my ears. "You kind of suck at singing," he said.

I pulled back, staring into his violet eyes—pupils still larger than normal—smiling at me between his hood and scarf. "It's not me; it's the song. It was the first thing that popped into my head."

"It has a way of doing that."

"Are you going to be all right to go on?"

He nodded and grabbed my hand. "Let's go."

Now that it appeared Adrian wouldn't rampage through the depot, I looked around self-consciously. To my relief, there weren't that many people at this time of night, and they seemed keen to avoid eye contact with me.

"Is this the type of people you associate with these days?" Alessandra asked Noire.

Noire shrugged. "Alphas have their own ways. We don't question it."

As we stepped out of the depot, I breathed deep the scents of Mysraina at night. This was the city I had spent most of my life in. And it was just as lively after dark as it was during the day. Taverns, clubs, and food stalls were open until the early morning hours, and there were plenty of fae to patronize them.

We stood at the base of the mountain, which rose up at the center of the city. A thick mist blanketed the mountain, swirling and swaying as if dancing, its tendrils reaching toward us. Yellow fae lights pulsed in lanterns along the winding path that led upward, fading in brightness the farther away they were.

"Follow me," Alessandra instructed, starting up the path.

I could still see the bright flame and fae lights of the city behind us, though I couldn't hear its bustle. Whether that was because of a spell or simply the nature of the place, I did not know. But the path was hushed, the only sounds our footsteps and our quiet breathing.

We passed a small sanctuary, not much more than a stone altar with a roof. Still, it was clean and held offerings of food and drink for whatever fae deity or spirit it was dedicated to. And it wasn't the only one. We passed several sanctuaries and shrines, a fae light glowing in a lantern outside each one, as we made our way upward. They got more lavish the farther we climbed, glittering with precious stones and metals with elaborate tapestries depicting the deities they honored.

The mist was thick, and it was difficult to see more than ten feet in front of us. But as we neared the top, it began to clear. I could see the crescent moon far above us, too thin to provide much light—not that anyone but Alessandra would need it.

The royal palace shone brightly in the distance ahead, its many lights making it sparkle like a polished gem. Spires topped silver domes, and terraces positively dripped with flowers and greenery kept alive by spells even at this time of year. Waterfalls flowed into glittering fountains, spraying mist that glimmered in the lights like so many stars.

My throat tightened, and I had a hard time swallowing. *Are we really going to try to sneak in there? This place has to be crawling with guards.*

But well before we even reached the elaborately crafted front gate, Alessandra led us down a branching path. "This is the way the servants take," she whispered. "Can't have us lowly librarians using any main entrances."

Every step pushed my nerves closer to the edge. Every scent and every sound seemed to demand equal attention. Was it an animal? Was it the wind? Was it some fae who would raise the alarm?

Adrian hissed beside me, and I winced when I realized I was squeezing his hand too hard. "Sorry," I mouthed.

The building that housed the archives was as grand as the Château de Chantilly. A wide staircase led to a courtyard with a fountain at its center. Columns on the second floor of the archives held aloft the arched openings of a gallery, which wrapped around the courtyard.

All seemed quiet. Fae-light lanterns were hung every so many feet, but I could hear and smell no presence nearby.

Approaching a very imposing set of arched double doors with no handles, Alessandra turned to us. "I'll wait for you at the shrine at the bottom of the mountain. If you're not back by sunrise, I'll assume the worst and leave."

Glad to know she has her priorities straight.

Then placing her palm flat on the wood of one door, Alessandra simply pushed it open. "Good luck."

61

"I'll be the lookout," Noire said, stationing herself near the entrance.

I nodded and turned to Adrian. "You know what you're looking for?"

"Yeah, as long as Heiden's information was accurate, it should be this way."

The archives were massive. Huge shelves stuffed with books and cubbies with scrolls slid in neatly atop each other stood in rows that stretched to both ends of the large room.

It was dark and quiet as Adrian led me along the rows. Feeble light filtered through the arched windows—so feeble a fae likely wouldn't even see it. There weren't any lanterns in here, but we didn't need them. Floorboards creaked beneath our soft steps, and Adrian's breathing sounded loud in my ears.

Approaching the end of the wide room, I eyed the stairs that were straight ahead. I didn't want to go to the second floor; it would be that much harder to escape from up there should something unexpected happen. I was relieved when we took a sharp turn before reaching the stairs, following the angle of the building.

Adrian's eyes scanned the shelves as we went, attempting to recognize some pattern he'd been told to look out for.

"Here," he whispered, stopping in front of a shelf that looked exactly the same as the ones around it.

He ran his fingertip along the spines of the books and folios, his lips moving silently. But just as he bent his finger to pull one out, a distant hum of magic, like the soft murmur of electricity, made us both freeze.

The hum was followed by a creak and the sound of steady footsteps.

I held my breath, each footstep a pinprick in my ears. "Check it to make sure it's the right one," I whispered, hurrying Adrian in his task.

He fumbled, and the folio made a loud thud as it hit the floor.

My heart screamed in my chest, and I clenched my jaw, waving my hand for him to pick it up.

As he knelt and opened the folder to verify its contents, I stuck my head out from between the shelves. A light that hadn't been there before bounced off the wall at the far end.

Noire appeared a second later, materializing from the darkness beside us. "Someone is here," she whispered.

"Hello? Who's there?" a woman's voice called, the footsteps increasing in volume and frequency.

"This is it," Adrian murmured, rising to stand.

"Great, now we just have to figure out how to get out of here."

Noire stared at us seriously. "I'll lead her away from the door. Take that back to Alessandra as quickly as you can. I'll join you at her place shortly."

I grabbed her wrist as she moved away. "No, I can't let you do that. What if you get caught?"

Noire gave me a tight smile, a gesture I wasn't used to seeing in her expression. "I'll be all right. Fate is on my side. She wouldn't give him back to me only to take him away."

What kind of wishful thinking is that?

I wanted to argue with her, but she would need that optimism if we had any chance of getting out of this.

Noire melted into the shadows of the shelves.

Farther back the way we'd come, another thud echoed off the high ceilings. This one was much louder than Adrian's. The light on the wall stilled, then the footsteps retreated.

"Hello?" the woman called again, her voice farther away. "Father, is that you?"

I snatched Adrian's hand and crept toward the bend in the room. We needed to get past whoever this was if we had any hope of getting away unseen. But as I peeked around the corner, I saw that that wasn't possible.

A fae woman, lantern in hand, had her back to us as she walked toward the other end of the room. She was between us and the door, and if she turned around, she would certainly see us.

Another book dropped from a shelf at the far end of the room. I bit my lip.

Noire knows what she's doing.

The woman looked over her shoulder, and I jerked back. Her footsteps halted, and all I could hear was my own heartbeat.

"Marisa." Noire's voice was quiet but steady as she stepped out from behind a bookshelf at the other end of the room.

The fae woman tilted her head. "Yes? Who is it?" She walked toward the sound of her name, passing the door and giving us an opening.

"How could you?" Noire asked.

"I'm sorry?" Marisa clearly didn't know what the voice was referring to.

I crept toward the door, Adrian at my heels.

"You betrayed your own brother."

"Who is that?" Marisa demanded.

"How does it feel to know that he died by slowly being drained of his life's blood, and it was your doing?"

"How—Noire?" The light of Marisa's lantern reached Noire's face.

Adrian and I slipped out the door and made a break for the path that would lead us to Alessandra.

The mist was thick, and it seeped into our clothes as we ran. Our footsteps were quick but not as quiet as I would've liked. Finally, my heart pounding while I gasped for breath, I saw Alessandra.

She stood beside the shrine, a fae light glowing in her hand as she squinted into the mist. She breathed a sigh of relief when she recognized us. "Where's Noire?"

I shook my head. "She'll join us later," I assured her, hoping every word was true.

Alessandra nodded, and we headed toward the depot.

We were back in Alessandra's cozy cottage within the hour. It had cooled since the sun had set, and the fire in her hearth had burned down to embers.

We stood around the messages table with its sigils and runes carved deep into the wood, the folio detailing the fae's treachery at its center. Alessandra rested her fingers on the edge of the table and closed her eyes. Words of ancient elvish danced on her tongue, and a yellow light flashed.

Her green eyes shined like a cat's when she opened them to stare back at me. "It's done. Every messages table in Faerie now has a copy of this. Everyone will know the truth by morning."

I picked up the folder and handed it to Adrian. The wolves and fae who lived in the human realm would want to see it just as much.

Adrian's eyes, still mostly black, met mine. "Should we wait for Noire?" he asked, his words muffled by his scarf.

I bit my lip, glancing out the window at the still night outside Alessandra's cottage. "Let's wait until sunrise."

The hours passed slowly. Alessandra built up her fire and retreated to her bedroom. Whether she slept or not, I didn't know. I stood at the window, watching for any sign of Noire.

How am I going to explain this to Lia? And to Ashwin?

Adrian stayed by my side, sometimes wrapping his arms

around me and sometimes simply holding my hand. The longer he stayed in Faerie, the more the violet returned to his gaze.

I sighed heavily as the sun started to light the eastern horizon, shaking my head as grief weighed down my heart. I hadn't known Noire very well. But this seemed too sad an ending for such a tragic life.

Glancing at Adrian, I nodded, telling him it was time to leave. We tried to go quietly, not wanting to disturb Alessandra. Our footsteps were nearly silent on the stepping stones of her cottage path, and the gate made only a soft rattle while I closed it behind us.

But when I looked up toward our path into town, I squinted at the silhouette of two figures walking our way.

"What...?" Words failed me as I stared at Ashwin grinning while he walked beside his sister.

"Did you really think I wouldn't find out what trouble my sister was getting into?" Ashwin asked when they reached us. "I can't let her have all the fun."

I huffed a laugh, my breath frosty in the morning air.

"Come on, sis." He wrapped his arm around his sister's shoulders. "I believe you have someone waiting for you."

Noire let out a full smile, her yellow eyes brighter than the rising sun as she leaned her head on her brother's shoulder.

"What do you think?" Adrian whispered to me. "Do you think a werewolf and a vampire can make it work?"

I laced my fingers with his. "As far as I'm concerned, there's no better pairing in the world."

EPILOGUE

The sand was warm between my toes, heated by another perfect day of sea and sunshine. The gulls called above my head, riding the breeze to new horizons.

I hummed "Kokomo" to myself as I stared out at the setting sun dyeing the summer sky all the hues of pink, orange, and yellow.

The salted sea breeze carried a familiar scent my way: clary sage, iris, and a campfire of lemon and pine. I glanced over just as Alasdair appeared farther down the beach.

He smiled at me, his orange eyes bright as he dipped his head in respect.

"I knew you'd find me eventually," I told him once he reached me.

He shook his head sadly. "Ah, you've caught on. Now I'm going to need better tricks to impress you so you'll let me into your pack."

I groaned. "Give up. There's never going to be a pack."

He snatched up my hand, my gold band—a symbol of Adrian's and my vow—shining on my third finger. "What's this? Don't tell me you actually mated that thing."

"Hey," I snapped, "that's my husband you're talking about."

He dropped my hand and stood beside me, gazing out at the ocean. "Well, you certainly won't have many wolves trying to join your pack now. He's werewolf repellent."

"Is he? So you'll stop asking?"

He gave me that lopsided smile. "Don't get your hopes up. I made a vow of true friendship, remember? I'm in it for life."

At this point, I could admit that some small part of me did, in fact, want to lead a pack. My inner alpha and her instincts were part of me. But even in acknowledging that, I knew I wouldn't form one. There were many gives and takes in life. And to live the life the majority of me wanted, I had to let that instinct go.

That was fine. It was enough for me to be friends with Alasdair rather than his alpha. I could still be there for him and protect him as a true friend. I bumped Alasdair's shoulder with mine. "I guess you can go ahead and start calling him 'brother-in-law' then."

He curled his lip. "Ew. Stop that. I just ate."

I chuckled, and we fell into a companionable silence.

"Your territory is beautiful," he said after a while. "The ancestors whisper that you'll be happy here."

I don't need to hear that to know it's true.

"Thank you. And what about you? How's your research going? How are you dealing with your family? What happened to Amelie and Lolly?"

"Lolly had her baby before Jean-Henri showed up to evict everyone—a healthy little girl."

I smiled. "That's nice."

He gave me a sideways glance. "They named her Willow."

I pressed my lips into a line and sniffed. "Don't say that. You're going to make me cry. Did they really?"

He nodded with a chuckle. "They did. As for my research, I still have a lot to learn, but I believe my theories are sound. More wolves choose to leave Faerie every day. And, every day, the land and the ancestors speak a little louder. Some of the other mystics who have come through the veil feel it, too. My family was as shocked as everyone else by what you uncovered. The head of the Pink Moon Clan holds firm that the whole thing is a hoax. He's lost a lot of support, but we don't have another alpha to take the role from him yet. Still, there are whispers amongst the relatives, and some of my cousins have come here."

I resisted the urge to click my tongue. Our big reveal had certainly made an impact, but not nearly as much of one as we had hoped. It seemed that even in the face of great truth, people were unwilling to believe what was uncomfortable to them. Yes, some of the wolves had abandoned Faerie in favor of the realm of origin, but most had not. The wolf council had renegotiated the treaty; most of the traditions were still firmly in place. Though I supposed the fact that wolf pups were now only bound for the five years leading up to a faeling's awakening was a small victory.

"I'm sure you're a great comfort to those who are trying to settle here," I told him.

He glanced over at me. "I still have a long journey ahead of me."

"I wish you everything you deserve, Alasdair. I know a heart as good as yours won't search for long."

"Fate will provide me with whatever I need," he said with confidence.

I had long given up the question of whether I had won against fate. Maybe I was defying her by being with Adrian. Maybe I was her puppet all along. I didn't think I could ever know the answer, and I didn't really care. That wasn't even the right question. I loved him, and I knew that he would fight beside me whatever fate might throw at us.

"What about you?" Alasdair asked. "What have you been up to since you turned the whole world upside down?"

I scowled at his accusing tone. "I've been doing my part. I match those coming through the veil to packs here in the realm of origin. Actually, Adrian has been doing something similar for vampires. He helps newly turned vampires find families so they can learn how to control their bloodlust."

"I guess he's good for something."

"Aww, come on. You know you like him a little." I reached up and poked Alasdair's cheek.

He snapped at my finger playfully, and I snatched it away. "Never," he vowed with a grin.

Alasdair glanced over my shoulder and bowed slightly, giving me the respect that was my due as an alpha. "That's my cue. Until we meet again, captain."

Then he sauntered away.

Adrian arrived not a moment later. "Was that Alasdair?" He wrapped his arms around me from behind.

"Yeah."

"What did he want?"

"I'm not sure actually. Just to pop up out of nowhere to annoy me? How was your call with Ikaros?"

Adrian snuggled in closer. "Good. He's settling in with Korina's family. He seems to have come out of the worst part of his transition all right. I think he'll be very happy with them."

"That's good to hear. I know you were worried about him."

A tingle ran over my skin as Adrian trailed his lips down my neck. "What I'm worried about is how I'm going to resist your charms long enough to get you all the way home. I can never thank Yuti enough for buying you that bathing suit. She's the best friend a guy could ever have."

I leaned against him, reaching back to run my fingers through his hair. "Who says we have to wait until we get home? There's a very deserted patch of sand I know of."

"Oh yeah?" He nibbled my neck, careful not to break the skin.

But then he growled, a sound he'd no doubt picked up from all the werewolves he had acquaintance with, as his phone buzzed in his pocket.

"Ignore it," I told him, spinning in his arms to kiss him on the mouth.

He hummed against my lips, but the buzzing continued. Digging his phone out of his pocket, he answered it. "What?" he snapped.

His eyes flicked to mine, and he handed me the phone.

"I'm a little busy right now," I murmured as Adrian pulled me close again.

"Just because you're a lone alpha, doesn't mean you get to ignore the rest of us," Shri growled in my ear. "Why don't you ever answer your phone?"

"She's too busy with her mate!" I heard Damjan shout in the background.

"Shut up!" Shri snapped. "Listen, Willow, we have our hands full. We're going to need you to match some of these wolves coming through with alphas here in the realm of origin. We're too busy running our own packs. Isn't that what you're paid for?"

"Yeah, okay. Send them my way."

Shri sighed in relief. "Thank you. They'll be there in a few days."

I hung up Adrian's phone and handed it back to him. "How long do we have?" he asked.

I embraced him, nibbling his earlobe as his cock throbbed against me. "Long enough to make you mine many times over."

AFTERWORD

Thank you for reading! I do so hope you enjoyed it. If you have a moment, I would very much appreciate a review on the store where you bought it. Tell other readers what you thought and help them make a decision on this book.

If you'd like to stay updated on news about my books and events, you can subscribe to my newsletter on my website: www.dlieber.com

On my site, you will also find my blog, where I post all my fun little tidbits.

Thanks again! I hope you will travel through my worlds with me again in the future.

D. Lieber

ABOUT THE AUTHOR

D. Lieber has a wanderlust that would make a butterfly envious. When she isn't planning her next physical adventure, she's recklessly jumping from one fictional world to another. Her love of reading led her to earn a Bachelor's in English from Wright State University.

Beyond her skeptic and slightly pessimistic mind, Lieber wants to believe. She has been many places—from Canada to England, France to Italy, Germany to Russia—believing that a better world comes from putting a face on "other." She is a romantic idealist at heart, always fighting to keep her feet on the ground and her head in the clouds.

Lieber lives in Wisconsin with her husband (John) and cats (Yin and Nox).

Links:
Website: www.dlieber.com
Goodreads: www.goodreads.com/dlieberwriting
BookBub: https://www.bookbub.com/profile/d-lieber

Lightning Source UK Ltd.
Milton Keynes UK
UKHW012018250123
415976UK00016B/208/J